THE WESTERN STORIES OF CARROLL JOHN DALY, VOLUME I

TWO-GUN GERTA

Carroll John Daly

TWO-GUN GERTA

THE WESTERN STORIES OF
CARROLL JOHN DALY, VOLUME 1

CARROLL JOHN DALY
AND C.C. WADDELL

EDITED AND
WITH AN INTRODUCTION BY
DAVID LAURENCE WILSON

COVER BY
RICK GEARY

STEEGER BOOKS • 2023

AN EXTRAORDINARY WRITER

HE USED to be a somebody. Maybe now he is somebody again. He went from pervasive to obscure until finally not even the British or the French were keeping him in print.

He wasn't the luckiest or the most successful of writers but he was awesome.

If you're a fan or a scholar you may love him or hate him but if you're honest you've got to accept that Carroll John Daly was "somebody," and his legacy is an essential building block of contemporary American crime fiction. He was not among the greatest of American writers but he was certainly among those most influential.

He was not only the first hard-boiled detective writer, he is also the first to break through any number of walls to confer directly with the reader. He is so familiar a voice, so stream of consciousness, so self-conscious and unfiltered that the stories of his grim, relentless heroes take the form of quick, chatty memoirs, somewhere between emails and instructional handouts.

Daly was the forerunner. In 1922 and 1923 new characters and their stories gushed out of him like a great exhalation of purpose. He was the Godfather of every private detective character who has followed, over 100 years of influence. Daly was the prime domino.

Though Daly is primarily known for his crime fiction, he also had a secondary interest in western stories, particularly during the first ten years of his writing. Novel length serialized stories were published in the pulp magazines *People's* and *Western Story*. Novelettes were published in *Complete Stories, Northwest Stories,* and *Frontier Stories.* Years later he tried to write westerns for television but was unsuccessful.

The Western stories were an unfamiliar setting for Daly; he knew little about the west and what he knew seemed to come from the cinema. Despite this these adventurous stories are dry, dusty treats, and this essay will try to explain how they came to be. They are little known because they have never, ever, been reprinted. Some have never been cataloged, so the only way you could find them was if you stumbled into one of them by accident.

Beginning with *Two-Gun Gerta,* these western stories centered around a town of Yavisa in the great Sonoran desert. Yavisa was not far from the U.S. border, where in 1923 you could still ride a horse for hours without crossing a paved road.

In this year, 2023, the 100-year anniversary of its initial publication, Steeger Books is offering up *Two-Gun Gerta,* the first reprinting ever of one of Daly's western stories. You might like to think it was planned… like salesmanship! Actually it was just the roll of the dice: luck that it has taken this long… and no longer. At any rate, more of these rare cowboy treats will follow. Or… hold that thought. Actually there is a paucity of cows in this dusty cow-boy town.

It begins right here, at the end of what could be an ironic story. The creator of the Private Eye, the "fixer," the mercenary and outsider—happened to have come from a family of notable attorneys and jurists.

IN SOUTHERN California, in the rolling sunset hills of Forest Lawn Memorial Park, Carroll John Daly's grave is understated, like the man himself. The man died January 13, 1958, at the age of 68. According to his obituary he had been retired for five years. His earthly remains were boxed and nestled beside those of his wife Margaret, who passed three years before him, April 15,1955.

They were the parents of John Russell "Jack" Daly, an actor who in his 1935 White Plains High senior class of 418 was known and celebrated for his performances in the school's dramatic productions, particularly as "Francois," the comedic, crowd-pleasing Concierge of the Hotel International, in *The Prince of Pilsen*. Fifteen years later Jack was putting out big effort into a career of small movie and television parts as bartenders, clerks, drivers and dogcatchers. He died ten years after his father, June 2, 1968, at the age of 54.

Daly pére's gravesite demands no special attention. It is sparse, with no monument or pictorial theme, no clues for sightseers or essayists, just a name on a simple metallic plate and the years of Daly's birth and death. Just a simple description that produces a chill, in that bland, west coast setting, a haunting message, the words say "EXTRAORDINARY WRITER."

A N D I T was true. Daly had an extraordinary career, particularly if you don't mix the volume and influence of his writing with more complicated judgments about subtlety and character development. Daly's stories were lathered up with passion and entertainment and yes, his writing could push the limits and be controversial! He was not to be read within the best of homes. If language can be disreputable… well that was Daly.

There are hints about his early life, but not nearly enough is known to suggest his nature or ambitions. In *Black Mask* magazine, 1924, he sketches out a frequently-cited resumé:

> My first business venture was the opening with another chap, of the first moving picture show on the boardwalk at Atlantic City—came theaters at Ashbury Park, Arverne, and a stock company at Yonkers. After that the deluge—stock salesman, real estate salesman, manager of a fire-alarm company, and a dozen or more other jobs.

Beginning in 1923 Daly published nearly one short story

or novelette a month for twenty years, not including 14 novels that for the most part had already been published as serials. Hardcover or not, Daly was a pulp writer who ascended to great popularity and a long plateau that lasted, in a humbled form, until the end of pulp. Daly's career represented a nearly perfect three-act play, thirty years of missteps and preparation, a quick rise and accomplishment and then a fall-off into frustration, obscurity, but not quite defeat. Fashions might fall, wars were inconsistent, but Daly could keep writing. He did not give up even after he had admitted to "retiring."

Daly was a New Yorker who had followed the sun, all the way to Ninth Street, in Santa Monica. All the way west where he could watch the sun sink into the Pacific while his own career went south.

New York, Florida or Santa Monica, it was all moving south, as the pulp magazines folded or cut their rates to writers. One of the strategies was to move to California, where the movies needed lots of words. There's no need to second guess Daly's personal choices because the big changes had nothing to do with one man's house or his druthers or family life. In 1938 Southern California made sense. Daly loved the ocean and wished to live near salt water. His son Jack wanted to try the movie business, and Carroll was deeply invested in his son's ambitions.

Though Daly was unwilling or unable to step outside of his comfort zone—a personal rhythm and familiar brand of character, he tried to write screenplays. A screenplay seemed to be another art altogether, but something a good pulp writer could master, and many were able to do so, particularly in the omnibus years of *Playhouse* series, a simple matter of prose written for minutes instead of pages. How hard could that be? But Daly tried and failed. However grand a *Wagon Train* written by Carroll John Daly might have been… it wasn't.

Though Daly was not exclusively a first-person writer but even his third person stories carried the aura of "I—I—I—and then I" prose. He wrote step by step thoughts and movements but they worked better on a page than in a sequence of rolling pictures.

The first person story style works against suspense, doing it's best to kill it, basically. For one thing, you can make a rather secure bet that whatever his challenges, your narrator is going to survive until the last foot of film. With notable exceptions, a motion picture is only occasionally going to be narrated by a dead man.

Daly's 1934 story, "Ticket to a Crime," featuring the detective Clay Holt, was the source material for the sixty-seven minute B movie of the same title, also released in 1934. It is slow, dark, and difficult to watch and consequently the sixty-seven minute film did nothing to boost the lives or careers of any of its cast or crew.

And that was it for Daly, and right there was a thumbs down for any incipient Carroll John Daly Film Festivals or monographs, an unsatisfactory Hollywood experience at the length of a continent.

One strike and Daly was out. He was not going to be a screenwriter and his phenomenally successful character, Race Williams, was never going to be adapted to film.

Have any of Daly's stories been optioned?… Not recently.

Compared to Daly you could say F. Scott Fitzgerald and the paperback noir specialist Harry Whittington had lucrative, satisfying film careers. Today we know they didn't. They all had a fairly miserable time in Hollywood.

Daly was a New Yorker, and as much as Fitzgerald himself, you could say Daly was a man of a specific time *and* place. His art and career are their own glorious monument. There is still no Carroll John Daly credit attached to a single film produced during the last ninety years.

But here's the kicker: His writings have never been more in print, more accessible, than they are today. This is a climactic change. Seeger Books has published over twenty pounds of Daly's stories and they are all available right now.

FOR YEARS I have read Daly like a hungry sailor who has found a misplaced sandwich but I knew no details about his life, nor much of what he looked like before… before I found his family's photo album.

No posed and studio lit cabinet cards in this family record; it was a photo diary of playful times. Before this discovery there only seemed to be two photographs of Daly; these new pieces of a captured soul were almost as rare as a pic of Billy the Kid. Actually not nearly as rare as they were two years ago.

One of those two photos was printed in an early issue of *Black Mask* and now it fits perfectly with the photographs I held in my hands, like a piece from a jigsaw puzzle. Suit, tie and cap on the beach? Check. Rumpled, black hair and glasses and a dress shirt escaping over his belt? Check. This was our Daly. On this occasion he was thirty-two years old and taking a break from writing while he vacationed on Nantucket island. That was the way the early readers of *Black Mask* knew him.

The second photograph was posed with dramatic lighting and from the chest up. Daly appears to be caught in a moment of listening, as if he wished to cup his ear, an older man in his forties, godfather of the hard-boiled idiom. He almost looks like James Joyce. This is the way the readers of Daly's novels knew him though it lacks the spunk and spirit and the sense of easy-going friendship he had between, say, 1917 and 1924, when he was beginning his adventures in writing.

Now here were twenty-seven more photographs of the writer, not counting a few similar ones that escaped the album and are now lost again. It represents a new and unexpected insight into the life of a late-blooming pulp writer from 100 years past.

But no matter. At this house Daly will always be a young man, a sturdy-looking fellow on the beaches of Nantucket Island and Atlantic City, a man who shows promise.

The identifications written on many of the photographs were wrong enough often to make all the captions suspect. Can that be Daly's signature? Another rarity? Possible, but probably not.

*Carroll John Daly
at the ocean, 1919*

Often, Daly is seen with his wife and son at the beach, watchful and impassive. He looks incomplete. Is this the writer at rest? There is certainly no evidence of him at work. No typewriter, no pen and paper. Sometimes we see him wearing a hat. We never see him holding or signing a book. It was not an age of self promotion.

Daly's uncle, John Brennan, figures prominently in this album of photographs. He looks as strong as a statue of Balzac but in the photographs of this lion Brennan is frequently misidentified as Daly's father. There are no photographs of the father. At the time Carroll's father—Joseph Daly—Brennan's friend, partner and brother-in-law, had been dead for ten years.

John Brennan, ca. 1915–16

Almost all these photographs were taken outside, external in every way. The only shots between walls were taken beside a public swimming pool. Were these photographs taken by Daly, by his wife or son? This was another mystery. At least one of these early snapshots is absolutely the work of the author.

The discovery of the photographs was timely, readymade for my own deadline and something to be thankful for. Given the

Carroll John Daly on 190 Street

circumstances, they seemed like a gift, a mutual hundred-year old commitment between Daly and this observer, a commitment surpassing generations and baffling time. It was literally the rediscovery of a celebrated and then forgotten writer.

If you want to get close to a writer, how's this? For over a year, every day, I've been seeing the world as Daly and his family saw it, through a camera's viewfinder as lights and darkness passed through their eyes to mine. Carroll, Margaret and Jack… all with cameras in their hands, recording moments in their lives as I kept going, following the route allowed here, looking into this family's long-ago future.

I have literally been looking through or looking at Daly's eyes every time I've flipped open my laptop computer. I see Daly's world, a city of brick and mortar, masonry that spreads out like stacks of cold grey waffles stacked on end. These photographs are old, and a battered photo album is no archive. Sometimes there is only a dull contrast. We could be looking through a dirty window. There are all these relatives, grandmothers and kids that look like twins but Daly stands out distinctly.

His wife, Margaret Daly, appears vampish and Bohemian,

*Carroll John Daly with his son,
Jack, at the beach (1918)*

an early Goth, domestic, gawkish, usually with a scarf over her head or a hat leaning over her right eye, peek-a-boo style. Daly himself seemed to have a full wardrobe of awkward suits, particularly when he wore them at the beach. He seemed to have a hobby of looking rakish or bemused but was sometimes only awkward.

Son Jack is a wide-eyed and stylish young boy and early adolescent, already a performer. He is four or five, and younger, at the beach, forever laying in the sand, the youngest amid an army of cousins, jostled and gentled.

Sometimes Daly would pose on the roof of his apartment, where he could hang his wash and enjoy the view of the city surrounding him, resolute beside the drying garments of the tenants at 601 190th street. Like a member of the Rushmore Quartette.

At the beach a medallion hung from a ribbon around Daly's neck; He wore a black tank top over black shorts. He was not particularly muscled but he looked like he could swim as fast as he wanted. It was a body sufficient to his needs. In other pictures he is dressed for hiking, suit pants tucked into boots and a puffy Gatsby cap. Daly is centered, balanced, and usually smiling. He is standing straight and at attention, but with his hands behind his back.

Right or wrong, the date on many of these pictures is 1917. When Daly registered for the World War One Draft that year, on June 5, the registrar looked him over and decided that he was of medium build, medium height, light-colored hair and blue eyes. His habits seem to have been moderate.

The early Daly, the man I see in these photographs, appears an active individual, hiking and probably swimming, too. Carroll was still on the quick side of thirty, though usually it looks to be Uncle John and young Jack who are most often in the water or lying in the sand of a beach while their nephew and father tries to look thoughtful, as if he's conjugating a sentence.

There are more posed photos at the seashore: Carroll and

Margaret, Carroll with a very young "Jack" Daly, sitting on top of him… Carroll in a suit: separate shots with his son and mother-in-law and in these, he wears glasses, as he is unlikely to swim in that suit.

There are two photos where he looks as a writer would like to look, a dark suit, tie and vest. Glasses with perfectly round lenses—spectacles, you might say. A bowler hat and a surly expression. In another photo he looks like Ahab, but with two good legs. The typewriter would be his whale.

I sent some of these pictures to Tadie Benoit, a French scholar, professor and translator who has written about the author. He wrote back to me that this was not what he had expected from Daly, this father of the hard-boiled idiom. He looked like—Benoit noted—a myopic Groucho Marx. Daly had thick, unruly hair and a bushy mustache that allowed such a comparison. I suppose James Joyce, too, looked a little bit like Groucho.

AN ANECDOTE by Erle Stanley Gardner, Daly's long-time friend and colleague, was relayed by Dorothy Belle Hughes, in her biography of Gardner, *The Case of the Real Perry Mason.* Gardner suggested that Daly was not particularly keen on physical fitness:

> Daly was tough in spirit but slender in physical build. He once said to Gardner: "You think I don't get enough exercise and that I'm not an outdoor man. I want you to know that on some sunshiny days I think nothing of going out and walking the full width of this lot on the sidewalk—and this is a fifty-foot lot!"

Then Dorothy B. Hughes offered another back-to back story from Gardner, concerning his later home in White Plains:

> Daly lived in one of a row of identical houses and always found his difficult to identify. On one occasion, he rang the bell of one of the houses on his block and asked the lady if she could tell him where Carroll John Daly lived. She started to reply and then said, "Why you're Carroll John Daly."

Margaret Blakeley Daly at the
Blakeley beach house (1913)

Jack Daly at the beach, 1919

As Gardner told the story: "Daly bowed. I know who I am, Madam. I am only trying to find out where I live."

Daly didn't have a better friend than Gardner.

WHEN I think of Daly I want to see him with Marge and Jack on the beach at Atlantic City. And I want to see the rest of them, all the family members. There are brothers and sisters and there are plenty of nieces and nephews to dress the scene. In these early years Daly appears to be an athletic man, not a trained athlete, but he's a man outside who looks to be comfortably enjoying the season. It is a ironic pose, for a writer of pulp, and later, in the summer of Daly's success, there are no photographs to dispute the image of C.J. Daly we see here, save for the default setting, the studied pose of an author on a book jacket.

THIS IS how it started, and to say Daly came from an influential, loving family is both insufficient and presumptive. The extended Daly family was filled with politicians, attorneys and educators whose early deaths occasioned ritualistic mourning and the fall of flags to half-mast. On a personal level Daly had a much more cordial relationship with the forces of order and governance than his readers might suspect.

Joseph Daly had been Justice of the Peace in Yonkers, then Acting City Judge and its City attorney. He was an expert on municipal and civil law and served as a member of the Board of Education.

For our purposes Carroll John Daly's story begins on October 21, 1885, when the high-profile attorney Joseph F. Daly married Mary L. Brennan, at the Church of the Immaculate Conception, in Yonkers, New York. Mary was the sister of Joseph's law partner, John F. Brennan. The two brothers-in-law were close friends, first professionally, than by family ties. Both families were the sons and daughters of Irish immigrants. They lived on south Broadway. On August 30, 1886, Mary and Joseph welcomed their son Joseph Russell Daly into the world.

Their second son, Carroll John Daly, was born September 14,

1889. The family's second son would be the writer in this family, a well-loved contrarian.

In 1894 the Daly household included three servants. That was the year they moved to 476 Warburton Avenue, a newly built two-story Queen Anne home across the street from Trevor Park and the Hudson River in Northwest Yonkers. (In later years the home would be divided into apartments.)

During the summers the young family enjoyed extended vacations in the Catskills, near Haines Falls, and at Ashbury Park, New Jersey. Uncle John made his own pilgrimages to Europe.

On one memorable occasion, the boys' Uncle John arranged a "trolley party" for his nephews and twenty-three of their friends. Between two and six p.m. the cheering children rode through Yonkers and into New York City for lunch and ice cream.

On another occasion, April 22, 1901, Joseph Daly, President of the Westchester County Bar Association, presided over the organization's fifth annual dinner at the Murray Hill Hotel in New York. Both Daly and his brother-in-law were reported to have delivered witty speeches.

Some say the original trauma is birth, to be evicted from a comfortable, loving home, surrounded by the sounds of life and warm during all seasons. Truly the Garden of Eden.

For Carroll John Daly the day of trauma was June 11, 1901. He was eleven years old when his life changed completely. Both of his parents died unexpectedly at home of natural causes on the same day from unrelated heart ailments. Joseph Daly was 43, his wife Mary just 39. Only a week before this Joseph had been arguing—and winning—a highly publicized case in court.

Mary died at one o'clock p.m. Joseph died at 4 p.m., truly the victim of a broken heart.

Shortly after Mrs. Daly's death her eldest son graduated from elementary school. After receiving his diploma he was informed of his mother's death. He was rushed home where he found his father unconscious and dying.

Mary, 39, had contracted the flu during the previous winter and her symptoms had lingered. Just a week before this Joseph had felt the first touch of the grippe. He collapsed after being told of his wife's death. The couple was given a double funeral.

Joseph Daly's unexpected death was a big blow to Yonkers, a system-changing event within the city's legal and political communities. Ten years later Joseph was still being referred to as one of the Yonkers' most prominent citizens.

According to the *Eastern State Journal*, in White Plains:

> There seemed no occasion for alarm in the condition of either of them until Thursday afternoon, when Mrs. Daly died, and upon Mr. Daly being informed of his wife's death he lapsed into unconsciousness and died exactly three hours afterwards.
>
> He was probably the best known trial lawyer in Westchester County, being identified with the most important cases before the courts here.... His common sense application of legal maxims, the soundness of his advice, his brilliancy as a pleader gained for him the respect of the bench and the admiration of his colleagues.

The following day Yonkers was at half mast—schools, pumping stations, water towers and the City Club—all the flags had been lowered in honor of Joseph. Mary's brother John F. Brennan, was booked to sail on a two month trip to Europe just two days after her death. Of course he canceled. According to the *Yonkers Statesman*, Mary's brother, "a prominent lawyer, says that the boys are to be his kids, henceforth, for he is to take care of and provide for them." On July 13 Brennan officially became guardian of the two boys. The stolid attorney was as good as his word. Brennan and his wife Margaret A. Brennan were without their own children.

Joseph Russell Daly and his younger brother Carroll moved into their aunt and uncle's home at 190 North Broadway, near downtown, Yonkers, a large estate.

Two years later, in September 1903, Joseph Russell Daly

left Yonkers to attend Georgetown University, graduating in 1909. He began working at his uncle's law office while studying at the New York Law School. Illness prevented him from completing his studies but he continued his employment with his uncle's firm.

On December 4, 1911, Joseph Russell died of a sudden onset of pneumonia at the age of 26. As recently as the week before he had been motoring with his uncle and attending—but not participating in a marathon race. After what was described as a "hearty meal" he complained of shortness of breath and the family physician was summoned.

We don't know how Carroll John Daly reacted to his brother's death but we know the circumstances and outcome... sudden... and unexpected loss. Again.

At the age of 22, Daly's uncle and aunt were the only survivors of his immediate family. It is difficult for many of us today to assume the attitudes towards mortality of a hundred and more years past. The closest we can come to an understanding of the fear of an untreated common cold during those years is to recall the years of COVID, "the years during which this present volume was prepared. Was it a shock or had Daly become accustomed to the deaths of his family members, not just one or two but almost all of them? It was terror, the terror of an illness that has no defense, just an endpoint.

IT WAS now 1912. We don't know Daly's goals, his hopes or dreams; we can only follow his steps, dust his fingerprints. Maybe it was just one step after another. There were a series of jobs that did not translate to long-term employment or satisfaction.

He didn't make out very well as a manager—or an entrepreneur—that's something we know.

His greatest interest seems to have been the theatre. He had tried to become an actor. There were certainly plenty of references to stage productions in the stories that came later.

In July, 1912, Daly took passage on the steamship *Finland* for a tour of Europe.

On December 11, 1913, Carroll married Margaret Blakeley and honeymooned in Atlantic City. Blakeley, was born May 27,1891, and named after her mother. She had two brothers and one sister. Her grandfather had been a State Senator representing New York City.

On September 28, 1914, Carroll and Margaret's son John Russell was born in Nantucket, Massachusetts. The baby was named after his doting great uncle and his father's brother Joseph Russell, an uncle the boy would never know.

Perhaps frustrated or disillusioned by his interrupted efforts on the stage, at the time of his son's birth Daly described himself as "retired." In 1917 and 1918 the Daly family lived at 260 Valentine Lane in Yonkers: Carroll was now employed as a law clerk at the Brennan and Curren Law Offices.

THEN CAME the big move, a short geographical adjustment that changed every bit of Carroll John Daly's life.

In 1920 the Daly and his family moved to 601 West 190th street, a newly built, five story, 75 unit apartment house in the Fort George area of Upper Manhattan. On the block of Wadsworth Avenue, between 180th and 190th Street. There were three five-story structures, five suites on every floor with four or five rooms each. Rent averaged $8 to $10 a month.

Daly was working at his father-in-law's real estate firm. He was 30 years old with four years of high school, no big success behind him, and no signs of achievement in the future.

Margaret's oldest sibling, Samuel Gillespie Blakeley, lived in Mount Vernon, Westchester. After the seventh grade he enlisted in the Army infantry, where, after nine years, he had ascended to the rank of corporal. He married Ethel Violet Nosher in 1906 and they ultimately produced nine children, five daughters and four sons. Their children included the many young girls who appeared in the Daly family's photographs of the streets outside their apartment house and the bathers in photographs from their Atlantic City vacations. Margaret was probably the most frequent photographer of these gatherings.

On reflection, given time, many unlikely paths become obvious, when we consider them from their end and look back. In retrospect Daly's own path is clear, including a low-key existence with a small, close family. Sometimes he seems to have lived in a vacuum, a space devoid of matter. It seemed that a career as a writer might suit him.

He had read Mark Twain and Edgar Allan Poe and later he referenced both writers in his own fiction. We can guess about his apprenticeship. He made a successful attempt to copy Poe and sold stories with a horror or occult angle.

Then came one of those fantastic, fortuitous encounters when you meet a new friend and you know it right away and sometimes it even turns your life around.

Daly encountered the near-celebrity Charles Carey Waddle, who since coming to New York had become "C.C. Waddell," not so much a pseudonym as an adjustment.

When Daly moved to the wilds of upper Manhattan, to the block of Wadsworth Avenue, between 180th and 190th Street, he was thirty years old and his skills had not yet matched his need for employment. He was not a professional writer. Several years later, when he left the apartment and moved to White Plains he was well established, a sudden, miraculously popular and an innovative performer in American pulp writing.

His rise was complete—his career stretched ahead of him while his inventions were in place and capitalized upon by other authors.

If Daly had a mentor, it was Charles Waddle.

Waddle was a successful writer of adventure fiction who produced stories like "A Mysterious Motorman" *(The Argosy,* 1904), "The Scarlet Warning," *(The Argosy,* 1905) and "Hell and High Water" *(People's Favorite Magazine,* 1921). Ultimately Waddle published more than 120 short stories, serials and novelettes. He wrote several Nick Carter novels. He was comfortable with collaborations, partnering with seven different writers during his short story and serial career. He even produced an Instructional Writing Course.

Waddle was born in Chillicothe, Ohio on March 3, 1868, the youngest of nine in the family of Dr. William and Mrs. Jane McCoy Waddle. He was more than twenty years older than Daly, his talented but unknown neighbor.

Like Daly, Waddle had come from an accomplished family of Irish ancestry. He had even found time to graduate from Marietta College in 1889, the accomplishment of which was not necessarily a requirement for future newspaper bylines or a mayoral campaign.

After graduation Waddle worked as a reporter for the *Chillicothe Daily News*, where his sister Nancy Mann Waddle, also worked as an assistant editor.

William Waddle, Jr., an older brother who specialized in sports stories, contributed to *The Spirit of the Times*, a leading sports magazine, but died of typhoid fever in 1889, at the age of 39.

Charles Waddle became the young, energetic mayor of Chillicothe for two four-year terms, 1889–1897, a position which had also been held by his uncle, Angus Langham Waddle, a two-time mayor between 1869 and 1875, following the Civil War.

In 1895 William Waddle, the patriarch of the family, a well-known Ohio physician, died at the age of 83 after suffering multiple strokes.

In 1896, before losing his second re-election contest, Waddle had raised enough money to purchase a half interest in the *Chillicothe Daily News*. He intended to return as both editor and reporter. In the line of duty, in an editorial, he termed President William McKinley, "a sawdust Napoleon."

He subsequently published *The News* until 1901, when it merged with the *Chillicothe Advertiser* to become the *Advertiser-News*.

In his memoirs, the Cincinnati newspaper veteran E.S. Wenis summed up Waddle's newspaper career:

> Charles C. Waddle was a rare genius... a brilliant young writer, but he loved the bizarre and the comic too much to build a solid foundation for future success. He was too intermittent, if I may use that as a descriptive phrase, and he passed on.

In the year 1900 Waddle resolved to become a free-lance fiction writer. Along with three of his sisters he moved to New York and began working in the publishing business.

According to E.S. Wenis, they "formed a Chillicothe colony, all from one family."

Eleanor Waddle, the first to make the move, became an editor at *Vogue* magazine and then editor of *The New Idea Magazine*. She had dabbled in fiction.

Jane Waddle Guthrie became a historical research writer, first in Duluth, Minnesota, then in New York.

As a writer Waddle was consistently overshadowed by his sister Nancy, two years his senior and a home-schooled student. She had been contributing articles to the *Ladies Home Journal* since June, 1896, and would ultimately publish over 100 short stories, poems and articles, primarily for the more prestigious slick magazines.

Her book-length fiction, which ranged from Western wilderness to the ultra-fashionable society of New York, included *The Bird of Time* (McClure, Phillips & Co., 1907), *The New Missioner* (McClure, Phillips & Co., 1907), *The Silver Butterfly* (Bobbs-Merrill, 1908), *The Beauty* (Bobbs-Merrill, 1910), *Sally Salt* (Bobbs-Merrill, 1912), *The Black Pearl* (D. Appleton & Company, 1912), *The Hornet's Nest* (Little, Brown and Company, 1917), *Swallowed Up* (Brentano's, 1922), *Burned Evidence* (A.L. Burt Co.,1925), *Come Alone* (Macaulay, 1929), *The Moonhill Mystery* (Macaulay, 1930), *The Second Chance* (The Archer Press Corp., 1931), and *The Pawns of Murder* (R. Long and R.R. Smith, 1932). She wrote one play, *The Universal Impulse*, in 1911.

LIKE DALY, Charles Carey Waddle was a late-blooming fiction writer although he also possessed a substantial background as a non-fiction writer. Along with his newspaper writing, articles for *Cosmopolitan* magazine were published in 1890 and 1891 using his full name, "Charles Carey Waddle." In August, 1894, he wrote "Ostrich Farming in South Africa" for *The Strand Magazine.*

Charles Carey Waddle

Waddle began publishing his first fiction around the age of thirty-two. Step by step, he became a successful writer of genteel mysteries and pulp adventure. He seemed to enjoy manufacturing a surprise, a "twist ending" to his stories not dissimilar to some of the short stories written by Ray Bradbury fifty years later.

Waddle and his sister Nancy contributed fiction to the Hearst and McClure newspaper syndicates. Their short stories and articles appeared in issues of *Metropolitan* magazine, along with other contributors including Stephen Crane, Rudyard Kipling, H.G. Welles, Jack London and Paul Laurence Dunbar. For the regular feature, "A Leaf in the Current," which was presented as the journal of a "Private Secretary," Ms. Woodrow referenced her mother and her grandmother with her pseudonym "Jane Wade."

One hurdle was the honored (in Chillicothe, at least) name "Waddle," which evoked the locomotion of a duck, as well as other barnyard animals, as per Oxford Languages, a leading publisher of dictionaries: "waddle; verb: to walk with short steps and a clumsy swaying motion," ... "three geese waddled across the road." Both Charles Carey and Nancy Mann Waddle early-on transitioned to pseudonyms.

In 1902 Waddle began writing as "Charles Carey," publishing 57 stories under that name.

The Van Suyden Sapphires (Dodd Mead & Company) 1905)

was published as "Charles Carey." He began writing as "Carey Waddell," and, more frequently, as "C.C. Waddell" in 1910. *The Girl of the Guard Line* (Moffat, Yard & Co., 1915) was published as Charles Carey Waddel. *Midnight to High Noon* (Whitman Publishing Company, 1929) and *Juror No. 17* (Albert King, 1931) were both published as C.C. Waddell.

Nancy wrote as "Mrs. Wilson Woodrow." It was her legitimate name because in 1897 she married James Wilson Woodrow, a mining engineer and cousin of Woodrow Wilson, the man who in 1913 would become the twenty-eighth President of the United States. The President's mother had been born in Chillicothe.

Though she divorced Woodrow in 1905, Nancy Mann continued to use "Mrs. Wilson Woodrow" as her professional name, provoking occasional confusion with the President's wife. When she was challenged by the First Lady, Woodrow Wilson's second wife, the former Ms. Waddle retorted that she had used the name "Mrs. Wilson Woodrow" longer than Mrs. Wilson had been married.

Mrs. Woodrow had lived in the Colorado Rockies during her marriage and her first fiction sale was a story about women's lives in a mining camp. She would often return to the subject but she would never again write as "Nancy Mann Waddle."

Ms. Woodrow was the most eclectic of writers, penning popular fiction, and direct, straight-talking advice columns about romance, honesty and personality while lobbying for equal rights for women and other liberal positions. Another column debated the question of which sex is the most emotional.

After the turn of the century she wrote frequently for the satirical humor weekly *Life* magazine, the only woman among the magazine's contributors. Typical of her stories for *Life* was "As Others See Us," from June 9, 1904, which began: "A distinguished woman instructor of a Martian college was recently sent to Earth to make an especial study of woman, her manners and peculiarities, upon this globe."

Mrs. Wilson Woodrow was also engaged in the early film industry in New York. Along with several other notable authors, including Irwin S. Cobb, Zane Grey, Rupert Hughes and Louis Joseph Vance, she received story credit on Universal's 1915 20-episode serial, *Graft*, starring Harry Carey and Jane Novak.

In 1916 Mrs. Woodrow wrote twelve separate stories starring Anna Nilsson and Tom Moore for Arrow's "Who's Guilty" series, distributed by Pathe. The stories for these episodes were also published in the local newspapers in the towns where the films were shown.

According to the *Indianapolis Star,* April 19, 1916: "Mrs. Wilson Woodrow, one of the few really great woman writers of the present time, recently delivered to the Pathe Exchange the last of the (twelve) scenarios and the novelettes based on them."

Mrs. Woodrow declared this to be the biggest theme she had ever considered. She declared that it would give her the chance of creating another such multi-varied microcosm of life as Honore de Balzac had created in the forty volumes of his *Human Comedy.*

Ultimately, she was credited with the stories for 26 films, all but one of those credits coming before the arrival of synchronized sound.

According to Mrs. Woodrow, in "Reasons Why I Like Men Better Than I Do Women," writing for the Metropolitan Newspaper Service, in 1925: "My subconscious mind may have been strongly impressed by the words of an old gypsy who read my palm when I was at an impressionable age, about twelve, I think. She fixed her dark, glittering eyes on me and said, 'Beware of women. Men will always be your best friends; stick to 'em.'"

Readers were said to imagine that the rather dense, uber-literary author was a man masquerading under a feminine pen name.

ON AUGUST 16, 1906, Charles Waddle became only the third most celebrated writer in his family when he married Louise Foster (born March 13, 1873), a delightful young woman who used her Swedish emigre father's original surname and wrote as Louise Forsslund. Her novels included *The Story of Sarah* (Bretano, 1901), *The Ship of Dreams,* (Harper & Bros., 1902), and *Old Lady No. 31* (Century Co., 1909). In *The Story of Sarah* Ms. Forsslund was credited with writing about the seafaring people of Long Island and a phase of women's history which had been previously unexplored. It was predicted that her novels would one day be considered classics.

According to Ms. Forsslund: "If the only man in the world—where is he?—were to come tomorrow and say, 'Only woman in the world, let us lock hands,' I would do it."

On the occasion of the marriage, and with their rival safely out of Ohio, the *Chillicothe Gazette* described Waddle as a "newspaper writer, literateur, author and jolly good fellow."

On February 2, 1907, Forsslund's father, Andrew D. Foster, who in the California gold fields had been a close friend of Mark Twain, died at his home in Sayville. His widow and five daughters survived him.

LIKE DALY, Waddle also experienced a life that was touched deeply by keen, indelible tragedy. This is what the two writers had in common. On May 31,1908, Louise Forsslund Waddle gave birth to two twin girls at their home in New York City. The babies died within hours.

Almost two years later, on March 5, 1910, the couple's son, Charles Forsslund Waddle, was born.

Two weeks after giving birth, May 2, 1910, Louise Forsslund died of heart failure at the age of 37.

One month later on June 4, 1910, the writer with a baby but no wife, married Stella (or Adele) S. Harrington (records are mixed), eight years his junior. William Waddle was born March 25, 1911, and daughter Nancy Waddle Waddle two years later. They lived in New York city with a butler, a maid and cook.

In 1916 Ms. Forsslund's novel, *Old Lady No. 31* was adapted as a play that ran for 160 performances on Broadway, with a portion of the royalties set aside in an educational fund for her bereft son.

According to the *San Antonio Light,* November 12, 1916: "Both playwright and star are rejoicing over the play's prosperity and the fact that the absent mother's mind has accomplished so much for her little boy."

Unfortunately, the announced recipient of that generosity would be unable to take advantage of it. On August 17, 1917, Charles Forsslund Waddle, the surviving son of Waddle's first, ill-fated marriage, died at the age of seven after contracting measles, followed by pneumonia. Charles Forsslund was buried beside his mother in the St. Ann's Episcopal Church Cemetery, Sayville, Long Island.

Later Forsslund's novel became the basis for two Hollywood films, *Old Lady 31* (Screen Classics, Inc., 1920) and *The Captain is a Lady* (MGM, 1940).

IN 1920 C.C. Waddle became a tenant at the 190th street apartment house. He lived there with his children, William, nine years old, Nancy, seven, and Elizabeth Dunlap, a 70 year old live-in housekeeper from Canada. Ten years later, this housekeeper was still a member of the family.

Both the Waddle and Daly families were among the first to move into the big new apartment house. On the undeveloped fields around them there were the debris of construction—pallets and boards and, undoubtedly, nails and splinters. It gave the appearance of an urban wilderness though, it was a wonderful place for the children to learn sportsmanship. There was lumber and other building supplies to repurpose for play. There were rocks to sit on. Young Jack Daly was a favorite within the neighborhood.

The writers—Waddle and Daly, journeyman pro and the rookie—lived just down the stairway, or down the hall from one another, close enough to borrow a cup of words, or for the kids to play with a dictionary.

There is no way to know when the idea of becoming a professional writer took hold of Carroll Daly. His apprenticeship is unknown, though he wrote in a variety of genres for the back pages of several esoteric publications. It is also impossible to sketch the parameters of Waddle's influence on the fledgling author. It just seems like—zing—suddenly Daly was a writer, all there at once, a completely formed savant, a pivotal figure who was contributing to a new post-industrial vocabulary. His prose was conversational, with the veracity and the easy, know-in all attitude of a New York city newspaper columnist. It had immediacy, it dealt with subjects which fascinated his readers and they enjoyed the surprises in his prose.

Daly had never before written for a newspaper. He'd never been a journalist. He wasn't leaning towards the obscure occult literary stuff either. His north star was set on F. Scott Fitzgerald and Edgar Allen Poe. Daly claimed to have written over 100 unpublished stories before his first sale, but in 1920 his writing career began a quick ascent.

The first of his published stories were short vignettes for national pulp magazines,. At the age of thirty Daly's first story, "Moral: Never Trust Spirits" was published in *Saucy Stories*, July, 1920. Next came stories in *10 Story Book*, edited by the eccentric author Harry Stephen Keeler.

Daly published as L. Carroll Daly and John D. Carroll, but he soon settled on his full name, writing only as "Carroll John Daly." This distinguished him from another "John Daly" who was a successful theatrical actor in the Northeast.

Between 1920 and 1922 Daly published eleven stories. In 1921 he began a series of "Chester Robinson" stories, in *People's Magazine*, and later in *Argosy*. These were gently amusing tales of pre-teen courtship with boasts and casual chivalries, contests over which boy could spit the farthest... and other feats. Young Chester played a gallant but subversive influence. The object of his affection was an admiring twelve year old neighbor, Marg Blakely, named after Daly's own wife.

Nineteen twenty-three was Daly's pivotal year as he began

to find his own literary voice, one quite distinct from that of Waddle. In his third year of writing he published a stunning 23 stories that year, in *Argosy, Black Mask,* and *People's Magazine.*

In *Black Mask* magazine, Daly created the character of Race Williams, a figure who was not a representative of law enforcement or of criminal element, but as someone who served as an intermediary, a broker in issues of crime and its consequences. He is more a concept and a force than a man exhibiting human characteristics. He was not over-sensitive.

Williams would become Daly's mainstay; he would be with him for the rest of his life and beyond. His other characters were variations of this one, this original icon, a hero of many names.

Williams was what would come to be known as a private eye, not necessarily a detective, but he could deduce when necessary. A lot of time he was just muscle, a smart, resourceful and lucky muscle, as relentless as fate. He was also indifferent and detached, a risk-taker whose faith was fatalism, a drifter with an office.

New York City was a stage where Daly's characters fought inconclusive battles between good and evil. The city is flat, stiff, and shadowed. It looked more like the idea of a city than the great city itself, a silhouette or the stage of a city. This is what he saw. He wrote about corruption and the desire to control, loot, and take advantage of the weak. There is no morning in Daly's stories, scarcely a night, little sleep, few meals, only a steady *now.* It is always twilight in Daly's crime stories, always shadows, always atmosphere.

This was Daly's New York, a city Daly could picture as gloomy or dignified, sinister or... well, usually sinister. He could write chase scenes on these streets and know exactly when the hunted should take a quick turn.

Race Williams was an accurate knight with a gun.

For the writer it seemed best to cultivate an isolated quality of indifference, a Zen-like solution to pain and frustration. This was the lesson Daly himself had learned in his early years. You couldn't take anything for granted and death was always at your shoulder, waiting. Daly knew death.

Survival of the fittest had nothing to do with this. Daly was very much aware of the finality and arbitrary character of death.

ESSENTIALLY WADDLE was both a mentor and a competitor. They were two riders on parallel career paths, twenty years apart. They worked the same factory and used the same tools, mostly words. They both contributed to prominent pulp magazines. In retrospect, Waddle was another exceptional writer who had no meteoric success but he had enjoyed a career that was a clearer and longer professional pathway than the one given to Daly. It seemed, when Waddle entered the field of writing, that it was an easier gig.

Through luck, skill, and probably Waddle's influence, Daly followed Waddle into several of the top pulp story showcases: *People's, Complete Story Magazine,* and *Argosy.*

In the early 'twenties both Daly and Waddle (beginning with the short story "Mose Cushenberry, Toreador" in February 1902) were particularly frequent contributors to *Argosy.* In one iteration or another *Argosy* was one of America's longest-running fiction magazines throughout the length of the twentieth century. Waddle had already produced 42 stories for the magazine before Daly cracked the contents page with his third Chester Robinson story, "Not Reel Life," on the March 3, 1923 issue.

For both writers *Argosy* was a particularly steady market. Ultimately Waddle published over fifty stories in *Argosy,* almost a third of his total magazine fiction. Many of his serialized stories were illustrated on the magazine's covers.

Daly would total ten stories in *Argosy,* including his second western effort, "Marty From Arizona," March 29, 1924.

Daly was published in 63 issues of *Black Mask* magazine, mostly due to the popularity of his character Race Williams. Waddle never made a sale to the magazine. He had only one sale to the mystery pulps, and that was "Juror No. 17" a 1930 serial in *Detective Story Magazine,* co-written with his sister. In 1931 it was published as a novel credited solely to Charles.

IN JUNE of 1922 the big John F. Brennan estate on Broadway, in Yonkers, was sold to the city, with a new high school scheduled to be built at the location. John and his wife, Margaret A. Brennan left for a summer home in New England. When they returned to Yonkers they began living at 11 Delavan terrace.

Two years after this move, after a succession of illnesses related to pneumonia, John Brennan died on June 22, 1924, at the age of 71. Once again flags were lowered in honor of another member of this family. All along Daly's uncle had been his friend and champion and Brennan had lived to see the tip of Carroll's success with the serialized *Two-Gun Gerta.*

Brennan's last words, it was reported, was that he "felt nervous." At the moment of death his eyes closed and a slight smile spread over his features.

With his uncle's passing Daly's family had become even more limited. He had no more elders, no one to share his coming triumph except his wife and son. Like his characters, Daly was becoming known as a loner. He worked at night, slept during the day.

Now Daly was more than ever on his own, though he now had a profession, a track record and standing, and most of all, he had Race Williams and New York City, a malleable neighborhood that Daly could picture as gloomy or dignified, a line as thin as that between two sides of a coin.

"There's a false air of respectability to the staid old buildings," Daly wrote.

DALY AND Waddle, the two big producers, began working together and there had to be a reason. One of them might have said: "Let's write a western," and the other one must have agreed. Or maybe it was a favor, and one of them was sick or overwhelmed with deadlines or opportunities. Maybe they just couldn't get away from one another. We still don't know why they took this single co-credit. *Two-Gun Gerta* was Daly's longest, most challenging effort during those early years and in 1925 it would become his first book, credited to both Daly and Waddle. Because of his association with Daly, his junior partner, *Gerta* would become Waddle's best known work.

It was first published in 1923 as a serial in *People's Story Magazine*. It represented a change of locale, a "western," albeit a contemporary story, dealing with prohibition racketeering rather than cattle rustling.

One hundred years later the pace holds up. God forbid it should drag. As far as style in concerned, there are fewer dashes at the end of quotations, and a lot more semi-colons. Everything accept the vocabulary and the punctuation reads like Daly.

Waddle was basically a flowery writer—Daly's words were shorter, direct and high-contrast. Daly worked his vocabulary to the nub. He didn't reach to the top shelf for adjectives and obscurities.

Gerta also has more humor, and for Daly, a rarity… a back story. Also interesting is how Daly veers into horror-pulp territory.

For the most part *Two Gun Gerta* is not demonstrably different than the crime stories which preceded it in *Black Mask*. There are two ways to perceive this continuity: either Waddle contributed little to the finished product or that he was indispensable, mentoring the younger man, nurturing his talent from the beginning. Waddle was comfortable as a team-player, with frequent collaborations. Now he was in a position (professionally *and* geographically) to inspire Daly, to teach him much about the job of writing stories.

If it difficult to say that Daly emulated Waddle. Even conceding the more than twenty years that separated them, it would take an effort to find two more dissimilar crime novels than Waddle's *The Van Suyden Sapphires*—and *The Snarl of the Beast* (Edward J. Clode, 1927), the first Race Williams novel, published more than 20 years later. Though the latter is often described as the first hard-boiled novel ever published, *Two-Gun*

Gerta was equally hard-boiled, with a western style of hat. Even the titles draw out the distinction—and indicate the vast differences in style and vocabulary.

Waddle wrote with a flowery, sometimes with an elliptical, teasing style. Daly was short and direct. Even their vocabularies came from opposite ends of the dictionary. Daly had a limited vocabulary. Waddle did not. He used words that don't exist anymore.

One hundred years later, on this big occasion, does *Gerta* stand out distinctly from the rest of Daly's first five years of fiction?

Not really. I see a lot more commonality than anything that makes the novel distinct. It is longer, of course, but the pace holds up. I don't see that much difference in the Daly prose with or without Waddle.

The sentences in *Gerta* favor the terse and objective style of Daly's emerging talents, rather than the more elegant and florid prose of Waddle. Waddle wished to fully describe a scene, framing it with words that were not necessary. Daly cut to the chase. He was simply blunt.

There were enough deficits in Daly's writing that he relentlessly had to play up his assets, like the simple beauty of much of his phrasing, that cadence and timing! Speech, attitude and location, it all worked together, along with the cheap paper it was printed on. It all fits and it's a mistake to dissect it today.

When Daly assayed the small town of Yavisa and the American west he wrote: "The sun was hot and the street was dirty." And that, too, was elegant. But not so florid as it would have been in Waddle's description of the same scene. Unlike Daly, Waddle was not phobic when it came to a sentence that capitulates, that turns up with the sound of a question at its end. Why would you want to use the word "queried" when a question mark will do? That seems redundant to me. Race Williams would tell you that you can't really be a tough guy if you use the word "query," right?

Daly was clearly ascendant and Waddle a writer emeritus and well established, still a featured fiction writer when he died unexpectedly of heart disease on June 10, 1930, at the age of 62, just five years after the publication of *Two-Gun Gerta*. His body was returned to Chillicothe for burial. His obituary in the Chillicothe Gazette called him "a true optimist."

Nancy Mann Waddle, a.k.a. Mrs. Wilson Woodrow, died September 7, 1935, 65 years old in New York City..

IN 1924 in "Devil Cat," the fifth of Daly's Race Williams stories, Daly described the apartment house and neighborhood where he had met Waddle and he began to blossom:

> "I took one quick look at the situation of the apartment— turned and dashed up the stairs to the roof.... The roof door swung easily open—I stepped out into the moonlight, gun in hand.... Across the traveled tar I sped, hardly noticing the sharp pricks to my stockinged feet. I didn't have to guess at the ladder of the fire-escape leading to the roof. I knew these buildings and knew where it would be. Thirty seconds in all and I had swung down and onto that straight narrow iron ladder which leads from the top floor to the roof. Six, seven, eight rungs and I faced the closed window of Apartment 5C."

Daly's readers, the lucky regulars who had to wait for his monthly surprises, perceived his stories viscerally. Do you hear the jagged stop-start of the words and the pulse of blood? This was Daly's singing voice. He wrote with a terse but rhythmic timing that gave the reader an unusual first-person immediacy. Daly and his characters were like bludgeons tumbling down a wild river. They just rushed out of the starting gate and they broke things, including the conventions and expectations of modern crime and mystery fiction.

Two pages later the "Devil Cat" case was completed, and it is here that Daly works up to one of his best-known lines: "I wanted my check and I wanted to drop this doll and drop her quick. If I ever do get married, I want to settle down quiet and peaceful-like—not sleep with a gun cocked every night. Why,

Carroll John Daly, 1921

this dame might take a notion to cut me up because I thought the coffee a little cold."

These were the words that melted in your mouth.

In the end, this is surely an exaggeration. This is not life: these are just words on paper and for many years they were lost, or out-of-action. For now, in this twenty-pounds plus of publications from Steeger Books, they have been given new life, continuing this story and becoming one more clue into the man who was Carroll John Daly.

In another story that apartment 5C might not have burned, in another plot Race Williams would have simply walked to the door of the apartment and knocked, and C.J. Daly would have been writing at home and the two men could have talked for hours.

There is no way today to prove occupancy. It is not known if Daly lived in apartment "5C" but I choose to think he did.

CHAPTER I

HIRED

THERE ISN'T much to say about Yavisa except that it
is hot and dirty. But then all the towns in Mexico are hot
and dirty; so I'll put it that Yavisa is a shade hotter and dirtier
than anything else along the border.

Still there I was in Yavisa's heat and dirt, and prepared to like
it there, not because I was a bootlegger or a deserter, or down on
my luck, or because of any of the usual reasons that take a man
into Mexico, but just because I was a kid with a kid's fool itch
to go poking his nose into places where he's got no business—
seeing the world, they call it.

I had nothing on my hands but time, and enough jack in
my jeans to see me through. I wasn't exactly looking for work,
although of course if a job came along that paid good money
I wasn't going to toss it over my shoulder. There'd be plenty of
chances, I figured, if I cared to take 'em up; it ain't so easy to get
a fellow from the States down there any more, since the bump-
ing-off of any gringo that happens to be out alone has become
a sort of national pastime, with major and minor leagues and a
box score posted up every evening.

The pay was bound to be big. Any American is the kitten's
patent leathers in greaserland; and for an all-around, high-class
guy like myself—well, they'd have to bid some if they wanted
my services. As for any incidental gunplay, I can twirl a fairly
mean gat myself; and in case things did get too hot for me, I
could always beat it to God's country.

That's one reason I picked on Yavisa. It's only a night's ride from the border—a good, fast ride to be sure, but with the proper incentive behind you, it could be made.

On the whole, Yavisa looked pretty good to me. It was a sort of Tia Juana, I judged, on a small and rougher scale. There was a little, old half-mile track out on the edge of the town where you could burn up your money against a bunch of outlaw skates and crooked bookmakers every Sunday and Thursday. Big, yellow bills were hung up in the windows announcing a cockfight for that evening. The only street was lined with wine shops and saloons, and looking in through the swing doors I could see about every kind of a gambling layout.

As I strolled along on my way from the corral where I had left my horse, and observed the abundant evidences of personal liberty, I began to get all set for a large evening.

"Old-timer," I says to myself, "you've probably come to the right place."

Most of the native population were inside at that hour, taking their siesta; but as I swung along toward the general store I saw a big goofer crouching at the side of the doorway like a cat watching at the edge of a household. He gave one look around at me as he heard my footsteps, and I stopped right where I was.

Half Mexican and half something else, I took him to be, but all murder. He looked like the bad man in the movies, only more real. A yellow, splotchy face under his broad-brimmed sombrero, with eyes as cold and deadly as a rattlesnake's, and a cruel, crooked mouth that ran halfway up his cheek on one side as the result of an old knife scar. He had on a black frock coat, white riding breeches, and high patent-leather boots and spurs, and I noticed a big diamond ring flashing on his little finger. A saloon-keeper or boss gambler, I places him, but also he might be one of the local big bugs, mayor or chief of police or something like that. As a stranger, it was up to me to watch my step.

After that one look, he paid no further attention to me, but centers all his interest on that store door; and I edges sort of nonchalantly over toward a big locust tree that would be handy to jump behind in case of trouble. For I had a hunch that trouble was apt to come stepping out that door.

Well, it did; but not in just the shape I expected. What showed up was a woman.

At first, I thought she was only a half-grown girl, she looked so young and slender in her riding togs, and, besides, things happened so quick that I didn't get a clean slant at her. I saw, though, that her arms were full of bundles and that she was heading for across the street, where a pretty fair-looking pinto was tied to a post.

But as she crossed the doorstep, that big gorilla's arm shot out and caught her by the shoulder, swinging her about and making her drop her parcels. Then quick as a wink he grabbed her by the other arm, and held her so—face to face with him, powerless to move.

I saw the storekeeper who had followed her to the door scuttle back out of sight like a scared rabbit as soon as the thing happened; and outside of me, the street was deserted. I knew that I would be wise to duck, too. It wasn't any of my mix, some personal affair of the big greaser's; maybe the girl was his daughter. But I was always a nosey fool; so I stayed there and watched 'em.

He had shifted his grip now and was holding her two wrists with his one hand. It threw her a little away from him, and I could get a better look at her.

She was young all right but not so young as I had thought. And I decided, too, that she wasn't his daughter. In family row there is almost always a certain amount of tit-for-tat; your folks can get your goat so much harder than any outsider, that you can't hardly help slapping back. But this girl didn't even sneer. She was playing poker and you couldn't have told from her face whether he was wishing her many happy returns of the day, or slathering her with Spanish abuse, which last was what he was really doing. I knew that from the movement of his shoulders. A man who is in a temper will often give himself away that way.

I saw, too, now why he was holding her so tight. She had a couple of heavy Colts strapped about her waist, and for all her sweet-sixteen look and her quiet manner, I figured that they weren't just a bluff. Give her half a chance, and she'd use 'em. Anyhow, Mr. Greaser wasn't taking no risks with her; them thick, yellow fingers of his was clamped down over her two wrists same's an iron vise. She couldn't make a move.

Nosey I am, as I tell you, that's my middle name. So I just couldn't help slipping up a bit closer to find out what it was all about. I sure got an earful.

"Little devil-cat!" The guy was jabbering in Spanish, but I didn't need no interpreter; you could 'a followed him if he'd been speaking in Chinese. "You boast that you play a man's part around here, do you? Well, then stand up and take a man's punishment. Tell again what you have done to 'old Crooked Mouth,' will you? Por Dios, your mouth shall be crooked on both sides. Look, I will put my mark upon you—a slash up and a slap down right across your face!"

As he spoke, he ripped out a wicked-looking knife from somewhere at the back of his neck. But he never got a chance to use it. 'Cause why? Well, I was standing right behind him, tickling his ribs with my automatic. Quick as he was in drawing that knife, I had been just a split-second quicker.

"Drop it, mister!" I says persuasively.

Him being a lad that was open to argument, he done that same little thing; and I kicks his knife out of the way with my foot.

Course I ought to have bored him; would have saved myself a lot of trouble if I had. But, remember, I was a stranger, and butting in on something I didn't know a hoot about. I didn't want to start wrong in a new town; and this bird might be the whole works in Yavisa, for all I knew. It certainly looked funny that not another soul in the burg besides myself had interfered to help the girl; they couldn't all be asleep.

So I just contented myself with running my gun friendly-like up and down his spine, while I relieved him of some other weapons, and meantime handed him a few well-meant words of advice.

Or rather, I started to give him the advice, but didn't get very far.

"You lousy, yellow bum!" I says. "What's the big idea, jumping on—"

Then my attention was attracted to another quarter; for the fair heroine of this drama had yanked out them Big Berthas of hers, and was evidently preparing to go into action. I learned afterward that she was a bit tardy on the draw on this occasion, 'count of her wrists being stiff from his grip on 'em; but I'll tell the world, it wasn't no slow-motion-camera stunt at that. With anybody on hand less quick-minded 'n me, it'd have sure been "curtains" for old Crooked Mouth.

"Cut that out, you!" I snaps at her out of the corner of my mouth. "If I was playing for a funeral, I could have fixed it up myself. You leave me handle this little affair my own way."

I didn't bend my gun on her. I didn't have to. She looked at me hard a second, sizing me up; then she tucked the forty-fives back into her belt, and bust out a-laughing.

When I turned back to the greaser he was gone—hot-footing it for an alley about thirty yards away so fast that I'll bet them patent-leather boots of his were smoking.

"*Hola*, Crooked Mouth!" she shouts after him. "See the gallant Colonel Crooked Mouth, hero of a thousand battles!"

I didn't try to stop him; but when he reaches the alleyway he halts and peeps back as if to get a better look at me. If I was of a nervous temperament, that look wouldn't have made me feel any easier. Being as I am, though, I just grins and, sliding my gun back where it belongs, started to picking up her scattered bundles.

But she wasn't through with the gentleman yet; not by a long shot.

"Listen, half-breed swine!" she hollers at him. "If you ever lie in wait for me again, be prepared to finish what you start. For at the first suspicious move I'll commence to shoot, and you know I don't miss. You won't always have a chivalrous stranger to protect you. So be on your guard."

He started to answer her with string of vile, Spanish oaths, but I jerks out my gun again, and he fades from the picture *muy pronto*. I finished picking up the parcels, and hands them to her. All this time, though, I was keeping an eye peeled toward that alley, in case our little playmate should come back; for I didn't need any seventh son of a seventh son to tell me that he was going to get me if he could.

"Never mind him," she says, catching me at one of those side-wise glances. "He won't show up again, while I am around. He has too much respect for my skill with these," slapping them miniature cannons of hers.

There wasn't much I could say to this. 'Twas me that ought to be telling her not to worry about the big brute, I'd take care of him if he pestered her any more. But here she was, playing my hand. This thing of mixing up with a lady gunman had me kind of confused.

"You're a Yankee, aren't you?" she asks, as I walks over with her toward her horse. When I nodded, she gave an odd, little, twisted smile.

"I knew you must be," she says. "None of this native scum would have taken such a chance. Colonel Manuel Esteban—old Crooked Mouth, I call him—is a bandit leader, and holds the whole region in fear of him. You saw how the cowardly vermin of the town took to their holes during out encounter; not one but you would raise a hand to help me."

This was the first mention she had made of the favor I'd done her; and as thanks, you could hardly call it gushing. Pretty matter-of-fact I'd say, for a girl who'd just been saved from the clutches of a bloodthirsty villain.

But she couldn't put anything over on me. "A bandit leader, is he?" I says, careless as herself. "Pity, he didn't have his gang with him. That might have made it sort of interesting."

She had vaulted into the saddle by this time, and was leaning over, looking at me; and I was looking back at her—kind of placing each other, you might say. Not but what she was worth looking at for her own sake—slim and graceful as a tule reed, with a round, firm chin, and a sassy cock of her head, and eyes that sort of dared you and yet held you off, deep and shinning under her long lashes. I seen now that, for all those black eyes, and her heavy tan, and crinkly black hair, she wasn't no greaser, but of the same breeding as myself.

"I'm betting there's an O'Toole somewhere in your pedigree, young lady," I says, hardly knowing I was speaking out loud; that's where the black of your hair and your eyes comes from."

She laughed.

"What might your name be?" she asks.

"Roger Francis Conners, ma'am, but mostly they call me 'Red.'"

"Red Conners?" she repeated. "Well, now, do you know, I have an idea that the one thing most needed in my outfit at present is someone with the name Red Conners, and hair the color of yours. You're not tied up with anyone in this country yet, are you?"

"Not yet," I says. "But you better speak quick."

"All right," she snaps. "I'm on my way now to take these supplies to my brother out in the hills, but I'll be back in Yavisa tonight. Be at the Cafe El Toro about ten o'clock, ready to go with me to the ranch."

With that, she dug her spurs into the pinto, and whirled off up the street in a cloud of dust; while I stood staring after her, with my hat on my head like I didn't know enough manners to take it off.

But you could hardly blame me at that. Here I was hired, but for what I didn't know, or where, or at what wages.

Why, come to think of it, I didn't even know the critter's name.

CHAPTER II

THE TRAP

IT FINALLY dawned on me, that I wasn't going to learn very much, standing there staring and scratching that carrot top-piece of mine; so I turned and walked over to the store.

And then it struck me all of a sudden, that since my new boss had lit out, the town had come to life again. While the argument was on 'twixt her and the colonel, the place was like a deserted city, not a soul in sight. You might have been in the middle of the Sahara desert. But now heads was sticking out of every window, and the order of the day was being resumed at the bars and wine shops.

The storekeeper, a half-portion Dutchman with scraggly, yellow whiskers, had come out of his gopher hole, and was standing in the door blinking kind of nervous through his big, horn-rimmed goggles.

I asks for a sack of Bull and some papers as an excuse to start a conversation; and then while I am rolling a fag, inquires casual who's the little lady.

"V'at liddle lady?" he growls. "I didn't see none."

"No?" I shifts my gun. "Danged if I mustn't be having one of them nightmares again. The trouble about 'em is, that if anybody tries to get gay with me while I'm in 'em, I always start shooting. Cur'ous," I says, "but I'm dreaming that I was chatting with a little lady what just come out of here."

"Ach!" he says, quickly recovering his memory. "I know who

you mean. *Ja, ja,* a very nice lady, und a goot gustomer by me. I do anydings for her."

"Sure," I nodded. "You just about broke your neck to help her, I noticed, when that big false-alarm grabbed her out at the front door."

"Aber, mein herr!" He grabs me by the arm, and gives a scared look around. "Dot vas Colonel Esteban. You have heard of him, *nicht wahr?* Very bad man. He kill me in a minute, if I interfere."

"Bad man, huh? Well, I'm worse"—no harm in establishing a reputation—"and none too patient. Which reminds me that you ain't answered my question yet."

But this Jerry was too plumb rattled to get me. He kept whining that he had a wife and children, and that Esteban would have croaked him sure if he'd took a hand.

"Pesides," he went on with his excuses, "dot lady need no help. She can take care of herselluf."

I slams my hand down on the counter to shut him up.

"Name, please?" I says. "I ain't interested in none of these other details, nor in yet what would happen to your wife and family if they was fortunately relieved of your presence. Listen now—third and last call. Who's the lady?"

"Dot lady?" He stared at me like it was the first time I'd asked him. "V-y, dot's Señorita O'Beirne, the owner of de big Voreza ranch. 'Two-gun Gerta.'"

I looked at him to see if he was joking. For some time past, tales of a skirt who was carrying that label, and who was said to be just about running things down in her neck of the woods, had been coming across the border; but I'd heard too many greaser lies to take much stock in it. Furthermore, this Two-gun Gerta, according to all accounts, was as big as Jess Willard and meaner than seven rattlesnakes; not no slim, little girl that you wanted to take on your knee and tell not to cry."

"Quit your kidding, Butch," I says. "You can't put over nothing like that on me."

"But I speak de trut," he swears. "De lady is Two-gun Gerta.

Das ist recht. She haf seven noches on dose guns of hers. She de only one dat efer got anydings back from Manuel Esteban. His men dey requisition some of her cattle, und she raid his camp for it und at de point of her guns maig him pay a hundert und sixty dollars for efery dam' steer dey took.

"Dat's for v'y," he explained, "dat she und Esteban is enemies. Maybe, in de end, he kill her. Maybe she kill him. I don't know." He shrugged his shoulders. "But dey is bot' customers of mine; I take no sides.

"I tell you, d'ough"—he dropped his voice—"you want to watch oudt for yourselluf. Dot Esteban, he try to get you sure now for v'at you done. Und he is a bad hombre, I'll tell de vorld."

He shut up then; for a couple of greasers had drifted in, probably to see what him and me was chinning about. I figured that they'd likely dope it out that he'd been tipping me off as to the general characteristics of their countryman, my late adversus; so I gave a sort of a careless toss to my head, rolled another pill, and then, easing my gunbelt a bit, strolled out.

I wanted the impression to get out, you see, that I wasn't side-stepping nothing. You can pass for most anything, if you put up the right sort of a front. If this Esteban got an idea into his head that I was something of a killer myself, I judged that it might cool down his ardor.

So I swaggers up and down the street, trying to give a correct imitation of Bill Hart when he defies a gang of bloodthirsty supes, and bids 'em all come on. But all the time the sweat was running down the back of my neck, 'cause I didn't know just when that vengeful half-breed might take a pop at me from behind.

Course I knew that I was a dern fool. What all this dress-parading was going to get me, if I imbibed a slug of lead betwixt the shoulder blades, wasn't no question at all. If I was anything less than a triple-plated dumb-bell, I told myself, I'd be already on my horse and trying to see just how good time I could make back to the shelter of the Stars and Stripes.

But somehow I couldn't do it. I never run yet from anything the color of smoked side meat, and neither did I ever fail to keep an appointment with a lady. As between a bullet and the scornful look that I knew'd be in Miss O'Beirne's eyes if I didn't show up at our rendyvoo, I decided I'd chance the bullet. She was relying on that Irish name of mine, and the color of my hair; and I couldn't let her think they was false pretenses.

So I kept on ballyhooing around the burg, treating the natives to what I fondly hoped they would think was a murderous glare, and holding my face so straight in front of me that I almost sprained my neck.

But Yavisa ain't so big but what you can cover every hole and corner in it in the course of an hour; so by the time I had sauntered from the race track at one end to the Last Chance Saloon at the other and back again, and still wasn't plunked, I made up my mind that I'd either thrown the fear of the Lord into Esteban, or else that he wasn't so venomous as they made out. At any rate, it seemed idle to wear out any more shoe leather; so I retired to the hotel and went up to my room to decide on the next move.

"Be at the Cafe El Toro at ten o'clock," the little lady with the death dealers—which goes double for both her guns and her eyes—had told me. So along about nine I wanders over to that justly christened resort. Bull by name, and bull by nature, it was for the liquids they called whisky, rum, wine, gin, ale and beer was anything but, and the games that was running had every element in 'em except chance.

Play, however, was strong at both the bar and the tables. In fact, it seemed quite a night in the bright-lights district. A couple of near-by ranches had driven cattle over to the railroad that day, I found, and now the outfits was back for a celebration. These boys was mostly greasers with a sprinkling of border-jumpers among 'em; and after casting an eye over the lot, I decided there wasn't nobody I especially cared to pal up with.

One little, squint-eyed ex-burglar did sort of sidle up to me and try to get sociable.

"You're the guy that had the run-in with Esteban this afternoon, ain't you?" he says.

"Esteban?" I looks at him. "Oh, you mean that yellow cockroach I brushed out of my path this afternoon. Is that what they call a run-in down here?"

" 'Fraid you don't know what you're up against, bo." He shakes his head. "That ain't no cockroach you're fooling with, it's a tarantula. He holds a high hand in these parts. For you to linger around here is just the same as suicide. If I was you I'd backtrack real sudden for wherever you come from."

Well, that sounded friendly all right, but it struck me he was overacting a bit. I figured that he was either trying to shake my nerve, or to drive me outside where somebody'd be laying for me.

"Oh, I guess I'll stick around a while." I hunched my shoulders carelesslike "Fact is, the doctor recommended tarantulas to me as a diet. He said I was getting too fat on them scorpions and horned toads and Gila monsters I'd been browsing on."

"All right." He sheers off. "But I'll be obliged if you keep a reasonable distance away from me. I ain't aiming to be in no line of fire."

"Never fear," says I. "There's one insect I don't yearn for no close proximity to, and that's a louse."

But there must have been something in what this weinerwurst said; said; for I noticed that I was just about as popular in that assemblage as the smallpox. If I stepped up to the bar, they'd edge away and give me plenty of room. If I looked on at one of the games, interest would flag, and the winners would start to cash in.

There was a dance platform a the back, with an old tin-pan piano going and a pretty fair bunch of skirts. But could I grab off one of those Consuelas for a fox trot? Nothing doing. They was off like a flock of quail, if I so much as slanted a look at 'em.

Nobody seemed to want to talk to me or be in my neighborhood. I could have any part of the dump where I was to myself; when I started to move, the crowd scattered like I was a skunk.

Funny thing was to me, that I didn't get put out. I kept expecting it; for I didn't miss the sour looks the proprietor kept shooting at me from where he sat at the head of the bar. But he never
made a move; only sat there, chewing on the end of a cigar and
watching me.

Then about half past nine, Esteban prances in. I seen him as
he comes through the swing doors, but I'd have known who it
was even if my back had been turned, from the way the crowd
sort of tenses up.

I was ready for him, if he's planning to start anything; but he
don't. He don't even give me a tumble; just swaggers over to the
bar, and begins chinning with the proprietor. They have a couple
of drinks together, and two or three others come up and join
them. And still no attention paid to me. I can't make it a-tall.

Just the same, though, I knew that Esteban was up to mischief.
He was there to get me, and he was simply scheming to do it in
some treacherous greaser way.

And then I figures that it's time for me to make a move. I've
always found that in a scrap the first lick counts for a whole lot,
and I thinks to myself that I'll force the gentleman's hand.

So I jumps to my feet, kicking over a chair as I did so. At the
crash, the music stops, the players at the table turn around, the
line at the bar jumps back, and Esteban and his crowd swing
around quick toward me.

There's about twenty-five feet between him and me, a clear
lane; for the crowd, expecting immediate gun play, was pressing
back to give us room.

We eyed each other across that open space, him and me. Then
he set down the glass he still had in his hand and folded his arms,
with a sneer on his lips.

Smooth, wasn't it? He'd got the edge on me. There ain't no
place—not even in Mexico—where it's justifiable to shoot down
a man that stands up to you with his arms folded. If I tried it, I'd
be bumped off by some of his friends before I'd even got a hand
on my gun. Probably there was twenty-five cannisters trained

on me at that minute in the hope that I'd make a fool move of
the sort.

But I ain't so slow on the thing myself. Quick as a wink, I
flings out my arms wide to show that I'm empty-handed; and
then, matching him sneer for sneer, folds 'em across my chest.
I've got him whipsawed.

Course, I was taking a long chance. Somebody in the crowd
might have dropped me, claiming to have misunderstood my
action. But then if I'd made a draw, they'd have certainly did it.
I judged that I could hold 'em a second or two by the surprise of
the thing, which proved correct.

But what was I to do now? You can only stand and sneer for
just so long, and already my nose was beginning to tickle. If I
sneezed, I was lost. I was too far from the door to strut out. I'd
have to go slow and contemptuous, and on the way some of his
gang was sure to get me in the back. I had to make a play of
some sort. Maybe, I could taunt him into going for his rod or
knife. Then it would be up to the quickness of my hand and eye.

"Listen, Crooked Mouth!" I digs at him. "You've been
making your half-breed brags that I couldn't stay in this town.
Yet when I face you, you're afraid to shoot it out. You fight with
women, I see, and not with men. So, you big, yellow cur, since I
can't kill you, I am going to pull your nose."

Still, with arms folded, he stands and looks at me. I didn't like
it. There was murder in his eyes all right, but not the red rage
I'd expected from my taunting. There wasn't a quiver in his face,
nor no change of color; his lips didn't tighten or go white. All I
saw was just a sort of cold, gloating triumph.

But, having announced myself I had to go through with it.
Slow and disdainful, I starts toward him, head up, arms folded,
but watching him like a hawk.

One step, I takes two, three, four, five. I was about ten feet
away from him now, and still he was steady as a rock. Not the
shift of a muscle in him, not a change in that gloating sneer.

Then suddenly his arms unfolds, and I am looking into the

muzzles of two guns. One of his hangers-on had edged up close behind him, and slipped 'em into his hands.

All too late, I seen the trap I had walked into. I didn't dare turn my head, but I could feel some of his bunch pressing in on me on either side. And I knew what would happen next. Someone behind me would jerk one of my arms down, and—well, there would be plenty to swear that I had tried to draw. Please omit flowers.

I thought of a thousand things in a second, but none of 'em seemed to fit. As the cards lay, my life was worth just about the price of a sand-flea in Senegambia.

Then, all at once, the swing doors of the Cafe El Toro jerked open. Bang! Bang! Esteban's guns clatter to the floor. I see him clutch out with his empty hands, and crumple down in a heap. And through the smoke of the two revolver shots, I saw the genteel little lady of that afternoon, my new boss, standing in the doorway.

She had took in the situation as she stepped inside, and pulling both her guns, had fired so quick that it sounded like a single shot.

CHAPTER III

BEWILDERMENT

HOW I got there, I'll never be able to tell you; but before the echo of those two shots had stopped, and while Esteban was still lurching to the floor, I was over at the girl's side, and had my own gun out and ready for business.

I hadn't no other idea, you see, but what the gang would rush us as soon as their first surprise was over.

"You get out," I jerked to her over my shoulder. "I can hold 'em until you make your get-away."

But she only laughs at me.

"Don't get nervous, Red," she says; "and put that gun of yours away. None of this rabble is going to take the chance of a return shot from me. They know how quick I am on the trigger."

As she spoke, she was stuffing her own artillery down into her belt; and then, bold as brass, she pushes past me and saunters over toward the bar.

Esteban was rolling around on the floor, cursing and groaning, and all the rest was holding back as if waiting to see what she was going to do. She looks down sort of regretful.

"It was an awful temptation, Crooked Mouth," she says, "not to have given you your finish that time, and probably an error on my part. But I've always planned to have you facing me when I did it, and besides, you might have got Red before you went. So I had to aim at your hands. You won't be using a knife or gun for some time, I'm thinking."

I seen then that she'd merely punctured him very neat through both wrists. Some headpiece on that dame, I'll say—to figure it all out just so in no more than the flicker of a cat's eyelash.

Esteban don't make no answer to her at all, except just about all the rotten cuss words in the Spanish language, and that ain't a few.

She stands it for maybe thirty seconds; then she stiffens up.

"I am accustomed only to the society of gentlemen," she says, looking around at the crowd, cold as ice. "Some of you pick up that foul-mouthed brute and get him out of here—over to the medico's. Any of the rest of you who can't control his speech in a lady's presence can follow."

She was certainly playing a high hand. Here she swanks into a dump that is Esteban's especial headquarters and filled with a mob of his followers; and she not only cracks down on him, but defies the whole bunch and tells 'em how they got to behave.

I was plumb nervous, I'm free to admit. Many's the ugly look I seen cast at her, and I knew that only a spark was needed to start the fireworks. Our cue, as I seen it, was to mosey while we had a chance. But she kept on dallying there, as unconcerned as if she was in her own parlor; and not a yegg among them dared so much as spit. I guess it was just the unadulterated gall of her that done it.

Over to the bar she prances, and tosses a yellowback peso note across to the proprietor.

"Give the boys what they want on me, Tony," she says, and as the gang crowds up, she pours out a big hooker of whiskey for herself.

"Here's to crime," she says, and swings the glass up to her lips. But I was watching her, and I noticed that she kept the drink well covered with her hand, and furthermore, that a minute later while the rest was naming their poison, she emptied it into the spittoon.

The proprietor brought her back her change.

"Oh, give us another round." She pushed it away.

Then her voice suddenly dropped. Only her and me and him could hear the words.

"Listen, Tony!" She was smiling, but her remarks certainly had a razor edge to 'em. "You can be as friendly with Esteban as you like, but don't you ever let him stage another affair here with one of my men or I'll wipe your robbing joint off the earth."

The proprietor cringes and commences rubbing his hands.

"I did not know, señorita that the stranger was—"

"Well, see that you do know the next time," she cuts him short. "And now I've got to be going." She swings around to the crowd again. "It's a long ride to the ranch. Drink hearty boys, and bueno noches. Come, Red."

It's funny what a couple of drinks will do. Five minutes before that bunch was ready to murder her for interfering with their gentle pastimes, and there wasn't no guarantee they wouldn't lay for her the next time she went out; but just then she was the kangaroo's tiara.

"*Viva, la señorita!*" they kept shouting as we went out. "*Viva,* Two-gun Gerta!" You'd have thought she was just elected mayor, the racket they made.

She kept waving her hand and joshing back at 'em until we got through the swing doors. But what do you know about women, anyhow? We wasn't hardly outside before she says:

"Red, I believe I am going to faint!"

Darned, if she didn't flop over on me, dead as a mackerel.

Nice position for a law-abiding guy in a strange town, wasn't it? Nobody to call on for help but that crew of carousing cutthroats we'd just left; and a unconscious lady on my hands.

"Here, you can't do that!" I says, giving her a kind of shake; and either that or something else brung her to.

She opens her eyes and looks around kind of dazed; then as she realizes that she's reclining on my manly breast, she straightens up sudden, and I can see her blushing in the moonlight. She's still weaving on her pins, though, and I stand ready to catch her in case she keels again.

"Give me your arm, Red," she says, "and help me over to the horses. We can't linger here; for I miss my guess, if most of that cheering multitude won't soon be off to waylay us."

I convoys her across the street to where her pinto is hitched, and I lifts her up into the saddle. Gosh! She didn't weigh more than the pinfeather of a hummingbird.

"All right?" I asks.

"Oh, quite," she says.

But when I'd mounted my own cayuse, I edges him in close beside her'n, and I rides with one arm around her. I told her it would be safer that a way until her faintness wore off; and she thought so, too—at least, she didn't pull away from me none.

Pretty soon, though, she says she's plumb herself again, and that we got to be making some speed. With that, she draws away and starts to ride. But we ain't gone more than a quarter of a mile before she stops sudden, and gives me the office to keep quiet.

"Did you hear that?" she whispers sharplike.

The only thing I could hear was the breathing of the horses and the rustling of the chaparral in the wind; but I nodded just the same. I wasn't going to let her think I was any less of an Indian than she was.

"They are taking the other trail to head us off," she mutters. "There! You can hear them again."

I did get it now—a faint, far-away thudding of hoofs.

"Come!" she says, jerking up her pony's head. "We can beat them to the ranch, if we take it as the crow flies."

Blamed if she didn't turn off the trail, and go crashing right into that mess of thorn bushes that was all around us. Nothing for me to do but to follow. I didn't like it a little bit, and Henry Ford, my horse, seconded the motion, which made it unanimous; but what else was there to do? When Henry Ford tried to swerve, I give him about a inch of spur; and in we went slap-dash, helter skelter after her.

Talk about the great, open spaces! If there was any opening in that patch of chaparral, me and Henry certainly failed to find it.

We had to make ours. Them branches was wove together as tight as a Navajo blanket, I tell you. And thorns! It was like wrastlin' with a army of fretful porcupines.

The girl and her pinto seemed to have a knack of twisting and turning and getting through without much damage; but me and poor Henry, we banged against everything that was there to be banged into. Vivisection would 'a' been soothing and restful, compared with it.

Still and all, we managed to keep right at her heels. I'll tell the world she was fanning some. If there's a world's record for sprinting through chaparral, I'll bet it was smashed that night.

But nothing don't last forever. After we'd cantered through about two hundred miles of that devilish stuff—or maybe it was only about two miles in fact—we came to a arroyo.

"All right, Red?" she asks, half stopping and turning about as me and Henry lunged out of the tangle.

"Sure!" what was left of me lies heartily. "You didn't think those little bushes was going to stop me, did you?"

"Follow me, then!" she sings out. "And make it snappy. We've got to be moving, or they'll waylay us sure." And off she went again.

Gee! What a pace that little pinto set. Course he wasn't carrying no weight to speak of—she didn't heft no more than a wart on a mosquito's nose—and poor, old Henry was loaded down with one hundred and eighty pounds of me, and all my traps to boot. But, oh boy, if a horse ever had his work cut out for him, Henry had it that night.

Hard sand or soft sand, sagebrush or clear footing, up hill or down hill, it didn't seem to make no difference to the pinto. A airplane couldn't have skimmed along no smoother. And me and Henry kept nosing along right behind him, not more than half a length away.

Up a little rise we swept, and down the other side around a sort of corner of rock. And then all-round us dark forms popped up, and there was a banging of guns and a screeching and yelling fit to wake the dead. I didn't need no interpreter to tell me that we had run into a nest of old Jazzbo Esteban's merry men.

Naturally I reached for my gun. But—would you believe it—"Brown Bess" wasn't there. Empty was the cradle, the baby gone away. I figured that it must have been jerked loose from me while I was roughing it through that darned chaparral.

Also I seen that, for all her boasts, she wasn't making no move to bring her Colts into play. Too rattled, I supposed, by the unexpectedness of the attack.

So, from where I sat, it looked like the only thing to do was to be getting away from there, and not to lose no time doing it.

"Get a move on you, ma'am!" I yells back at her, for in the mix-up I had got separated from her and was now a little distance ahead. "Our only chance is to make a run for it."

But I was just about four seconds too late. The words wasn't fairly out of my mouth yet, when two of the gang had the pinto by the bridle and was holding him, while a dozen others dashed down at her from the rocks like a pack of coyotes.

Quick as a flash, I whirled Henry Ford on his hind hoofs and started to reach her side. I didn't have no very clear idea in my nut of just what I was going to do; but I guess I was sort of planning to scatter 'em by a charge, and then if I couldn't do any better, grab her up like young Lochinvar and ride off with her. Henry wouldn't hardly have knowed he was carrying double, with such a mite of extra weight on his back as her.

Anyhow, I was certain I wasn't going to let them rotten greasers get her; not unless they downed me first.

There was about fifty yards between us when I started for her; and as I settled Henry to the rush, I seen a sort of a snaky, black circle swing out overhead between me and the sky. I gave a jerk to his head, at the same time touching him in the flank with my spur; and straight up in the air he went like a rocket. Then, as we came down, he leaped forward; and where we ought to have been but wasn't, there was a loop of rope laying harmless on the ground.

A pretty little stunt, eh, what? But it wasn't the first time me and Henry had jumped through a cast lariat, and we didn't waste no time pluming ourselves over it.

Instead, we went right ahead to rescue the girl. I guess the way we went at it must have looked like business to them Mexicans 'cause what of 'em could get out of the way scattered like sheep, and the rest began throwing up their hands and hollering for mercy.

But I wasn't taking no chances with that kind of cattle, not with the odds they had against me; and, surrender or no surrender, I'd have rode right over 'em, if it hadn't been for the girl.

As I come whirling down at that panic-stricken bunch, I hears her let out a yell.

"Red! Stop!" she shrieks. "You mustn't hurt these men. You don't understand. This is my crowd."

At the same time, she pulls them two Colts, which hitherto she has been giving a holiday, and she fires a couple of shots which kicks up the dust about a inch ahead of Henry's forefeet.

Well, I was so flabbergasted that I guess I'd have kept going right on. But that Henry horse is a wiser bird than I am, Gunga Din. He knows that when a lady says "Halt!" and emphasizes it with a couple of Colts, it's etiquette to agree; and he done it so abrupt, that I almost went off over his ears.

Maybe I would have, if just at the same second another lariat, which we didn't jump through, hadn't settled over my shoulders and held me tight.

"That's more like it!" said Two-gun Gerta, giving a nod of satisfaction when she seen they had me fast.

Then she began spilling a mess of Spanish at 'em, which as near as I could follow it meant that they was to tie me tight, and bring me along to the ranch.

"A dirty Irish trick, isn't it, Mr. Red?" she says, turning to me with a funny sort of a smile.

But I'd have died before I let her see that I was sore.

"Far be it from me to question anything that a member of

your charming sex may do, Miss O'Beirne," says I. "Whatever the game may be, I'm still sitting in. It's worth all this," I says, "just to have had the pleasure of having you faint in my arms."

She turned red as a cherry there in the moonlight, and she gave the pinto a slash with the whip that sent him scooting.

So it wasn't my goat but hers that was got, after all.

CHAPTER IV

A PROPOSITION

IF THIS bunch that had me was the little lady's outfit as she claimed, there wasn't no doubt about 'em obeying orders. She'd told 'em to tie me tight, and they certainly done that little job to the queen's taste. When they got through with me, I looked more like a coil of clothesline than a human being, and I couldn't so much as wiggle a toe joint.

There was one thing, though, that they couldn't hogtie nor gag, to wit, my brains; and them was certainly having a busy session, only they didn't seem to be getting much of anywhere.

Leave it to yourself. S'pose now, you'd 'a' saved a fair maiden's life, rescuing her from a murdering bandit; and then s'pse she'd saved yours in return, and the two of you had rode off together in the moonlight? It would have looked kind of romantical to you, wouldn't it?

But all the romance I'd got out of it was to be dragged through a bunch of chaparral till I didn't have a whole rag left on me; and then have a bunch of *tamales* sicked onto me, that tied me up and brung me along to the ranch like I was a horse thief.

What could you make of it, I ask you? I hadn't done nothing to her except to keep Esteban from caving his initials on her face, and I was content to let that end the matter. 'Twas she herself that had offered me a job, and made me come along with her. Friendly enough, too, she had seemed; even a bit more. It wasn't altogether weakness that made her snuggle up to me, when we was riding together out of Yavisa.

No; figure it any way I tried, I couldn't make head nor tail out of it. She couldn't have sized me up as a spy, or an enemy, or nothing like that; not after she'd seen them two run-ins I had with Esteban.

Then what did she size me up for? And what was she planning to do with me? It was sure plum beyond me, and about all I succeeded in doing was to scramble my brains, puzzling over it. There wasn't no answer; and the harder you circled around trying to find one, the worse you got bogged.

Meanwhile, we was jogging briskly along, and in the course of about an hour we fetched up at the ranch.

Some dizzy joint, believe me. An old Mexican hacienda, it had evidently been in the days when them haughty old Dons would call one a piker who owned less than six counties; but at present, the layout reminded me more of an army post.

There was a high stockcade all around it made of sharpened logs, and laced together so tight that you couldn't hardly have slipped a postal card through the cracks and about every fifty feet or so along it, there was a sentry box and also an embrasure with a very businesslike machine gun sticking its nose out of it.

That all this wasn't just for show was proved by the fact that we hadn't hardly got within hearing distance of the place before there was a strong searchlight turned on us. They plainly weren't taking no chances on having anybody sneak up on 'em without knowing who it was.

Even after that, we was sharply challenged when we reached the gate, and Gerta had to ride ahead and give the password before they would let us in. Finally, though, a drawbridge was lowered, big doors of heavy planking was slid back, and we rode through.

The inclosure inside the stockade was about a half mile square, I should say; and it made you think of the place as a fort even more than the outside did.

In the center was the ranch house, built of adobe in a kind of Spanish mission style, but without no windows on the ground floor, only narrow slits for loopholes, from which I gathered that it had been put up in the old days when Injuns was plenty in the neighborhood and a massacre was the favorite local sport. Also, it looked kind of moth-eaten.

Originally, I suppose, like most of the houses of the sort, there was quarters for the horses in the cellar; but with all that bunch what Gerta had on hand, there wasn't room for that now; so there was a big corral back of the house, and also a row of rough stalls that served as stables.

Besides that, there was a lot of low sheds which from the gangs loafing about 'em, smoking cigarettes and et cetera, I sized up as barracks for the men.

All this, I sort of caught in a bird's eye flash as we galloped from the gate across a hard-baked parade ground up to the house; and the chief impression I got from the layout was that the business at this ranch was a whole lot more connected with guns than with plowshares, with fighting than with raising fodder.

If I was planning to go into the bandit industry, I wouldn't want a more complete and efficient plant than this appeared to be. Which at the time, and from where I was sitting, gave food for thought, as the poet says.

Still, at that, I couldn't yet figure out what they wanted of me. There wasn't no special reason that they should have mistook me for J.P. Morgan; and if they was banking on me being a American citizen and that the state department would put up a big ransom for me, I saw where they had likely disappointment coming to 'em. Any request of that kind, I felt, Charlie Hughes would just politely drop in the waste basket.

But, as I didn't have anything else to do, I naturally kept on puzzling. We had ridden through a big archway into the house, and I was now stabled in a big, inside patio, with balconies running all around it on the second floor, and the open sky overhead.

A couple of roustabouts jerked me off my horse, and set me

down on a bench, but they didn't offer to untie me. They just went off about their own business, and didn't pay no more attention to me.

So there I rested for an hour. An hour, did I say? It seemed like all the years since creation, with no time off for good conduct. And me fairly dying for a smoke; but without no chance to roll one, and the greasers only grinning at me, when I tried to make 'em understand what I wanted.

At last, though, about the year A.D.3089, a big mutt come over and began unwinding my ropes, and then when he'd got me back to normalcy, he took me by the arm, and marched me into the house.

"Well, here's where I probably learn something," I says to myself. But once more I was fooled. All he did was to lead me upstairs, to a room on the second floor, and leave me there alone.

Room, I said; but it was really more like a church—big as all outdoors, with great beams across the ceiling and little windows high up, and the walls all covered with tapestries and hangings. It reminded me of a set in a theater.

There was little tables standing around with lamps and handsome things on 'em, and easy-chairs, too, and divans; but I didn't dare set down. I didn't dare smoke, neither. I just stood there and waited.

No use to try for a escape then. I seemed to be alone all right; but I was pretty sure that somebody was watching me from somewhere, and I'd 'a' been a boob to start anything. Besides, I was kind of getting interested.

Then, all at once, the doors at the upper end of the room opened, and as I looked, I couldn't do nothing but just open and shut my mouth like a fish.

I realized at last what all the delay was about; for a woman never takes no 'count of time when she'd dolling herself up, and that's what this Gerta had been up to.

I couldn't believe at first that it was really her. I'd thought, just seeing her in her riding clothes, that she was pretty nice. But now, by gum, she was the bird of paradise's left ear! She was all in white, tricked out like she was a prima donna, with her neck and arms bare, and a black lace shawl over her white shoulders. Her hair was piled up on her head, and had a big red rose stuck in it on one side. There was diamonds sparkling at her throat, and on her fingers; but they wasn't no brighter than her eyes nor more heart-thrilling than her smile. If anyone ever wanted to know why men leave home, the answer was right there. By my halidome, she was a wow!

Well, she come down toward me, and waves me to a seat. I collapses onto this here divan just in time to save me from flopping to the floor. She had sure knocked me groggy.

"Surprised, Red?" she says, smiling, as she set down beside me.

It was up to me then, of course, to say something pretty but I simply couldn't do it. All I could do was just to slump there like a dumb Isaac, and goggle at her.

Still she didn't seem in no way offended. I guess, maybe, she was enjoying the knock-out she'd handed me.

"Now, I'm going to explain what all this means," she says. "This ranch and a lot of other Mexican property came down to my brother and myself as an inheritance from my father. It came into his possession when old Voreza died, as a result of heavy loans he had advanced upon it and when he himself died about a year later, proved to be practically his entire estate.

"It wasn't a good time to sell, probably it would have been impossible to find a purchaser; consequently, my brother and I decided to come down here and take charge ourselves. We have always been looked upon as interlopers by the native population; still we have managed to get along and make a fair return on the investment. That is, we did get along until this Manuel Esteban set himself up as dictator of the region, supporting himself and his army of cutthroats by levying tribune on every one he could force to pay it.

"I refused, and he then did me the honor to say that he admired my spirit, and proposed that I should marry him. For answer, I slapped him in the face. Since then, it has been war between us. He steals my cattle and ravages my crops whenever he gets a opportunity. I make such reprisals as I can. Meanwhile, the ranch is going to rack and ruin. The men chafe at obeying a woman.

"For a long while, I have realized that what I need is a capable man to act as manager for me. My brother, who is younger than myself, is unfitted for such responsibility. What I required was a cool, experienced, absolutely fearless and staunchly loyal person, who could combine in himself the qualifications of both a military leader and a crack ranchman. An article of that sort is not so easy to find.

"Then by lucky chance I meet you—an American, evidently familiar with every phase of ranch life, and a perfect Lancelot."

I kind of stiffens up at this, and breaks in on her.

"A which, ma'am?" I says coldly.

"A Lancelot," she says; "a gallant, courageous gentleman."

"Oh?" I stammers. "I thought you was calling me some kind of a sissy. Or, no: I remember now. That's little Lord Fauntleroy."

Well, there ain't no use in giving you all the rest of the interview. What I've told you will give you a line on what she was after.

Only, I wanted to know, of course, what was the big idea in trailing me off on a wild-goose chase through all those thorn bushes, and then having me took prisoner by her greasers.

"Oh, that," she says, "was all arranged as a sort of a test for you. I had to be certain, you see, that you were really the man I wanted. Probably, if I had known beforehand of the nerve you showed in facing Esteban there at the Cafe El Toro, I wouldn't have done it. But the stage was all set, and my men waiting; so I decided to carry it through, believing that it would be an excellent introduction of you to them, as showing them your caliber in an emergency. I certainly couldn't have asked for better results," she said, her eyes shining.

"Then 'twas you that got my gun, when you was leaning

against me there just outside of Yavisa, pretending to be all in?" I says.

She nodded.

"But you'll forgive me, won't you?" she says. "You'll forgive me for that, and all the rest, now that I've explained the reason for it—Red?"

When she smiled in that sort of coaxing way she done then, a man'd have forgiven her for stealing his last shirt.

"Sure," I tells her. "I don't really see how you could have done nothing else."

But at that, I'd have been better pleased if she hadn't told me that when she snuggled up to me, it was just to swipe my gun.

"And you'll be my manager?" she asks; and again I answers "Yes."

Well we talked for quite a spell longer; and then she says she's sure I must be dying for sleep, and she calls a chink servant and has me took to a bedroom that might have been fixed up for a king.

But with all I'd been through, my head was whirling so, that it wasn't easy to get to sleep.

I kept thinking over that story of hers; and although it had run along smooth enough, the more I thought about it, the more it struck me that she was holding something back on me.

Well, if she had, it was fifty-fifty. Here was I, engaged as a experienced ranch boss; and all the ranching I'd ever done in my life was as a cowpuncher in the movies.

I was just a plain counterfeit. A ranch boss? Why I hadn't never even seen a ranch. This here trip was the first time I'd ever been west of Fort Lee, New Jersey.

I tell you, as I thought it over, my conscience hurt me for stringing her along as I'd done, and yet I just couldn't make up my mind to give her the straight of it.

There was only one thing to do, that I could see; and that was—experience or no experience—to make good.

So, having made up my mind to that little thing, I turned over and burrowed into my pillow.

Then, just as I'd settled down, there pealed through the silence the most awful sound I ever heard—a long-drawn cry of someone in terrible agony—the voice of a woman!

I started up all excited and started for the door.

Again that awful cry rang out, seeming to come from far down in the depths of the house.

For a moment, I blundered in the darkness; then I reached the door, and flung it open.

But, as I did so, the chink who had showed me to my room jumped up from where he was squatting outside, and shoved a forty-five in my face.

"You go back." He grinned. "Missee say you not to be let out."

CHAPTER V

A MISTAKE

THERE'S A saying I've heard pretty often, that no one needn't ever be afraid of a Chinaman with a gun, 'cause a chink'll always turn his head away and shut his eyes when he pulls the trigger.

Personally I ain't never put the question to a test so I can't say for certain whether it's the truth or not. But there is a rule that I ain't never known to fail; don't take no chances with a guy that grins and speaks soft when he bends the old canister on you. And that goes for me, whether said guy is a slant-eyed heathen, or one of the Hudson Dusters.

Course, if there'd been a camera grinding, and a director bawling at me through a megaphone, I'd have done one of them showy stunts like kicking the rod out of his hands, or turning a somersault in the air and grabbing him from behind. But, believe me, your impulses is a whole lot different when it's blanks you are facing and when it's real honest lead.

What I actually done was to back up a hasty step or two inside the doorway, and temp'rarily at least, let the chink have his own way.

"Missee says I'm not to be let out, eh?" I repeats. "Well, of course, that makes it different. No one but a roughneck would fail to respect the wishes of his hostess. But if questions ain't also barred, kindly tell me, Confucius, what all the hollerin' was about?"

"Me no savvy hollerin'," he says.

"You didn't hear nothin?"

He looks at me straight in the eyes, and shakes his head.

"Then what's that behind you!" I shouts, pointing over his shoulder.

It's an old trick; but it hardly ever misses, if you can catch a guy off his guard.

The chink whirled around to look; and as he did so, I sprang for him.

Down he went under me, and I grabbed for his hand with the pistol. Anybody else would 'a' had the breath jolted out of their body. But gee, what a scrap he put up.

He hadn't barely touched the floor before he was arching up under me like a cat, and wriggling and squirming to get free of my grip. It was like trying to hold a boa constrictor, and all the time he was screeching and spitting like a nest of wild cats.

Over and over we rolled, first me on top, and then him; but me holding the barrel of that gun away from me all the time, and him trying to twist it around and pull the trigger.

Well, of course we didn't make any noise—not any more than a trunk full of bricks falling down five flights of stairs. We was banging each other's heads against the boards whenever we got a chance, and stamping with our feet, and throwing each other around pretty lively. I could hear voices downstairs asking excited questions and footsteps running.

Just about then, the chink got his free hand fastened on my throat in a grip I couldn't shake off. I could feel his long finger-nails digging into my jugular, and his thumb pressing against my Adam's apple so as to completely shut off my wind. Everything began to turn black in front of me. I knew that my hold on the pistol was weakening. Another ten seconds, and it'd all be over.

But at that moment, he sort of twisted over on his side; and my left hand was loose and up above his shoulder.

Using all the strength I had left, I chopped down with it sidewise on the back of his neck in the far-famed rabbit punch which is barred in all respectable fight clubs, but is continually used by pugilists when the referee ain't looking.

Did it work? I'll say it did. Mr. Chink didn't have no more fight left in him than a fishing worm. He just kind of relaxed like he'd been gave a whiff of ether, and laid there quivering.

I jerked the gun loose from his uncurling fingers, and got up to face the crowd of greasers that was piling up the stairway.

Probably I'd have commenced shooting in another second, for the bunch didn't look none too friendly, and I was still shaky and half dazed from the mauling I'd been through.

But just then, Gerta pushed her way through the mob, and came running toward me.

"Here! Here! What's the trouble about?" she demands, looking from me to the chink still stretched out on the floor.

"Trouble, ma'am?" I says sort of sarcastic. "I ain't seen none. As boss of this here ranch, I was just enforcing a little discipline. The chink tells me I can't come out of my room, and I had to show him where he was wrong."

By this time my late sparring partner had managed to sit up. The little rice birds was likely still twittering in his ears, but he had corralled some of his scattered senses.

"Melican man say, lookum behind," he tried to alibi himself. "Me lookee, and him jump. Me catchum; then we roll, one, two, three times, and him hand me a wallup. Here." He felt the back of his neck kind of tenderlike. "No more savvy. Me go to sleep."

His blue shirt was tore, and one of his almond eyes is closed, and he's otherwise pretty well scratched up. She looks at him sort of disgusted.

"One wallop?" she says. "You couldn't be much worse off, if you'd had a tussle with a catamount. Better finish out your nap," she says, waving him toward the stairs. "I don't believe, Wong, you'll be any good for several days."

At the same time, she turns to the crowd at the head of the stairs, and tells them in Spanish to make 'emselves scarce, too.

"*Vamos!*" she says. "I can handle this without any assistance."

Then, when they had gone, and we two was alone, she looks at me, coldlike and disapproving.

"Maybe you will tell me now the reason for this outbreak, Connors?" she says stiffly.

"Just what I told you, ma'am. I started to come out of my room, and the chink up and sticks a gun in my face and says for me to stay inside. Course, then, I had to show my authority."

"But why did you want to come out?" she asks quick.

"Why?" I gave a start; in all this excitement, I had half forgot all about that God-awful screech. "My Lord, ma'am. You didn't expect me to lay quiet, did you, when someone was being murdered?"

"Someone being murdered?" She frowns. "What on earth do you mean?"

"Well, it sure sounded like it," I muttered. "Such an unearthly yell I never heard in all my born days. T'was a woman, too—a woman in terrible agony."

"Oh?" she says. "I begin to understand." Then she starts to laugh. "What an absurd mistake! That was my maid, Dolores, in one of her nightmares. We have gotten so accustomed to those wild outcries of hers, that we don't pay any attention to them. Still, I can hardly blame you for thinking it a murder." She laughed again.

Well, that sounded reasonable all right; but somehow her laugh didn't ring just a hundred percent true. She was looking at me sharp, too, as if to see how I'd take it.

"All right, ma'am," I says. "Sorry to have caused trouble. Still that don't altogether explain why the chink was stationed at my door. When he bent the gun on me, and says that I've got to stay inside, he told me it was by your orders."

"But that was for your own protection," she insists. "You know what a cattle outfit is, when a newcomer joins up. I was afraid they might try to haze you, or annoy you in some way, and I thought you had been through enough for one night. So I posted Wong at your door with instructions that you were not to be disturbed; I told him you must be permitted to sleep. Don't blame me for his stupidity."

If it wasn't on the level, you sure had to give her credit for being a quick thinker. There wasn't nothing I could say; and yet I was far from being satisfied. Somehow, I had an uneasy feeling that I was being flimflammed.

"Nobody to blame but myself, Miss O'Beirne," I says. "Nobody a-tall. But, as I've got a settled objection to staying any place where I've made a fool of myself, I guess, if you don't mind, we'll call that deal of yourn and mine off. 'Twas a mistake of mine anyhow a-coming here; I ain't ready yet to buckle down to a regular job. I want to travel round a bit first, and see some-pin more of the country."

"Very well," she says, distant as the north pole; "if that is the way you feel about it."

I had been standing with my back against the wall, while I was talking to her, so as to get some support; for my old head was weaving and I was feeling weak and sick from the scrimmage with the chink. I was about all in. I realized that if I didn't get away mighty quick, I'd disgrace myself by flopping.

"So thank you kindly, ma'am," I says; "and if you'll please let me know where I can find my horse, and give orders to pass me out of the stockade, I guess I'll be on my way."

I was waiting for her to move on, 'cause I was sure I'd wabble and make a show of myself if I got away from the wall but she just stood there, looking at me. Nothing to do, but go ahead anyhow.

The floor was heaving up and down in front of me, and she seemed all funny and blurred-like. But I stiffened up my knees and took a grip on myself like a souse does when he's trying to play sober; and I starts very straight and dignified for my room to get my pack. Gosh! That corridor seems like a million miles across, and it was pitching and tossing something scandalous.

One step I takes; two, three. I kept my face toward her, cause I had a nasty cut on the back of my head, and didn't want her to see it. But I was so woozy, I forgot the blood would show all over the back of my shirt.

"Red!" she gasps all of a sudden, and makes a dive for me. "You're hurt! You're bleeding!"

She ought to have had better sense than to pounce at me like that. It sort of throwed me off my balance, I guess; for my knees gave way, and down I went in a dead faint.

The next thing I knew, I was laying on a bed, and someone was a-fixing a bandage round my head—someone with gentle fingertips.

I laid still, never letting on that I'd come to; for I hadn't been three years in the pictures without learning what'd be the next shot. Unconscious heroes always has to be kissed.

But somehow the touch of soft lips didn't come off per schedule. Also, although I sniffed for all I was worth, I couldn't catch no faint, delicate perfume. All I could get was a snootfull of arnica with a strong chaser of garlic to it.

So pretty soon I got tired of waiting, and I opened my eyes. And lo and behold, it wasn't Gerta that was bandaging me at all, but a skinny old Mexican hag with her teeth gone.

Gerta was standing over by the door and when she seen that I'd come around, 'twasn't love words she handed me, but a bawling out for giving her such a fright. She was all white and scared looking, and she sure took it out on me for upsetting her so.

"Why didn't you tell me you were hurt, you big booby," she raged, "instead of trying to carry it off in that silly way? You seem to have a perfect genius for creating scenes!

"Well, you don't need to be bothered with no more of 'em," I returns, good and sore over letting myself be pawed by that old garlic hound under a misnomer, as you might say, "You'll soon be rid of my unpleasing company." And I starts to get up.

But I ain't no more than swung my legs over the side of the bed, than she's over there, pushing me back on the pillows.

"Don't you dare, sir!" she says. "And don't let me hear another word about you leaving. You're going to stay right here, and be my ranch manager just as you promised. Oh Red!!" she says, her lips quivering. "I need you—even if you kill every darned Chinaman on the place!"

"Well, what else could I do?" I mutters. "I heard a woman scream, and the only thought I had was that it might be you. I had to get there."

"You thought it might be me, and you had to get there!" Her voice broke a little, and her eyes were shining. "Oh, if you only knew what it means to me to hear you say that. To know there is somebody I can trust, upon whom I can absolutely rely. You will agree to stay and help me out, Red?"

"But I ain't fit to be no ranch manager, Miss O'Beirne. I've got to tell you the truth. I—"

"Let me be the judge of your fitness," she breaks in. "Besides, you have done enough talking. What you've got to do now is keep quiet. Dolores says you're not seriously hurt, only suffering from loss of blood. So we're going to leave you alone to go to sleep. But"—she shakes a key at me—"to prevent any more wild forays on your part, I am going to lock you in."

She laughed like it was a good joke; but when I heard the key grating in the lock, I realized that she was in earnest, too.

She was sure bound to see that I didn't make a sneak on her in the night—maybe, also, that I didn't go roaming around and pipe off something I wasn't wanted to know.

CHAPTER VI

THE RESCUE

I T ' S F U N N Y about the difference between darkness and daylight. That night the old house seemed as full of mysteries as a dog is of fleas; yet the next morning when I woke up to find Dolores bringing me my breakfast on a tray, and the room flooded with sunlight, any such idea seemed pure foolishness.

The old mystery loose then seemed to be how I could have got so fussed up over nothing. It sure ain't nothing strange for a person in a nightmare to give a blood-curdlin' screech. Why, come to think of it, old "Idaho Joe," the real cow-puncher with our picture outfit, what learnt me all I know, he used to yell like a Comanche in his sleep.

As for the rest of it—the bandit-like hangout, and the chink at my door, and even the locking me in—Gerta's explanations was certainly straight enough to settle any suspicions. Trouble with me is I've always had too much imagination. Born actor, I guess; see a part open, and I've got to jump in and play it. Maybe, too, that's what makes me so nosey and curious—imagining things.

But as I say, the bright morning sunlight don't give much chance for make-believe; and the smell of the sizzling ham and eggs and the coffee what Dolores had on her tray was satisfyingly real.

I set up in bed, and lost no time pitching into it.

"The señor feel better to-day? *Si?*" grins the old wren. "But 'e mus' stay in bed. Señorita Gerta sys 'e mus' not get up."

"Stay in bed, eh?" I passes up a mouthful. "Not a chance. Does she think a little bump on the bean like that is going to put me on the hospital list?"

As soon as my fair waitress had gone out with the tray, I hops up and begins shaving. I'd just about got into my boots, and had knotted a new red-and-blue han'kcher round my throat, when Gerta herself comes storming in.

"What does this mean?" she says.

"Nothing," I observes. "cept it's a large, fine morning, and if I'm going to be ranch boss here, I'd better be getting on the job."

"Your job right now is to stay still, and get well."

"Huh!" says I, sarcastical. "If I was any weller, they'd have to tie sand bags to me to hold me down." Which wasn't strictly true, for my legs was still a bit shaky, and I'd had to set once or twice while I was shaving. But I wouldn't let on to her; she was one of the kind that'd have made a senile paralytic try to act like one of these, now, supermen.

"Come on," I says. " 'The lark's in the heaven, the dewdrop is pearled.' S'pose you and me takes a look-see round the place."

Well, after some argument which chiefly consisted of telling me how many different kinds of idiot I was, and saying that she refused to be a party to the suicide of even a pig-headed, Irish lunatic, I got my way. She ordered Henry Ford and the little pinto brought around to the door, and we started out.

Here was a time, I figured, where my natural conversational talents was best kept on ice. My play was a still tongue, if I didn't want to tip off that, so far as ranch business was concerned, I was a complete and congenital know-nothing. I'd just have to keep "Yessing" whatever she said, throwing in an occasional, "Well, I'd like to think about that," for the sake of variety. Believe me, there's many a dumb-bell I've seen get by with nothing more in his mitt than them same four flushing words.

But shucks! I hadn't been out with her a half an hour before I saw there wasn't any use in bluffing. So far as both technical and practical knowledge went, I had anything in that outfit outclassed a hundred to one.

I've seen many another ranch gang since that day, too; and I'm here to tell you that if you want to see real professional cow-punching, either plain or fancy, the place to find it is on a picture lot where they've been doing a series of "Westerns." Them bozos who make it a regular business is just rank amateurs. 'Specially if compared with a guy like me what had been for three years under Milt Leffingwell, a director who wouldn't stand for no fake stuff, not even letting you draw your punches in a free for all.

So, when I seen how ragged this bunch was at their work, I naturally starts to criticize, and thereby earns the firm friendship—not—of Jose Marengo, the foreman, who was riding with us on our tour of inspection.

As I began to express myself more and more freely regarding what I saw, this bird perceptibly clouded up, and more than one was the dirty glare he gave me when Gerta wasn't looking.

Presently, under pretense of showing me where he was figuring on putting up some branding pens, he got me to dismount, and while I was going over the ground, had himself called away. By a singular coincidence, just at this minute a bull, what I afterward learned was known as a dangerous critter, got away from one of the greaser hands, and come charging down the field toward me. There I was, right out in the open, with the fence a good hundred yards away from me, and no place to take shelter.

Gerta seen my fix, and with a shout she cleared the fence on her little pinto, and swinging her lariat, came riding hell-bent to save me. But as luck would have it, the pinto stuck his foot in a hole and down he went, throwing her clean over his head.

Half stunned, she lay where she lit. And the bull, which had been drawn away from me by her shout and her dash into the field, was heading right toward her. Ten seconds more, and he'd be goring and trampling her.

Gee! how I run! I'll bet I smashed all records for the distance.

I let out a yip as I came, that'd make the rebel yell sound like the squeak of a guinea pig.

It didn't stop the bull, but it slowed him down and made him kind of hesitate which of us to go for. That gave me my opportunity, for I reached him, and grabbing him by the horns, sort of slewed him around sidewise away from her.

To keep himself from going off his feet, he had to dig his hoofs into the ground and come to a pause. Then it was him and me for it.

Bulldogging steers was an old story with me. I'd done it many a time in rodeo scenes. But a bull, I found, was a very different proposition. First place, them little short horns don't offer no decent hand hold; secondly, that thick neck is like a stone wall. Fact is, for the first minute of it, I was more dogged against than dogging. Up in the air I went with the swing of his big head, and down to the ground—from one side to the other. I done a fandango that I'll bet would have made a eccentric dancer look at it and weep. But I held on. I had to.

But a bull's frontispiece ain't no light weight to carry around at the best, and when you add to it one hundred and eighty pounds of human jumping jack, which was me, even them thick neck muscles of hisn commenced to feel the strain. He wasn't built to carry so much heft for'rd, and what with them furious struggles he was making, he was getting tired out.

I felt him weakening on me; and although an ordinary man would have been wore out just wrastling with that two-thousand pound cyclone of bone and muscle, I was comparatively fresh. I'd let him use himself up, tossing me around, and now it was my turn.

Watching my chance, when my feet touched the ground again I braced myself, and give the old sidewise twist to his horns.

It didn't work the first time. He give a jerk against me that swung me worse 'n any time before, and nearly broke my wrists. But I still managed to hold on, and on the next trial I got him.

Round on his shoulder went his old muzzle, his feet skidded

from under him, and down he went with a crash to the ground, me on top of him.

Just then the foreman and a bunch of punchers that Gerta had been hollering to, galloped up; and while I held him, they roped the critter and made him harmless.

I got up, and began dusting myself off.

"Santa Maria!" gasps one of the vaqueros. "He acts like it was nothing. That redhead is not a man; he is a pack of lions."

Gerta was so white and shaky that at first she couldn't speak; but when she got her voice back, she immediately begins paging the bird that'ldet the bull get away from him.

"You're done!" she says. "Jose, give this man his pay. I won't have such a careless bonehead about the place."

"Hold on, ma'am!" I broke in. "If you please, I'm ranch manager here. Allow me to handle the men. I don't believe," I says, shooting a look at the foreman which I guess he understood, "that this fellow is rightly to blame. Anybody's liable to have a rope break on him.

"Pedro," I says, "go on back to your work; only, the next time you're escorting that bull anywheres, be sure you ain't got a frayed lead-rope."

'Twas all I could do to keep the poor mutt from kissing my feet. So, if I'd made one enemy that morning, I had also made one firm friend.

"And now," I says, waving my hand to the rest of the bunch, "show's over. No use standing around here any longer. Get back on the job."

Then, because I was feeling more done up by the scrimmage with the bull than I wanted to show, I told Gerta that she was looking pale, and I guessed we'd better call off any more inspection for the day.

The cut on my head had opened up under the bandage, and I reckon I had as many bruises on my shapely person as there is delicatessen shops in Harlem; besides which, the sun was doing its best to bust the top out of the thermometer. Still I managed to get back to the house and sneak up to my room for repairs without attracting special attention. I knew it would mean having Dolores sicked on me again, and I wasn't keen on such sympathy.

The rest of the day, though, I was well content to loaf in a steamer chair on one of the balconies overlooking the patio, with soft cushions around me, and an awning to give me shade, and ice tinkling I'm a long glass at my elbow. Some luxury for a old, hard-shell moving-picture-stunt man, what!

Pretty soon Gerta came out and joined me, and we fell to talking. At first, it was mostly about ranch stuff—fodder supplies, and how many calves was to be branded, and this and that—but after a while, she says I must be fed up on all them details, and didn't I want her to read to me.

So she got a book and she started reading to me out of it about this guy Lancelot, what she'd nicknamed me after, and a couple of janes named Guinevere and Elaine that was stuck on him. Poetry it was and mostly bunk; but I liked hearing her voice. It was soothing and restful and made you feel sort of drowsy. Probably I dropped off to sleep for a minute or two, for when I came to myself again, she had quit reading and was asking me a question,

"Do I think this Lancelot was interested at all in Elaine?" I repeated after her, sort of to get myself together. "Why, no, ma'am; not as I gathered. According to the scenario, she was just a pink-and-white onjenoo that he didn't take much stock in; this vamp, Guinevere, was the real tiger's tusks with him."

"I don't know." She shook her head, and looked away thoughtfully. "If, as Oscar Wilde says, 'All men kill the things they love,' then it may be that it was Elaine after all, who inspired the deeper passion.

"All men kill the things they love?" I sniffs. "Where do you get that sort of guff?"

"Wait. I'll read it to you," she says. And she fetches another book.

This was a poetry piece, too. It was all about being in stir, and the fellows getting hanged, and other cheerful subjects of the sort; and I couldn't see much sense in it. But she seemed to waller in the gloom of it, just like a woman'll enjoy herself most at a weepy show. Finally, she come to that line she'd pulled on me.

"All men kill the things they love, but all men do not die," she read, and then she paused.

"All men kill the things they love," she said again very slow, seeming to turn it over in her mind. "I guess that goes for women, too," she said.

Watching her there, I saw her eyes sort of narrow, and her lips set in a hard, thin line. What with this talk of killing and all, I thought of them two guns she carried with the seven notches on 'em, and of the way she'd plugged Esteban, and of the blood-curdling screech the night before, and of the kind of mysterious air over everything; and I didn't feel none too comfortable. 'Cause there wasn't no doubt in my mind that this Two-Gun Gerta had took considerable of a shine to me; and if her way of showing affection was to bump a guy off, I could see pretty plain that would be my finish.

Then all of a sudden, that cruel look was gone from her face; and there she was, just a girl again—the prettiest, sweetest, most tantalizing bit of calico on the round earth.

"Make her out, though? I simply couldn't do it. Times, I thought one thing; and times, another. Maybe, I figured, she's a Mrs. Jekyll and Doctress Hyde.

CHAPTER VII

MORE PUZZLE

FOR TWO or three weeks after that things run pretty smooth; mainly, I s'pose, 'cause I was watching my step like a hawk.

You see, I wasn't taking the entire credit to myself for all what had happened. Lady Luck had been stringing right along with me, and all the breaks had been in my favor.

But the only sure thing about a streak of luck is that it's bound to change; so for my part I wasn't taking no chances. I just went ahead, tending strictly to business, side-stepping equally all ructions with the greaser foreman and poetry sessions with my black-eyed boss, the which of the two I didn't know was the most dangerous.

Still, even if I did walk a straight and narrow line, and figuratively speaking—as Milt Leffingwell used to say—wore blinders. I couldn't always keep my mind from wandering, and out of the dull routine, I managed to pick up a few thrills.

For one thing, it didn't take me long to find out as I went over the accounts that the ranch wasn't nowhere breaking even, and hadn't been for a long while. Turning back through the pages of the ledger, there was mighty few of 'em you'd come across where the footings weren't entered in red ink.

Well, there was some reason for it. Weather nor markets hadn't been so good for several months back; and, on top of that, disease had broke out among the cattle and a sort of blight in the alfalfa. But mostly, I figured, the losses was due to greaser

shiftiness and lack of system—if not something worse. I wasn't
ready yet to accuse Marengo of deliberate robbery, but I was
beginning to have pretty strong suspicions.

Still, it wasn't the thieving, nor the losses, nor the waste what
I read out of the ledger that intrigued me most—that's another
of Leffingwell's highbrow expressions—but the question of
where the money come from that kept all the military part of
the show going.

That end of the business Gerta handled herself, you see: I
didn't have nothing to do with it. She paid the men, and bought
the supplies, and looked after the books of it herself. But I wasn't
fool enough to think that it was a self-supporting proposition.
It takes jack to hire fighters, and regular pay days to keep 'em
hired—'specially Mexicans. Also, chow three times a day. And
likewise, you don't buy machine guns, and rifles, and equipment,
and ammunition at no five-and-ten-cent store.

Yes, sir; that army of her'n meant ready cash, and lots of it.
And it was a cinch that the ranch wasn't providing no sinews
of war. Yet Gerta herself had told me, the ranch was all that she
and her brother had. What trees then was the mazuma being
picked off of?

Once or twice, I tried to pump it out of Captain Cosette, the
French cavalry officer that was commander of the bunch; but
he evidently didn't know no more than I did, and when I asked
him what he supposed, he just give me one of them made-in-
Paris shrugs which says, "I should worry," plainer than you can
dig it out of the dictionary. He was getting his—half a grand a
month, I'd heard—and getting it on the dot. What did he care?

Course, it wasn't strictly none of my affair. Gerta had told me
that for the present at least I had better confine my attention
wholly to the ranch. Later on, when I'd got things there licked
into shape, it was understood I was to pull a Pershing with the
military department also, and display some of the tactics and
strategy I'd learned peeling spuds on kitchen police at Camp
Upton.

For the time being, though, there wasn't much call for my services in that line. Esteban was still laid up with his punctured wrists, and until he got so's he could handle a gun himself, things'd likely continue dull. There had been a few run-ins between small parties of our respective outfits, but nothing that down in that country could really be called trouble.

So there really wasn't nothing to keep me from giving all I had to the ranch. God knows it called for someone to pitch in and look after it. If any little patch of ground ever needed its hair combed, and its fingernails trimmed, and to be washed behind the ears, it was that same Voreza ranch.

Gee, how I wrestled with it. In the saddle all day, turning up where I was least expected, driving them greasers like an old-time Southern overseer, salving Marengo so as to make him think I never suspected him and yet stacking the deck on him, head and hands and eyes and tongue busy as long as the light lasted, and then sitting up until late into the night poring over figures and accounts, and reading agricultural reports.

If I'd been the real thing and not just a ham actor, and had recognized what I was up against, I'd have probably caved. But being a fool, I rushed in where angels would have stubbed a toe. By luck, I got away with it.

Maybe it was dumb luck, maybe, because I was in a spot where I had to make good, and couldn't do anything else. But at the end of the third week I had the old ranch showing a profit, which was something it hadn't done for months.

I was as tickled as a Zulu with a plug hat, and I couldn't hunt up Gerta fast enough to tell her about it.

It was a Sunday morning, and I found her reading out on one of the balconies over the patio. That is, she was supposed to be reading, but the book was lying in her lap, and her eyes was looking off at nothing. There was a kind of mournful droop to her lips that I'd noticed more than once lately, although she always tried to seem snappy and smiling when she thought anybody was looking.

I'd kind of figured it out, that she was worried over the ranch
doing so badly, and probably getting frightened at the terrible
expense she was under; so I thinks to myself, here's where I give
her a pleasant surprise.

I don't let on that I'm none elated, but I walks over to her with
a pan on me like a undertaker, and lays the statement I'd made
out in front of her.

She don't even look at it; instead, she cocks an eye up at me
sort of indifferent-like.

"Ah, Red?" she says very cool. "You are still with us then? I
see you so seldom that I wasn't certain. I thought you might
have left."

And me wearing myself to skin and bone over her darned
old ranch!

"I guess that statement you've got will show whether I've
been around or not," I says, a little hot under the collar. "You
can't laugh that off."

She glances at it then, but it don't seem to rouse no special
enthusiasm.

"Very creditable," she says, and tosses it over on a table. Her
eyes don't light up none, and her mouth still has that discon-
tented droop. She's tapping with one foot on the floor.

"Poor thing!" I thinks. "She's so deep in the hole that the
little saving I've made for her don't count. It's like winning a
white chip on the high card at faro bank, and losing a stack of
blues on the play."

So I starts in to try and chirk her up.

"Listen, Miss O'Beirne," I says; "now that I've proved I can
make the ranch pay, I've got several ideas in my head I'd like to
talk over with you. Take this army of yours, for instance; it ain't
doing nothing just now 'cept eat its head off. If we'd set the men
to digging irrigation ditches and—"

"Oh no!" she sat up and gave a quick shake of the head. "My
plan has always been to keep the fighting men and the ranch
workers separate."

"But it's unnecessary expense," I argues. "Why should you be paying them loafers for nothing, when they could be made to earn their way? If you'd let me use 'em, I'd show you a statement that'd make this one look like a hobo's laundry bill. At the same time, the ranch—"

"The ranch! The ranch!" She flings up her head and her eyes flash. "Don't you ever think of anything except the ranch, and your irrigation ditches, and pinch-penny statements?" Her lip curled.

"Why," I stammered; I don't know that I was ever more took aback; "ain't that what I'm here for? To run the ranch for you, and save money for you if I can? I thought you'd be pleased with what I've done," I says. "But of course, if I'm not suiting you, I'll—"

"No! No!" She sees that I'm getting pretty well up in the air, and she shifts the cut quick. "I am more than delighted with your showing, Red. I think you've done wonderfully—simply wonderfully. But surely there's no need for you to keep your nose to the grindstone all the time; you don't have to be eternally thinking and talking of the shop. Come on," she says, jumping up; "let's play hookey this afternoon, and go into Yavisa to the races."

I start to look down my nose at that, 'cause I was sort of figuring on breaking a bunch of colts that day and doing some other little odds and ends; but she won't listen to nothing else, and so after luncheon her and me and Captain Cosette rides off.

Well, as I've already told you, there wasn't nothing on the level about that Yavisa race track, from the track itself, which was all hills and hollows, to the short-change artist what presided at the ticket office.

Every race was fixed, and the only way you could possibly win was to soak one of them crooked bookmakers with a section of lead pipe.

But in spite of all that Captain Cosette or me could do, this crazy Two-gun Gerta was bound to bet; and believe me, she wasn't making no piking plays, neither. 'Course she lost steady, and as the more she dropped the harder she plunged, I was beginning to get real worried.

Then, to add my peace of mind, along about the third race Esteban and a whole mob of his followers shows up. Crooked Mouth has both arms in a sling; but that ain't going to stop him, I figure, from getting his gang on us.

Soon's I sight the bunch, I hurries over to where Gerta was.

"We can get around the end of the stand and over to our horses before they spot us," I says. "But we've got to hurry."

"Oh, don't be scary, Red," she laughs. "You act like a fussy old hen with a lone duckling. Crooked Mouth isn't going to do anything here; the race track is regarded as neutral ground. Besides," she says, "you don't expect me to leave when I'm a loser, do you?"

"You'll be a worse loser, if you stay," I tells her. "If I was you, I wouldn't bank very strong on this neutral-ground stuff. When Esteban sees that there's only three of us against his sixty or more, he'll forget any handicaps of that sort."

But 'twasn't no use to talk; she simply refused to budge. In another minute or so it was too late. Esteban and his crowd comes pushing up into the stand and sees us.

Along with the boss bandit was an American, a big, square-shouldered fellow with iron-gray hair and a pink face under a broad-brimmed Stetson.

"Oh, there's Jeff Tyrell," says Gerta, and she begins waving at him. And right away this bird comes over to where we was.

"Well, well; this is an unexpected pleasure," he says to Gerta. "I had just about made up my mind to ride out to the ranch to-morrow and pay you a visit. I'm getting a little worried about Rose. She doesn't happen to be with you, eh?"

"Rose?" Gerta gave him a sort of startled look. "I was just going to ask you what had become of her. I haven't heard from her in over a month. You're not really anxious; Mr. Tyrell?"

"Well, of course"—he drew his mouth down—"a father nowadays has no rights that a daughter is supposed to respect.

You know Rose as well as I do; she's apt to go skylarking off anywhere, if the fancy seizes her. Still I've rather insisted that she should keep me advised of her whereabouts, and I haven't had a letter from her now in over two weeks. Also, if as I have reason to suspect she is down on this side of the border, I'm not sure that there isn't ground for some uneasiness. I had hoped," he frowned, "to get news of her from you."

"No," says Gerta; "the last I heard from her she was in El Paso, and that was fully six weeks ago. Oh, I'm sure she must be all right," she says; and then to prove how sure she was, goes to asking a lot of excited questions.

While the two of 'em was talking, Captain Cosette and me was kind of left off to one side.

"Who's the Big Noise?" I asks.

"Zat," says Cosette, "ees M'sieu' Tyrell from Texas."

"You overwhelm me," I returned. "I already knew that his name was Tyrell, and I could have guessed the Texas part of it from his lid. Furthermore, I notice," I says, "that the gentleman laughs a lot with his mouth, but not at all with his eyes, and also that he shows up here in dam' bad company, which facts make me perhaps unduly curious. Who is this Rose that appears to be lost, strayed, or stolen?"

"Zat ees 'is daughter," says Cosette. "Ver' pretty girl. She and Mees O'Beirne, zey go to school togezzer in New York."

"And Tyrell?" I says. "What does he do, beside wear a big hat?"

Cosette gave a shrug. "Zey say"—he dropped his voice—"zat Tyrell breeng mooch munitions across ze border."

"Oh, I see. A gun runner, eh? Well, that's a profitable trade."

"'E make heemself a millionaire at it, I hear," says the captain.

"And that's why he's palling around with Esteban, I suppose? They've got a stroke of business, on, perhaps?"

"Perhaps," Cosette nodded. "Ze tell me zat Tyrell 'ave been backaire to Esteban. Ze Crooked Mouth was merely a cheap cattle stealer; zen Tyrell come along, and Esteban become great man."

"He made him what he is to-day, eh?" I comments, looking with renewed interest at this gray-haired gink. "Well, I hope he's satisfied."

But before I can ask any more questions, Gerta calls me and the captain over to where she and this Tyrell is talking.

"I want you two to be witnesses to a wager, Mr. Tyrell and I are making," she says. "He fancies that black colt for the next race"—she points to the string of goats just then parading to the post—"while I prefer the bay filly; and we are backing our opinion for five thousand dollars apiece."

I seen it all now plain as if it was pinned on a banner across her chest. The poor kid was so desperate over her finances that she was trying any way to pull out—even to plunging on these skin game bang-tails.

"Look here, Miss Gerta," I says; "you don't want to go risking no money on them dachshunds out there, even if the racing was on the square."

She looks at me, and her eyes waver for a minute; but before I could persuade her any different, it was too late.

Well, even if they was dogs I got to admit that there was a horse race. The distance was five furlongs, and right from the barrier the black colt and the bay filly made the running. Neck and neck they come, leading the field all the way, and not so much as the thickness of a postal card between them.

As they swung into the stretch, both boys went to the bat; and whipping, shouting, riding for all they was worth, raced to the wire.

Tyrell was jumping up and down, waving his hat around his head, and hollering.

"Come on, you black!" he shouts. "Come on!"

"It's a dead heat," says Gerta to me. "Did you ever see anything like it?"

But just at the wire, the black colt was done; and the game little filly outlasted him by a fraction of a second.

I swung off my hat, and give a whoop that you could have heard almost to Canada.

"By a nose!" I yelled. "Clean as a whistle! We win! We win!"

But when the numbers went upon the board, it was the black colt that the judges had gave the race to.

For a moment I could only gasp; it was too raw to believe. Then I started up, reaching for my gun.

"Hold on there, Red!" Gerta grabbed me by the sleeve and jerked me back into my seat. "Be a sport. We can't question the decision of the judges."

"Judges!" I sputtered. "They're just plain burglars in the pay of Esteban and his friend, Tyrell. Don't you pay that bet, Miss Gerta. Cosette here and me'll back you up. Tell that crook—"

"Hush!" she says. "It's only five thousand, remember. Not enough to make a fuss over."

This girl I'd been pitying as a near-pauper pulls a roll out of her bag that a greyhound couldn't jump over, and carelessly peeling off five one-thousand dollar notes, walks over and hands 'em to Tyrell with a smile.

Well, I was graveled! I won't deny it. No wonder she hadn't shown any excitement over the picayune saving I'd showed her in my statement. Yet she seemed crazy to have the ranch made into a paying proposition; had told me again and again that it was all her brother and herself had to depend on.

Where, then, was all this money coming from?

It was like a puzzle where the pieces didn't fit. Nothing seemed to fit.

CHAPTER VIII

THE EXPLANATION

TYRELL IS certainly a good winner. As he comes walking back with Gerta, he is chuckling and spilling wisecracks in a way to make you murder your grandmother.

"It takes an old Texan like me to appraise horseflesh, Miss Gerta," he says. "Now I saw, as you did, that the filly was fast, but I also realized that the colt had staying power. That's what won his race for him. He outfooted her in the final strides."

Gerta listened to his disgusting blatt without turning a hair; even looked up at him like she was impressed.

"By the way, Mr. Tyrell," she coos, "speaking of your judgement on horses, what has become of that wonderful Morgan you were telling me about the last time I saw you?"

"Oh, I've got him with me," he says; "using him as a saddle horse while I'm down here. Ah, there's a horse, my dear! I think I may say without boasting that he can show his heels to anything between here and the Ozarks."

"Well now, that gives me an idea," says Gerta. "Of course you're too good a sport, Mr. Tyrell, to refuse me my chance for revenge. We've got a horse out at the ranch that we think pretty well of; he doesn't belong to me but I'm sure that his owner would race him. Wouldn't you, Red?" She turns to me.

"Against anything on four feet," I says. "But not with a lot of pirates for judges," still raging over the robbery that had been pulled on us.

"Oh, that can rearranged all right," she says, careless. "Suppose, then, we have a match race, Mr. Tyrell; say, of a mile, each man to ride his own horse. You two are about of a size, so make it at catch weights.

"Suits me," I says.

The grin had died off of Tyrell's face, and I could see he was sizing me up cold and hard. But he was kind of in a corner; there wasn't much for him to do except agree.

"Very well," he says, struggling back to his genial bluff again. "You seem to have covered all the details except the date, Miss Gerta. When shall it be?"

"Oh, make it two weeks from to-day," I puts in. "I'll need fully that long to get my horse into condition."

Henry Ford was fit to start in a Derby at that minute! But I'd sort of tumbled to Gerta's game, and was playing in with it.

Old Tyrell swallowed the bait all right. You could see he was feeling easier. The twinkles begin to come back to his face, and he kind of licks his chops at the prospect of easy money.

"What shall we make the wager, young lady?" he says. "Another five thousand?"

"Oh, no!" She gives a toss to her head. Let's have this for something worth while. Suppose we call it twenty thousand a side."

Well, he gulped a bit at that. Course, he was figuring on winning, fair or foul. But accidents will happen, and to lose twenty thousand would evidently be just the same to him as parting with one of his lungs. Still, he was into it now; he couldn't very well back down. So, in the end, each of 'em made a note of the amount and the date and the conditions, and had it witnessed.

That was that. But for personal reasons, I wasn't sorry that it was only an agreement what was put up and not no actual cash; for, otherwise, I had a hunch the bet would have been decided pretty pronto. It being in the terms that each man must ride his own horse, the odds was, as I doped it, that before leaving the race track I'd be rendered *hors du combat*, if not worse.

Even as it was, I didn't feel by no means certain that we were
going to get away from that arena for the sport of kings without
trouble of some kind.

Esteban and his gang hadn't made no hostile move, it is true,
beyond looking everything at us from daggers to meat cleavers,
and it might be that the presence of Tyrell would restrain their
natural impulses; but somehow I couldn't believe that they'd
overlook such a favorable opportunity.

Also, there'd been a long squabble before the fifth race was
pulled off, and it was beginning to get late. Half an hour more,
and it'd be plumb dark, with every chance for something to be
started as the crowd was leaving the grounds, and a knife blade
to be slipped neatly into each one of us in the mix-up.

More and more uneasier I kept getting, but Gerta wouldn't
listen to none of my warnings. She just laughed at me for a
Gloomy Gus; and says, for Heaven's sake to quit spoiling everybody's pleasure with my croaking. She was out to enjoy herself,
she said; and she wouldn't quit until the last horn blowed.

Well, there ain't no twilight to speak of in Mexico, you know;
and by the time the horses come to the post for the last race, you
could hardly see your hand in front of your face. Anywhere else,
the race would have been called off; but the darkness was tapioca
for them babies. The judges decided that it was still plenty light
to see; and the starter commenced lining 'em up with a lantern.

Even Gerta began to get a little nervous now.

"Maybe we had better leave, Red," she whispers. "Don't you
suppose we can slip out of the stand unnoticed, and get out to
the gate the back way."

I flicks a look over my shoulder. Not a chance. As I had more'n
half expected, Esteban's men had divided up, and was now on all
sides of us, watching us like hawks.

"Too late." I whispers back to her. "There's only one thing we
can do now. The minute the barrier shoots up and their attention is off us for a second, the three of us got to make a dash.
Maybe the surprise of it'll hold 'em for five or six breaths; and

if it does, we'll have a chance to reach the horses. But it'll be a tight squeak at the best, with considerable shooting, so be fixed to start at the word, and have your guns ready."

Then I tips off Cosette to the same effect; and the three of us sits there on edge for a jump, while the horses keep jockeying at the barrier.

There was one little, bullheaded sorrel, I remember, that wouldn't come up, and was causing the starter a lot of trouble, and that delayed things quite a spell. Gerta began to get uneasy under the strain.

"Don't wait any longer," she urges me under her breath. "Let's try it now."

But I shakes my head. We needed just that one second when at the yell, "They're off!" every eye would be turned to the horses.

Just then, though, there came a shout of a different sort, and a lot of new arrivals—fifty or sixty of 'em—swept whooping and cavorting into the grounds.

"Good night!" I says. "Esteban's whole outfit is here now, and we ain't got a Chinaman's chance. But I'm going to get old Crooked Mouth before they slough me," I says. I pulls my automatic.

Gerta grabs my arm as I draw.

"Red! Don't!" She struggles with me. "Can't you understand? This is my brother, Ted, and his men. We're all right now. I've been waiting for them to show up all afternoon."

Then I see that a kid with dark hair and eyes like hers was making his way into the stand toward us.

Some relief? I'll say so; for it didn't take but one look to see that the bunch with Brother Ted was a hard-boiled lot—real Yankee cow-punchers, most of 'em, with only a sprinkling of greasers mixed in.

That mongrel gang of Esteban's just kind of melted away at the sight of them. Old Crooked Mouth himself stayed on with a few of his immediate followers but they kept mighty quiet. Also, Tyrell, who had strangely disappeared for the last fifteen or twenty minutes, suddenly popped up again, smiling and shaking hands all over the lot. I noticed, though, that him and Brother Ted for some reason didn't seem to hit if off none to well; they spoke to each other, but that was about all.

Meanwhile the new crowd was just about running the show; they wasn't going to be debarred of their fun, even if they was late.

First thing, they notified the starter to hold the race until they got their bets down. Then a bunch of 'em invades the judges' stand, and mentions that it'll be better for all concerned if their decisions is on the square. Lastly, about twenty of 'em with torches strung 'emselves around the track at intervals, so as to make sure there wouldn't be no fouls.

Under them circumstances a straight race was run, which hadn't been done before that afternoon. Ted was a nice little winner on it, but Gerta hadn't helped herself none. For sentimental reasons she insisted on backing the bull-headed sorrel, and the contrary brute was left at the post.

She was bewailing her hard luck as our bunch and Tyrell walked over toward our horses.

"How much are you out on the day, sis?" asked Ted.

"Over six thousand dollars," she says. "Five thousand to Mr. Tyrell here, and about thirteen hundred to the bookmakers."

"You poor fish," he laughs carelessly. "I suppose you think because there's plenty more where it came from, that you're free to waste our substance that way in sucker bets."

Now where them two got off with that Vanderbilt stuff, I couldn't help but wonder; I hadn't heard of no buried treasure being dug up on the ranch, nor yet of any oil wells coming in. And it wasn't just chatter, neither; that was proved by the roll Gerta had flashed.

You may say, of course, that it was none of my business, and maybe it wasn't; but you want to remember that this girl had put up a poor mouth, and had sort of appealed to me to save the ranch for her, because it was all she had. So if she was really well heeled all the time, she'd been obtaining my services under false pretenses.

The more I thought about it, the sorer I got. I don't like to be strung.

Yet, on the other hand, and vicey-versey, as the lawyers say, I'm sensitive to atmosphere, and there was things about that ranch which didn't bear out no idea of affluence. Shortness of finances can't be concealed no more than limburger cheese; and until this afternoon I'd never doubted it was there.

No, sir I had to believe my eyes. That roll of Gerta's was genuine all right. And still—and still— Well, as I've said before, things didn't dovetail, no way you tried to work 'em.

As we rode along out to the ranch, I made up my mind that me and Gerta O'Beirne was going to come to a show-down. Far be it from me to keep wearing myself to a frazzle to save pennies for someone who could throw thousands to the merry songsters and never miss it.

But, owing to the fact that Ted and his bunch come along with us to the ranch, I didn't get no chance that night for a serious talk with her.

This was the first time the two of 'em had been together since I arrived on the scene; and naturally they had a good deal to talk over. On account of dry weather, the kid and his men had took a lot of steers over to some leased land in the hills east of Yavisa, where the grazing was better, and had just finished rounding 'em up and loading 'em at the railroad for the shipment that day. It was some delay in getting the cattle on the cars, I learned, that had made the bunch so late in reaching the race track. Also, I picked up that the kid, after spending that night at the ranch, was leaving the next day to go through to Chicago with the shipment.

Well, you can see for yourself that it wasn't just the time for an outsider to be butting in; so I leaves the two of 'em to theirselves, and I goes off to my room.

I wasn't just in the mood to work over my books and reports

like I'd been doing every evening; and consequently, as there wasn't nothing else to do, I turns in pretty early.

Probably, on that account, I sleeps lighter than usual; and along about midnight I'm waked up by the door being opened softly, and Wong peeping in. Just to see what he is up to, I lay perfectly still and pretended to be asleep.

He don't come in, though; just sizes me up from the door. Then satisfied that I'm dead to the world, he steps back into the hall, and pulls the door shut after him. A second later, I hears the key being turned very gently from the outside.

"So," I says to myself, "I'm being locked in every night, am I?" For it was plain from Wong's actions that this was a regular program. "And it isn't done either, until I am supposed to be sound asleep. Now what's the idea, I wonder?"

I laid there quite a spell puzzling over it, and yet not seeming to hit on any very good explanation. I was just about drowsing off again, when the answer came.

That terrible, awful cry of agony! The same as I had heard the first night I was there.

It brought me bolt wide awake, sitting up in bed, startled and listening. Before I realized what I was doing, I had my gun in my hand, and was out on the floor, headed for the door. Then I remembered. I was locked in.

Was that cry the reason for it? Did they lock me in, so as to maybe to keep me from investigating and finding out something I wasn't wanted to know?

If it was only old Dolores having a nightmare, as Gerta claimed, what was the need of such a precaution?

I set down on the side of the bed to try and figure the thing out. The more I thought, the stronger grew that sense of mystery I had felt the first night I was there, but which I had almost forgotten about in the rush of my work. All my early suspicions came back, with a lot of new ones to keep 'em company.

Yes, sir; sure as shooting there was something going on here that I hadn't been wised up to. What it was, I could only guess;

but I was certain it must be pretty bad, else they wouldn't take such pains to keep it under cover.

Then I thought of Gerta, and somehow I couldn't figure that she was mixed up in anything that was really wrong or criminal. Was she in the power, then, of someone else, forced by some scoundrel or set of scoundrels to lend her place here to their crooked work?

Some dark stories came back to me that I had heard on the other side of the border of this Two-gun Gerta. Maybe, under cover of her name, a gang of desperadoes was operating, and had compelled her to let them use the ranch as a headquarters?

Maybe, too, that was the reason she had been so anxious to have me come there—as a protection to her, and eventually to help her get the upper hand of these villains?

Then, for a jolt to this pretty theory, came back the memory of the rolls she had flashed that afternoon. If she wasn't in on the dirty work, and getting her cut out of it, where did that money come from?

I smashed one fist against the other. By God, I was going to know! She was going to tell me the truth. Somehow or other I was going to get it out of her.

I had just reached this decision, when I heard the pad-pad of felt slippers in the hall, and the turning of the key in the lock. I laid down quick, and when Wong peeped in, again pretended to be asleep.

Evidently the business of the night, whatever it was, was over. They didn't care now whether I snooped or not, so rolling over, I went to sleep in earnest.

When I came down in the morning I found that Gerta had gone to the station to see Ted off, and wouldn't be back until late in the afternoon. My interview with her would have to wait.

I hadn't no stomach for work, though, and just jimmed around the house. I was in the room we used for an office, making a bluff at going over some papers, when along about noon there was a clatter of hoofs in the patio, and a minute later Tyrell came busting in on me.

"Where's Miss O'Beirne?" he says.

"Not at home," I answers. "Anything I can do for you?" I thought he must have come to see something about the race we'd fixed up.

He glares at me a minute; then he jerks a paper out of his pocket. I guess he's so excited, he's got to blow off to somebody.

"Look at this!" he snaps. "My daughter has been abducted, and is held for a hundred thousand dollars' ransom. This is the filthy crew's demand."

"Who's got her?" I says.

"How the hell do I know? This letter simply tells me to leave the money under a stone on the trail. But they can understand I won't be held up." He banged his fist down on the table. "Not one damned cent do they get. That's what I'm doing this morning," he says, "broadcasting the word, so they'll be sure to hear it.

"I especially want," he says, looking at me with his eyes narrowed, "to have my determination reported to Miss O'Beirne. Tell her, not one damned cent do I give, but that I know who has Rose, and if she isn't returned safe and sound by to-morrow morning, I'll come with men and cannon, and blow her abductors and their rotten old hangout off the face of the earth."

CHAPTER IX

HER GAME

SAY, BOY! He had me winging for a second. There's just two reactions to a dirty dig like that. One is a swift punch on the jaw; the other is to behave very dignified and upstage.

Personally, I preferred the kayo prescription; Jeff Tyrell didn't guess how near he come to having his gray hairs brung down in sorrow to the floor. But on the other hand, I was only understudying for Gerta at the time, as you might say, and I figured I'd better play safe.

So I starts to ritz him. "Am I to infer—" I says, and then throws a wicked pause. If I'd 'a' had one of these now monocles, I'd 'a' been perfect.

"Infer what you damn please," snaps Tyrell. "Only see that Gerta O'Beirne gets my message."

"Hadn't you better put it in writing," I suggests. "You see, kind sir, I'm only the office boy here, and talk like yours don't make much impression on my memory."

I thought for a minute I was going to get the chance I was longing for. He commenced to puff out his jowls and get purple. Then he calmed down, and shot a kind of a sidelong look at me, sizing me up.

"You seem to be a pretty smooth proposition," he says. "They tell me you came here a perfect stranger a few weeks ago, and are now in complete charge of the ranch. Maybe you're open to doing a stoke of business on the side"

"Depends on which side it is," I answers. "Where I come from the rule of the road is, 'Turn to the right.'"

"The right side for a man of sense is always the side where the money lies" He shoves his hand into his pocket, and pulls out a roll that looked like a bale of cotton. "You've certainly been here long enough to see that this ranch can never be made to pay under its present insane management."

"That sounds to me a trifle personal," I says.

"Oh, I have no doubt that you are all right. I should have said, the present insane ownership."

"Meaning, I suppose, that under different ownership it'd start right off to paying dividends?"

He nodded. "These two babes in the wood, especially that headstrong girl, can never do anything with it. They have thoroughly antagonized local sentiment and have made an enemy of Colonel Esteban, who is practical dictator of the region. What is needed here is a man of experience who knows how to deal with the people and conditions. I myself have offered a reasonable price for the property; but the O'Beirnes, with their exaggerated idea of its value, seem to think I am trying to do them."

"Funny the ideas folks will get in their heads," I murmurs; but he's so full of his subject that he never notices my sarcasm.

"Meantime," he says, "they're headed straight for bankruptcy."

"Still sees to be a few pennies left in the old teapot," I remarks, "judging by the way the pair of 'em was throwing it around the track yesterday."

"That's just it." He frowns. "Where did that money come from? They ought by right to be down to their last jitney. Do you know anything about it?" He gave me a quick look from under his eyelids.

"Not for certain," I says. "But you couldn't blame 'em none, if they eked out with a little rough stuff on the side. When in Rome, do as the Romans do; and the hold-up game seems be the general line of Christian endeavor this side of the Rio Grande." If he was fishing, so was I.

"Exactly." He nods. "I've heard something of this before. Five or six people within the past few weeks have been seized by a mysterious band of night riders and carried off to ransom. I have talked of four of them who were released after paying the sums demanded of them; but so thoroughly were the precautions taken, that they can give only a vague idea of their captors or the place of their detention. The aggregate obtained from them, since they were persons of minor importance, was also not large. Just about enough, I should say"—he slants another of them looks at me—"to keep this establishment running."

"You interest me strangely," I says "for you raise a question of demand and supply. What's the prospect of my wages continuing to be paid on this basis?"

"Slim." He shakes his head. "Unless I am mistaken, the list of victims who can or will submit to extortion of that sort is about exhausted. To carry on, operations must now be levied against those of greater influence, who are in a position to retaliate. It looks very much as if the first attempt of the sort has been aimed at me—certainly a case of getting the wrong sow by the ear."

"Ain't you mixing things a little?" I asks. But the shafts of my wit slides off his burnished armor, as Milt Leffingwell used to say when I'd muff one of his hot ones. The bozo don't pay no more attention than if I hadn't yipped.

"If this crack-brained girl doesn't pull in her horns"—he pounded on the table—"I'll show her. I'll bring a force here to-morrow morning that'll knock her flimsy fortifications into matchwood.

"But"—he wags his head boastful—"she knows me. The silly chit will drop it mighty quick, when she gets my message and realizes that I am onto her."

"A word to the foolish'll be sufficient, you think, eh?"

He laughs at that one and under cover of it gives me another of them sizing-up looks.

"I reckon you and I understand each other," he says. "Since

you seem so fond of proverbs, how about the old stand-by:
What's sauce for the gander is sauce for the goose?"

"I'll bite," I says. "What is?"

"Well"—he edges up closer to me and drops his voice—"you
and Miss O'Beirne frequently ride out together, I understand.
Suppose on one of these occasions you manage on some pretext
to get her to an isolated spot where by prearrangement, a squad
of men would be waiting to seize her?"

"Yes? What then?"

"Why," he says, pulling out his roll again, "if you'll agree
to do that, and also to see that her guns are left behind, or are
unloaded, it'll be worth a thousand dollars to you."

There wasn't any more I could find out from him: he'd tipped
his whole mitt. Besides, there was a greaser hostler passing the
window conveniently at the moment. So I pulls another John
Drew.

"Hi, Sancho!" I calls to the hostler, kind of picturing myself
in a frock coat and spats. "Bring Colonel Tyrell's horse to the
door, will you? He is leaving *pronto*—damn *pronto.*"

Tyrell's eyes bulged out, and he looked at me like he didn't
get it at all.

"Of course," I says to him, "if you prefer to get kicked out, I
shall be glad to oblige. We strive to please."

He probably seen that I was itching for the chance, 'cause he
didn't lose no time in grabbing up that Texas maintop of his and
beating it. He didn't even stop at the door for an exit speech,
which was a thing I'd never have overlooked.

Still, as he galloped out of the patio and down toward the
gate, it wasn't hard for me to figure what he was thinking; and
what of it was fit to print was chiefly concerned, I imagined,
with the things he'd like to do to me.

Moresoever, he wasn't like the youngster crying for the moon.
What with the high hand he held with Esteban and others
in the region, there was reason to believe that he might at no
distant day be able to put some of them pleasant wishes of his

into effect. I could sure chalk up another enemy on my list, and one that wasn't no pork-and-beaner, neither. As Gerta said, I seemed to have a genius for getting into trouble.

At that, though it wasn't my personal prospects that was bothering me. It was what I had pumped out of the big bum, and which dovetailed in so exactly with my own suspicions that I didn't have no room for doubt.

The poor girl, up against it with the expense she was under, had simply took a leaf from the Mex handbook of etiquette, and was collecting from the neighbors. So far, so good; my heart didn't bleed none over the shake-down of a few greasers. Like the suckers at a county fair, they've got it coming to 'em; if somebody don't gyp them, they're disappointed. But trying to hold up Jeff Tyrell was a horse of another color.

Course, in our recent palaver, Jeff, old dear, had been bluffing to a certain extent; but there was certain points which had cropped out in his discourse, that you couldn't afford to overlook.

First and foremost, he wanted the Voreza ranch and when Jeff Tyrell wanted anything, I judged 'twas foul means rather than fair that appealed to him. This kidnapping of his daughter gave him an excuse he'd probably been waiting for to use his strong-arm methods.

Secondly he wasn't doing no kidding when he said that he could blow us off the face of the earth. The stockade of Gerta's was good defense against rifle fire and bow-an'-arrers and bean-shooters, maybe; but what a piece or two of modern artillery would do to it—oh papa! Costette had told me only a day or so before, that he'd heard Esteban had got hold of a couple of French seventy-fives.

Yes, sir; there wasn't much doubt that Jeff could Bosco us, if he had to. Naturally, since him and Gerta and Ted was all American citizens, he'd rather do the job along diplomatic lines and avoid any chance of a kick-up at Washington; but if Gerta didn't jump through the hoops like he wanted, this kidnapping stunt gave him, as I say, pretty fair license to cut loose. Somehow I couldn't picture Gerta jumping through anybody's hoops; she was a charter member of the Yougoplumbtohell Society. Didn't make no difference whether she'd overplayed her hand or not; she'd see it through to the showdown.

Consequently and lastly, seeing that such was the layout and there wasn't nobody else to shoulder the responsibility, it was up to me to do something.

Now, of all the seventeen ways of settling a question, that there is the easiest—just make up your mind you've got to do something. But what to do ain't always so easy to dope out.

As I tell you, there wasn't no illusions on my part as to what was going to happen, if it got down to actual hair-pulling. We'd be licked to a frazzle.

You can see I'm honest. Some guys'd be claiming that they never turned a hair. But me? Well, I was goose-fleshing so hard that it rumpled my clothes. I'm good, too; t'would be idle to deny it. Ten, or even twenty greasers, I could attend to single-handed, and think nothing of it. But a whole army of 'em equipped with all modern conveniences is something else yet, 'specially where it was bound to be a one-man battle on our side, for any support I'd get from that busher outfit of ourn wasn't really worth counting. To my mind, it was over already, all but the shouting. There wasn't but one answer to that argument.

Furthermore, no matter who else decorated the casualty list, I had a strong hunch that my name would be No.1. Cosette and the garrison, and maybe Gerta and Ted might be treated in a way as prisoners of war, but the best I could hope for was a section of stone wall and a firing squad. Esteban and Tyrell would both see to that.

Common sense whispered to me that it would be the proper play to terminate my little jaunt into Mexico, while the terminating was, so to speak, still open. As I've already mentioned, those dear United States wasn't so derned far away but what me and Henry Ford could probably make it. If you must know, I actually got up out of my chair once with the full intention of starting. Just then, though, I caught a glimpse of that cerise brush of mine in a mirror on the wall, and it stopped me like a punch in the nose.

By all the red-headed fighting Connerses of Kerry, Limerick and Clare, I couldn't do it. I couldn't run out on a girl that'd picked me for her protector, not when she needed protecting probably just about six hundred and thirty-two times harder than she ever would in all the rest of her life.

No; it wasn't legs that was my long suit in this fracas; and I'd already figured out that strength of arm or fighting ability wouldn't do me any good. It was a time when I had to use the old bean.

What's all the shooting about anyhow, I says to myself.

About a squab, ain't it, which Gerta has pinched off with the idea of cashing in on her?

Also, it don't take no mathematician to calculate how it all happened. This Rose filly is a school friend of Gerta's, and was no doubt coming to the ranch for a visit. What easier than to waylay her on the road, and pretend that it was being done by a roving band of brigands? Blindfolded, and brought in over a circuitous trail, the girl wouldn't never dream that she was at the very place she had started out for. She could be held there a prisoner until papa came across, and then restored the same way she was took, without ever suspicioning nothing.

Not so bad, eh, for a smooth little scheme to raise the wind? Not so good, neither—the way it had worked out. For, instead of copping off a hundred grand as she'd planned, all I could see was that Gerta had given Jeff Tyrell his long-awaited chance to take her ranch away from her.

If his daughter was held there a prisoner, you couldn't blame Tyrell none for coming there and getting her, even if as a consequence Gerta got gypped out of her property. But if when he come, the daughter wasn't there—

"Aha," I says to myself; "that's the crucible point! It's up to me to see that she ain't."

CHAPTER X

SUBORDINATE

S O T H A T was all straightened out. Wonderful, how easy you can rope and tie the answer to most any question if you just put your mind to it.

Course that answer wasn't throwed yet. It was still running pretty free, you might say, considering that 'twasn't nothing but a guess on my part that the girl was at the ranch at all, and that before I could figure on getting her away, I had to locate her, which was just about as simple as finding a collar button under the bureau in a dark room.

There was something like sixty thousand acres in the Voreza property, comprising about every known kind of landscape except coral islands, and to comb all over that for one female answering to the name of Rose would take too long. Tyrell and his gang, you see, was due to show up the following morning, and the chances was they wouldn't keep banking hours either.

But once more I used the old bean. If 'twas the plan to restore the girl on payment of the ransom, she'd have to be kept meanwhile in some snug harbor that she couldn't recognize or describe; and about the only spot that filled them specifications was down in the cellar of the big house.

"Let's have a look-see," I says to myself, and I strolls out across the patio, and down through the archway where they took the horses.

But, snoop around as I would, all I could discover was stalls and a saddle room and a general livery-stable smell. That and a few horses was every blooming thing down there, except for a greaser sentinel roosting on a box by the doorway, with his head tucked under his wing and a cigarette dangling from his lower lip; and I wouldn't have thought nothing of that, except that I caught the son of a gun watching me.

Now a greaser sentinel that's awake is a object of suspicion; it ain't natural. That goes double, if the egg is pretending at the same time to be asleep. So when I gets back to the office, I sits down and starts to try and puzzle out the reason therefore.

Then, all of a sudden, something struck me. Likely, I'd never had given it no heed if the abnormal behavior of that sentinel hadn't sort of handed me a jolt. But it flashed on me now that the dimensions of the cellar was considerable smaller than the size of the floor above.

"Well," I argues to myself, "what of that? Maybe the old shack was built that way."

But when I cooked up an excuse to tramp back over the floor, I couldn't see that my footfalls made no different sound at one part more'n at another. 'Twas the same hollow echo to 'em all the way along.

Only one explanation to that, so far's I could make out. The cellar ran clear through all right but the hind end of it beyond the horse stalls was walled off into a secret chamber. And that, of course, was where the Tyrell girl was being kept.

Pretty smooth, what! A Sherlock Holmes couldn't have worked it out no slicker. But I was still a long way from knowing how to get into that secret chamber; I couldn't very well project around down there, with the greaser piping off every move I made. I was a longer way still from prying the fair captive—if such there was—loose from her dungeon cell and off the ranch. All of which had to be effectively disposed of, as we say in Wall Street, before Tyrell commenced to do his stuff in the morning.

However, I wasn't as much cast down as you might opine. In this here business dope that they print in the magazines, I'd

always read that the test of a great executive is to leave details
to his subordinates; and that cheered me up a lot.

Course, strictly, speaking, I didn't have no subordinates. The
authority I had at the ranch come to me through Gerta, and
on a private job like this didn't rate deuce high. The gang was
either for or against her; I didn't figure. If I went to topping off
my mitt to any of 'em, the fat'd be in the fire. They'd either pass
the word along to her, or else try to crab the play.

Then I happened to think of this Pedro, the guy whose job
I had saved for him when he turned the bull loose on me. He
wasn't exactly a tower of strength, being a cross-eyed, undersized
cholo, with the quick intelligence of a defective sheep but he had
two points in his favor. He was almost offensively grateful to
me and since I had outpointed the tricky foreman he placed me
only about one peg lower than his patron saint. So in default of
having anybody else, I elected him as my general staff, and went
out to round him up.

He had a pail of swill in each hand when I found him, preparing to serve an *alfresco* luncheon to a bunch of hogs, which in
their noisy impatience reminded me of a party of small-time
bohemians. You could almost imagine that they was squealing
"garcon" and "kellner" at him.

"*Amigo*, can I count on you?" I says.

He sets down his swill pails and wriggles up like he was going
to kiss me.

"To the death, señor." He puts his hand on his heart. "You are
my father and my mother, more to me than my wife and children. All that I have is thine." By which he probably meant that,
if he had plenty of tobacco and papers, he wouldn't begrudge me
the makings of a cigarette, provided he didn't have a grouch on.

"Good." I steps to the windward of him. "I think I am going
to have use for you. I don't know just what yet. But you had
better stick around so as to be handy when required. Meanwhile," I says, "after you have finished feeding your pets yonder,
you might mention casual to Marengo that me and the señorita

is riding to Yavisa early to-morrow morning. Don't say that I told you to tell him, understand; just pass it on as a bit of gossip."

He nodded to show that he was on, and I went back to the office to wait developments. They wasn't long in coming. About fifteen minutes afterward, I seen Marengo, the foreman, streaking it away from the stockade; and I didn't need no crystal ball to tell me, he was carrying the message to Garcia.

I reasoned, you see, that if Tyrell was willing to pay me for a jaunt of that kind with Gerta, he'd be more than tickled to learn that it was going to be furnished him free, gratis, for nothing. I'm a firm believer, as the song says, in scattering seeds of sunshine as you go—only, I was planning that when the denouement came, it'd be an understudy in the role of Gerta. In short, it'd be his missing daughter. Just how, I wasn't altogether clear but that, as Milt Leffingwell used to say, was a matter of stage management.

It was at this interesting juncture that Gerta herself came loping home. There'd been considerable of a question with me, whether or not she oughtn't to be tipped off as to what was in the wind; but her first words as she slid down from her pinto settled me in my conviction that she was best kept out of it.

Women ain't reasoning beings no how; they only pretend to be when it suits' em. Gerta was in one of them moods, 'twas plain to see, where she was apt to do something plumb foolish. T'wouldn't need but a word to start her off.

"Red," she says, flopping down into one of the office chairs. "I'm so fed up on cows that I'm afraid to open my mouth for fear I'll moo. Nothing else have I heard since morning; that kid brother of mine talks like the *Breeder's Gazette*. If anybody says another word to me about the ranch or stock or any duffel of that sort, I shall foam at the mouth. What I want to-night is to be deliciously feminine. I want to put on fluffies, and sing 'O Promise Me.' and flirt devilishly. Can you flirt, Red?"

"Well, I ain't never posed as no he-vamp," I grins. "But at a pinch I s'pose I could accommodate you."

Better act like I took it for bidding, thinks I, and josh back at her.

She was a-setting there all hunched up, slapping at her dusty riding boots with her crop, and looking for all the world like a sulky boy that was trying to make up his mind whether to run away from home or not—kind of milling, don't you know. Just a hint about Tyrell, and she'd be off to call his bluff and probably slap his face. Then there's be hell to pay.

So I plays up to this lead she's given me, and treats her to the once over like I was a casting director.

"H'm!" I says, meaning to be jocular. "Strikes me, you might make more of a hit as a siren if you was to wash your face."

Now I ought to of knew better than that, 'cause she had a smear across one cheek where she'd rubbed it with her glove. But I wasn't really throwing it up to her, only trying to be funny.

What does she do, though, but look at me like I'd pasted her one; and then she ducks her head down into her arm, and busts out a crying fit to break her heart.

"Now, now, Miss Gerta!" I pleaded with her. "Don't take it like that. I'm just a big roughneck. No use paying no 'tention to what I say."

I was hopping from one foot to the other, wallering in apologies; but it didn't seem to do no good. Fast as I'd work to the nigh side of her, she'd switch her head over to the offside, or vicey-versa, and go to sobbing harder'n ever.

She looked so little and pitiful-like, that you couldn't help feeling sorry for her. Gee! If anybody was ever made to feel like a unfeeling brute, it was me. And "there-thereing" her and patting her on the shoulder didn't seem to accomplish nothing, neither.

I got so upset and flustered, that I hardly noticed it when swinging her heels around she gouged me twice in the leg with her spurs.

"Why honey," I flounders, "you ain't got no call to be sore. A little smudge like that ain't nothing. You could have enough dirt on your map to plant potatoes, and still give odds to anything on the magazine covers."

The old salve. Tell 'em they're pretty. That's always the one sure-fire bet to smooth a woman down. It's vittles and drink to 'em. And, eight or eighty, no matter what their looking glass shows 'em, They'll believe you on that, where they'd doubt the Ten Commandments.

Also, I ought to say that, without savvying it exactly, I'd slipped my arms around her and had sort of drew her up, like you would with a kid you was trying to comfort.

Right away she stopped trying to make shredded codfish of me with them spurs; and for just a second, if I ain't mistaken, she clung to me and burrowed her cheek in the front of my shirt. Then she wriggled away quick, her face as red as a rose, and set down on the edge of the table. She was still sniffling, but I could see the flicker of a smile glinting from under her wet lashes.

"When knighthood was in flower!" she gulped. "Enough dirt to plant potatoes on my map! Believe me, Red, Philip Sidney or Walter Raleigh never turned a more courtier-like phrase than that."

"Sidney and Raleigh?" I says. "Who's them? Some Percys you knowed back East? I ain't never heard you speak of 'em before."

She laughed outright at that, allowing, I suppose, that she'd made me jealous. There ain't nothing, I've noticed, that tickles a dame more than to feel that she's stirred up the green-eyed monster. They'll take a licking just for the satisfaction of doing it.

But a fat chance she had of getting me worried over a couple of Fifth Avenue Johns.

"Say," I says; "I'll bet they's a pair that wears spats and carries a hand'cher in their cuffs. If you like their style of conversation bettern mine, why don't you have 'em come down here?"

"Well, I would," she says, turning her face away kind of shamed-like. "Only—only I don't know how to address them."

"Just as I thought," I nods. "Them hyenas'll make a girl think she's the elephant's nightshirt as long as she's around with 'em, but the minute she's out of sight they forget all about her. Has either of 'em wrote you a line since you've been away? Not so much. I'll be bound, as a picture post card of Grant's Tomb, with, 'Wish you was here' on it."

Poor kid, she crumpled up at that. She drops her face in her hands, and her shoulders starts to heaving.

"Don't rub it in, Red," she begs in a sort of muffled voice. "I was hoping for a letter to-day, and none came; and—and I'm miserable. And now you're cross with me, too—just because I spoke about Phil and Walter."

"Not cross," I says kind of stiff. "I don't deny that I'm surprised, even a bit disgusted at a girl as smart as you are in most things grieving over such trash. But I'm far from sore. 'Tain't for me to question who your friends is—even if they is bums. I'm only a hired hand."

I starts rolling a cigarette, indifferent-like. But I sees her peeping up at me through her fingers.

"Red," she coaxes, "if I promise not to have anything more to do with Philip Sidney or Walter Raleigh—or even to think about them—will you be friends?"

The little devil! Kidding all the while, and me never finding out till long afterward that them lizards she was talking about had been dead for something like three hundred years.

"So now," she says, when I'd agreed to make up, "the nights shall be filled with music, and the cares that infest the day shall, as you might say, do a Mustapha Kemal. As I disclosed to you, Red, I have a yen to play the guitar and yowl sentimental ballads; and you with your barber-shop tenor are elected as accomplice."

"Come on!" She jumped up off the table, and grabbed my hand. "We'll have dinner together, and then we'll go up on the roof and bay the moon with every mushy old chestnut, from 'Annie Laurie' to 'My Rosary.' But not a mention of business, remember," she warns me. "This is a society event, and cows are strictly taboo. To-night we'll eat, drink, and be merry."

"Merry—hell!" I thinks to myself.

I'd saw that line she pulled used once for a subtitle in a picture; and tacked on to it was, 'For to-morrow we die,' which was entirely too close to the facts to strike me as comedy. Knowing what I did, this proposition of hers seemed to me a good deal like old Pharaoh fiddling while Rome was burning.

Still, what could I say? I didn't dare tip my hand, for fear she'd get desperate and start something that'd cook us worse'n we was. Besides, I'd been laying for a private interview with her to find out what 'twas all about; and here was sure a opportunity made to order.

So in the end I consents; and she skips off all smiles, telling me to show up on her balcony in about fifteen minutes. "We'll eat there," she says, "count of it being cooler."

CHAPTER XI

ME AND GERTA

GERTA, I am bound to say, contrary to most of her sex, didn't waste no precious moments in prinking up. There is girls I've knowed, that'd keep you waiting a full hour while they fiddled with a eyebrow. But she was as quick with the powder puff and the old rabbit's foot as she was on the trigger.

My own preparations for the party wasn't none too extensive, being just to wash my face and hands, run a wet comb through my hair, and slip into a coat. Yet, will you believe me, when I reached the balcony she was there ahead of me, her riding suit changed to a dress and her hair done up a different way.

Some picture she was, too, if anybody should ask you. When I'd seen her in women's clothes before, 'twas either like on that first night when she was rigged out like a princess, or else she was in sports things same's any other flapper.

But, how come she managed it, to-night she was all girl— kind of sweet and innocent-looking and Mary Pickfordy. She made you think of Sunday school picnics and apple blossoms, and of being afraid of spiders and all old-fashioned things like that. And you felt bashful, and like it'd be awful to say "Damn" in front of her—Gerta, that I'd heard cussing out the cowhands like an old-time steamboat mate.

Well, I just stood there gasping, my eyes bulging out on my cheeks. 'Twasn't ten minutes before that I'd seen her in boots and breeches and a khaki shirt; yet here she was a ringer for commencement day at a young ladies' seminary, all in tulle and chiffon and silk stockings and slippers, and with her hair parted in the middle and hanging in two long braids down her back.

Only way I could figure it was, that she had her harness hung on hooks like a fire-engine horse's, ready to drop on her when she run under it.

But she knowed what she was doing all right. Ain't no man on earth can stand up against that real-girl stuff. It lays 'em quick and painless like a shot from the needle.

"How do I look, Red?" she coos, shy-like, casting her eyes down and wriggling her cheek toward her shoulder, just like a squab of that sort would do.

"Hel-lup! Hel-lup" I shouts. "Ain't you got me cuckoo enough already? What do you want me to do? Say my prayers to you?"

Well, there ain't no saying what mightn't have happened. All sorts of crazy thoughts was running around in my head, like picking her up and carrying her off, whether she'd go or not, so as to get her safe across the border and away from Tyrell. The garrison, nor the gates, nor nothing didn't cut no ice with me. Anybody tried to stop me, 'twould be the worse for them, was my idea. She had me just plain loco.

But before I could gather myself together, half dazed like I was, to start anything, the greasers commenced rustling the chow; and that sort of broke the spell. I stumbled into the seat Gerta motioned me to, and she sat down opposite to me.

What we had for dinner, nor yet whether I eat anything or not, I couldn't tell you. Vittles for once didn't seem to mean anything to me. All I wanted to do was to feast my eyes on Gerta.

That's a funny thing, too. Here, I'd been seeing Gerta every day, and we'd been darn good pals; maybe something more, especially on her part, 'cause right from the start I seen she was pretty well interested in me. Nor I ain't denying that I was interested in her, likewise. But it was a sort of superior feeling like you'd have for a horse or a dog that follers you around. I can't rightly say that I was in love with her.

Now all of a sudden she knocks me for a goal. I'm down for the count. No doubt about it being the real goods, either. I realize that I'm just a big, ignorant slob that ain't got no right even to live on the same earth with her. Why, I'm that humble, that I'd think it was cute for her to wipe her shoes on me.

Yet I knew she was acting, just like she was that night in Yavisa when she swaggers up to the El Toro bar and orders whiskey. She wasn't a onjenoo no more'n I was John D. Rockefeller. So what did I fall in love with? The girl, or her trimmings?

Blamed if I could tell you to this day. I only know that I was there. As I tell you, I don't remember whether I eat anything or not. I couldn't say whether I was on my head or my heels. I was floating on golden clouds one minute and down in the pit of despair the next, seesawing 'twixt heaven and hell, 'cording as I looked at her or thought of my own unworthiness.

I recollect dimly that we had champagne, and that I lapped up scuttle after scuttle of it like I had a raging fever. But it didn't have no more effect than so much pink lemonade. Champagne! The fix I was in, I could have drunk cyanide of potassium, and never batted a eye.

For our coffee we went up on the roof where she had a corner awninged off, with oleanders all around it, and piles of cushions to set on, and a hammock. And as she's promised, she tuned up her guitar, and we sang all the old fav'rites together, "Silver Threads Among the Gold" and "Way Down Upon the Suwanee River" and "Sweet Alice, Ben Bolt" and "White Wings" and "Loch Lomond" and "My Bonnie Lies Over the Ocean."

The moon came up—a moon about twice as big around and twice as silvery as the one what shines up North—and the breeze sprinkled the scent of the oleanders over us, and—oh, it was just heaven!

You get close to a person somehow when you sing them old sentimental ballads with 'em in the moonlight, a sort of a feeling that you don't get no other way.

Maybe it was that, and maybe it was the champagne; but I

forgot all about Tyrell and Esteban and the danger we was in and the mystery and all the other things that had been worrying me so. None of them things seemed to count. Nothing seemed to count, 'cept just me and Gerta, and the miracle of being alone there together.

We was like two people off on a desert island or some-wheres—in a world of our own. Not a sound came up to us. All you could see through the oleanders was the sky and the moonlight, and they belonged to us. It was our hour.

After a while the songs give out; and then somehow—whether she asked me or not, I don't just recall—I got to talking about myself.

I told her about how my father and mother died when I was just a little shaver, and how I'd been took by my Aunt Margaret to be brung up in her gloomy old house in Boston. I described Aunt Margaret's old house in Boston. I described Aunt Margaret's black coal-scuttle bonnet and her grim, set face, and her rules and how nothing wasn't to be touched, and how finally I couldn't stand it no more and run away when I was only twelve years old.

"That's why I'm such a dumbhead," I says. "She was rich and she'd have educated me; she was set on making me into a lawyer so's I could look after her property and not fritter it away, she says, when it come to me. But I couldn't see it that way. Staying there was just the same to my mind as ten years in the penitentiary. So I lit out, and started off to see the world.

"I've never been sorry until to-night," I says, "and I don't really know that I'm sorry now to have quit Aunt Margaret. A hell of a lawyer—if you'll excuse me—I'd probably have made. But it does seem a shame to grow up as dumb and worthless as I am. If I'd have stuck with her, I'd have money and a education, and I wouldn't feel so hopeless about—about—"

"Hopeless?" Gerta cut in quick. "Why should you feel that way? The education of books is only a veneer. The education of self is what counts, and you have that. Certainly you have shown yourself far from dumb or worthless in the way you have taken hold here. I don't know what I should have done without you.

"But you broke off at the most interesting part of your story, Red," she went on. "What did you find when you started off to see the world? I have felt that same adventurous urge, but I never had the courage to try it. I have often wondered, though, if it would be as full of romance as I expected. How was it with you? Where did the Gypsy Trail lead you?"

"Mostly to farms up York State," I says, "where I done chores for my board and keep. Then when I was eighteen, I put in a year working in a livery stable. After that, I just jimmed around New York City at one thing and another. Lots of hard work and a empty stomach fairly frequent, but not no especial romance that I can remember."

"But, Red"—I glanced up, and seen her looking at me kind of puzzled in the moonlight—"that takes no 'count of your range experience. When did you come West?"

"Oh, that?" I says. She had me cornered, but I could still have lied out of it. Somehow, though, I couldn't do it, not this new way I was feeling toward her.

"Well, I'll tell you, Miss Gerta," I says sort of low and shamed-like, "I've been imposing on you. I ain't nothing but a false pretense. The only ranch I ever worked on 'fore I come here was a make-believe one in the moving pictures. Being as how I knowed horses almost from the time I could walk, I got me a job with the Deadwood Dick Fillums, what makes a special of Westerns over at Fort Lee, and I stayed with them nigh onto three years. 'Twas there I learned cow-puncher talk, and how to handle a rope, and all things like that from old Idaho, who was leader of our outfit and had been the genuwine article. I was always nosey, you see, and I picked up a lot, just chinning the old man while we was out on location or at times when we was waiting for the camera.

"I worked up to be head stunt man for the company," I says, "doubling for the leads in all the dangerous situations, and even having parts specially wrote in the scenarios for me, where I was billed as 'Reckless Rudolph,' which Milt Leffingwell, our director, give me as a stage name. Maybe you've saw some of the pictures, 'The Looped Peril of the Cañon' or 'Within an Inch of Eternity.'

"Then," I says, "I had a spill. Not nothing that ordinarily'd have made me do more than jump up and dust off my clothes. I've had a hundred worse. But this one busted up most of my ribs, and jumbled me quite a bit inside. Ain't it funny," I says, thinking of how she'd bowled me over with her apple-blossom play that very evening, "how somep'n unexpected like that'll come along and change the whole course of your life?

"Well, the company acted darn' decent about it," I resumes. "I'm bound to say that. I was in the hospital ten weeks, and they paid all bills and give me every attention. Then, seeing as how one of them broken ribs had punctured my lung, and it was acting kind of suspicious they handed me a thousand dollars and shipped me off to Arizona. A couple of months there, camping out on the desert, fixed me as good as new, and I was thinking about going back to work. But that old urge you talk about, and which I hadn't never gratified, came over me. I had picked up this Henry Ford horse at a bargain from a feller which didn't know how to handle him, and I says to him like you talk to a horse:

'Old-timer,' I says, 'now that we've got the chance, let's see a bit of the world 'fore we go back East. We can probably make expenses while we're knocking around' I says, 'and no doubt we'll pick up some experience that'll be vallyable to us on the lot.'

"So, Henry offering no objections, we started off. And that's the way," I finishes, "that I come down across the border to Yavisa—and to you."

She'd been setting in the hammock while I was talking, touching a low chord now and then on the guitar in her lap; but now when I ended she tosses the guitar aside, and jumping up, stands in front of me.

"Do you mean to tell me, Red Conners, that you came here and undertook the control of this big ranch, an absolutely green man?"

"I'm telling you," I says. "I know it was a terrible thing to do, Miss Gerta, a low-down trick to play on you, but you'd kind of put it over on me with that fake capture, and—and—"

"You thought you'd get even with me? Yes; I can understand that. But what floors me is that you made good. You not only succeeded in taking me in completely, but a lot of old-time ranch men as well. There wasn't one of them, that even so much as raised a question. I can still hardly believe it."

"Well, that was the only alibi I could give to myself for doing it—to make good. I just had to. I seen, too that you really needed someone to handle these lazy Mexicans. I suppose you think I'm a awful crook, ma'am; but I honestly did try. Course, I had the the'ry of the thing in a way from listening to old Idaho; but I ain't denying it's kept me on my toes to—"

"An awful crook?" She flops down beside me on the pile of cushions where I'm setting, and grabs my two hands. Her eyes is shining like a pair of Klieg lamps in the moonlight.

"Why, Red," she says, "I think you were wonderful. To have dared such a thing, and to have gotten away with it. It was positively Napoleonic. I understand now, too, why you were always so busy and absorbed, when I wanted you to talk to me and be amusing. The idea! When it's I that should be bowed down with gratitude over what you have done for me."

She was so near to me there that some of her hair blowed over against my face; and that, and her praising me, and the moonlight and all sort of turned me half crazy for a minute. There was a lump in my throat that almost choked me and my heart was back-firing and thumping like a balky flivver engine.

"I'd do anything on earth for you, Gerta," I says huskily, and my arms went around her.

I drew her toward me. Her face was upturned to me, her eyes closed. Then she puts out her hands quick, and pushes me back.

"Wait! Wait just a minute, Red," she says. "I, too, have a confession to make. I am a false pretense, as you call it, as well as you. No! No!"—fighting me back, as I tried to tell her that nothing made any difference. "You must listen to me first. I want to tell you the secret of this old house and all that goes on here."

But just then we was startled by the sound of shooting from out beyond the blockade, and then the machine guns at the gate set up a rat-a-tatting.

"My God!" thinks I. "Tyrell and Esteban has come ahead of time."

"It's an attack!" says Gerta, jumping to her feet. "Come on, Red!"

She grabs my hand, and together we raced across the room and down the stairs.

CHAPTER XII

PASSWORD

A S W E reached the patio, there came a clatter of hoofs, and the next minute Cosette galloped in through the archway at the head of a bunch of his men.

They wasn't holding no very close order and as there was one or two riderless horses running with the rest I drew Gerta quickly back to one side to keep her from getting trampled on.

Cosette seen us standing there in the lamplight, and, wheeling his mount, came back to us, waving his hand meantime to his men to keep on. They went down the ramp to the stables in a sort of scrambled rush, but not so fast that even in that dim light I could see, if there was some saddles empty, there was also four or five which was carrying double.

"What is it, captain?" Gerta asks sharp, as he comes to a stop and swings down beside us. "An attack?"

"But no, mamselle." He shrugs careless. "Just a skirmish. A little brush wiz a small party of Esteban's men. Quite insignificant. We encountered zem on ze road coming from Yavisa; a surprise mutual, I apprehend. Shots are exchange', and a running fight ensue. Zey 'ave ze superior force, but we give a good account of ourselves. We lose two men, Alfredo and Sanchez, killed; zey lose eight, four killed, four prisoner. Zey follow us to ze gates; zen ze machine guns drive them off."

"Very good, captain," she says. "You will want to look after your men. I shall ask for the rest of the story later."

He saluted, and started to walk off, leading his horse; but I stopped him.

"Hold on a minute, cap." I says. "How many was there in the Esteban bunch?"

"About twenty, I would say," he answers; "we 'ave but t'irteen."

"Ought to have knowed better'n to start out with a hoodoo number like that." I waves him on his way. "You're lucky to have got through at all."

But what I was thinking was that I still had time to put through the move I was planning. Tyrell wasn't commencing operations ahead of schedule as I had feared. This was probably just a stray scouting party that Cosette had run into; not no part of the main forces. My spirits riz; I felt like a feller on the scaffold that's been granted a reprieve.

"Come on," I says to Gerta; "let's go back on the roof."

But she shakes her head.

"Our perfectly gorgeous moonlight evening is spoiled, Red," she says. "I've got to drop the sentimental maiden now and play commander in chief."

She tried to speak lightly, but I could see that she was worried.

"It's a certainty," she muttered, more as if to herself, "that Esteban will never accept getting the worst of a battle, without attempting reprisals. He will think he owes it to his prestige. This is the first open clash in a long while, and I am afraid it means a lot of fresh trouble.

"No, dear boy"—she turns to me—"I'll have to go into the situation thoroughly with Cosette, and see what is best to be done; and by the time I am through, the moon will be down. You'll excuse me for to-night, won't you, Red? Philandering must give way to the call of stern duty."

"But you were going to tell me something," I pleaded. "Can't you do that before you go?"

"Not now." She spoke curt. "The mood has passed, Red. Some other time—to-morrow, perhaps." And she turns and runs up the steps to her own quarters.

The very click of her heels was different. Funny. Up there in
the moonlight, she had been young. Young as April. She was
like a girl in second class of high school. But now all of a sudden
she made you think of the teacher, hard and bossy and superior
and you was just a sappy kid who didn't have no mix in really
important affairs.

Yet her hair was still hanging down her back, and she had on
that same commencement-day frock. So I guess it wasn't the
clothes that counted after all. It was, like she said, the mood
she was in. Although I may be a dumb-bell in some things, I've
learned this here: that a woman in a mood and a balky mule
is much the same; you can't drive 'em no way but the one their
head's set on, not even by lighting a fire under 'em.

Therefore and consequentially, I might as well give up hope
for to-night of Gerta spilling anything that'd be of use to me.
To-morrow, perhaps as she said. But to-morrow, if Tyrell kept
his word, 'd be too late.

If only that damn shooting hadn't interrupted us! If only it
had held off ten minutes longer!

But 'tain't no use crying over spilled milk; nor yet over
unspilled neither, which was more the case in this instance.
I just had to go ahead and dig up for myself what I needed to
know, same's I would if Gerta hadn't never offered to tell me.

The best time for digging up anything, I figured, was when I
was supposed to be tucked up for the night with the key turned
on me, safe from any attempts at snooping.

But first I had some arrangements to make with my more or
less trusty henchmen. Strange how history repeats itself, ain't
it? I remember we done a picture called "Ivanhoe" once—one
of them old-time things with knights in armor and the like of
that—and the hero of this piece, he was a good deal like me,
in a deuce of a fix without no one to depend on or to help him
out. So he has to make out as best he can, with a hog tender for
a esquire and a clown for his herald.

Exactly the same bill that I was putting on, you see, 'cept that

I was shy a clown. But then, as I didn't have no special call for a herald, that stanza could be omitted; if there was any need for clowning I could double the part myself. The main thing was to make sure that my esquire was on the job and wouldn't muff his cues.

So I saunters over toward the hog pens in search of this here Pedro, and pretty soon I locates him by his snoring and kicks him into semiconsciousness.

"Still standing by, are you, my hearty?" I asks. "Right on your toes, eh?"

"Aye, aye, sir," he says, or words to that effect. At any rate, he pulls his foretop.

"All right," I says; "but you may be needed to man the lugger before long, and I want you where I can put my hands on you quick. S'pose you continue this nap of yours over in the patio?

"But first," I says, "tell me how you get out of this here stockade, when it ain't expedient to give the password and go through all that red tape at the front gate? Where's the family entrance, so to speak?"

He gives me a quick, shifty look at that, and begins swearing by all the saints there ain't no such thing.

"Apple sauce!" I says, and chokes him a bit by way of refreshing his recollection.

Then he finally loosens up and tells me that over in the northeast corner of the fence behind a clump of yuccas, there is a couple of posts sawed off close to the ground, which when there is a friendly sentinel on guard can be pushed open wide enough to let a man and horse in and out.

"And who's the sentinel to-night?" I asks. "A sympathetic soul?"

"My brother." He shows his teeth in a grin. "He tell me, he go on at midnight."

Could you beat that for a *contretemps*, as Milt Leffingwell used to say? I begin to think that luck is coming my way.

"*Bueno!*" I says. "A couple of *buenos!* Now listen, amigo, You

go right out and hunt brother up. Show him this"—I slips a
silver dollar into his hand—"and tell him there'll be a couple
more of the same kind laying on the ground at the fence, if he
keeps his eye peeled for me to-night, and sets said secret postern
wide at my approach."

Then instructing him to report to me in the patio by rubbing
his sleeve twice across his nose if all is well I beats it back to
the house.

Pretty soon he shows up, and at the sight of me almost rubs
the nose off his face to indicate that everything is lovely. I'd told
him two rubs, but he was evidently one of them people think if
a little of a thing is good, a whole lot is better.

Fearing, however that if he don't stop, he may get quarantined
as a flu suspect, I nods him to a dark corner where he can curl
up convenient to the ramp, and having saw him comfortably
bedded down, goes into the office.

There I give an imitation of a man who is a weary, and wishes
he was in the hay. I starts putting things away for the night and
locking up, meanwhile yawning ostentatious and stretching till
I almost dislocated by shoulder blades.

Finally, having wound up the clock and put out the lights,
I stumbles heavy-footed up to my room. I takes off my shoes
and drops 'em one after another on the floor, thump, thump;
then, after rustling round a minute fixing a mound out of the
bedclothes so as to make it look like somebody was laying there,
I crouches down behind the door in my stocking feet, and waits.

Mebbe it's an hour, mebbe not so long, that I keeps my vigil,
as the title writers say; but at last I hear the soft slosh-slosh of
felt slippers in the corridor, and Wong comes to give his nightly
look-see.

Cautiouslike he opens the door a crack and peeps in; then as
there ain't no stir or movement from the mound of bedclothes
on the bed, he steps inside. But something seems to strike him
as wrong. He straightens up quick, and half faces around.

It's too late, though. Already my two hands is clutching his throat from behind; and kicking the door shut with my foot, I give a heave, and lands him over on the bed with me on top of him.

But even then I didn't loosen up none on him. Believe me, I knew better than to give that baby half a chance. I kept my two thumbs pressing into his windpipe until he went limp as a dish rag under me, and after that I choked him a spell longer just to make sure that he ain't pulling no Chinese trick on me.

Satisfied at last, I rolls him over to give him air; and while he's coming to, ties him up with the sheets, and relieves him of his gun and a bunch of keys that he's carrying. He's just beginning to roll his head and mutter, when I fastens a gag on him. I slips my feet into them felt dogs of hisn, jovially wishes him good night, and locking the door on him, pads off down the corridor.

Apparently I have the place wholly to myself, for not a sound do I hear nor a soul do I see until I reach the patio; and there the only thing that greets my eye is my faithful esquire sleeping just as I left him, with a butt dangling from the corner of his mouth.

Kind of uncanny-like, it was. That big, open square so empty and still and shadowy, where I was used to seeing it flooded with brilliant sunlight and a line of drowsy greasers propping up the walls and somebody always coming and going.

"It's like a circus lot when the show's on," I thinks to myself. "Everybody's in the main tent."

"Nevertheless, I don't ballyhoo my presence none. Silent as if I was a ghost of one of the old Vorezas, I slips along in the shadow of the wall, and rouses up Pedro.

"Time to up anchor, messmate," I whispers.

"Aye, aye, sir," he answers cheerily.

That was one beauty about a gink like this. His conversation was mostly grunts which you could translate any way you choose. He might be calling you a cross-eyed kangaroo, which he probably was; but you could always pretend it was an expression of fealty and devotion.

"But before we point for blue water, bos'n," I says, still sticking to the seafaring line, "let's take a peep down into the hold of the old brig, and see just what kind of cargo she's carrying."

Very quietly we snuck down the ramp, and made a observation. The visibility was low, owing to the fact that there was only one smoky lantern, but after peering round, I is pretty well satisfied that there ain't nobody here neither, 'cept'n' just the horses and a sentinel snoozing where tother one had been that afternoon. Might 'a' been the same one, for all I could say; there wasn't no difference in position.

"Go up and talk to him," I whispers to Pedro. "Tell him that when I was down here this afternoon, I dropped a purse with seven gold pieces in it, and ask him to help you search for it."

Where there's any cheating or chicanery to be done, a greaser'll show almost human intelligence. Pedro caught the idea at once, and stepping out into plain view, moves forward, casting his eyes here and there over the floor.

"Halt!" challenges the sentinel, swinging his rifle to a port. "What do you want down here, playmate of pigs?"

Pedro gets off the spiel I'd told him and immediately the sentinel is intrigued. After some jabbering in Spanish back and forth between 'em—chiefly relating to a division of the spoils— he gets up and starts to help looking. Pedro decoys him along toward the stall where I am lurking.

"Hah!" says Pedro just as he comes up to me, and jumps forward as if he'd spied something on the ground. Right away the sentinel dives after him; an I dive after the sentinel, landing on his shoulders and bringing him to the ground.

We ties him up with a couple of halters which Pedro fetched, and dragged him back into the stall. Then I eases out some of the straw that I'd poked into his mouth for a gag.

"A word out of you and you are a dead man," I says. "Now tell me where is this secret entrance you are guarding, and how does one get into it?"

But he was a stubborn devil, and we couldn't get a bleat out of him. Mebbe he didn't know; for he just kept shaking his head, even when we jabbed him once or twice with his own bayonet.

Anyways, I decided I couldn't waste no more time fooling with him; so me and Pedro goes over to the end wall and tries searching for the opening ourselves. But that was certainly one smooth little puzzle; without the combination you was lost. We passed our hands all up and down the wall, feeling for cracks and pressing every little knob or protuberance that we come to; but nothing budged.

Then just as I was figuring on going back and giving the sentinel another session, I seen a block of the pavement starting to rise, almost at my feet.

Quick as a wink, I doused the light of the lantern, and at the same minute jerked Pedro over to the spot where the sentinel had been.

"Play sentinel!" I hissed, thrusting the rifle into his hands.

As I tell you, these critters is natural-born flim-flammers. Wasn't it them that invented three-card monte?

"Halt!" bawls Pedro, without hesitating a second. "Give the countersign!" And he hands the fellow coming up out of the floor a poke in the breadbasket with the butt of his gun.

"Oof!" grunts the fellow. But he don't lose no time in giving the word. "Mariposa!" he sings out. "Mariposa!" I recognize the voice as that of Cortez, a pimply Peruvian, who was also one of Cosette's lieutenants. "Diablo! But you are impulsive," he grumbles. "Also, why is there no light?"

"Orders," says Pedro curtlike. "Orders from the señorita." I tell you this lad was there. He didn't need no prompting. And he's still holding Cortez back. "Why do you come out?" he asks suspicious, like a sentinel might.

"I seek that slant-eyed cat, Wong; he is wanted," says Cortez. "Do you know where he hides himself?"

"There is a game of fan-tan among his countrymen over at the far barracks," says Pedro.

"Good. That is where I shall find him. Let me pass."

"Pass," says Pedro, snapping up his rifle. The geezer climbs out of the hole, and hurries away up the ramp.

Soon's he's gone, I jerk out a flashlight I'm carrying in my pocket. There' a opening in the floor about three foot square, where the block in the pavement has lifted up. Easy enough, too, to see now how it's worked by pulling a innocent-looking ring in the ceiling.

Inside the opening is a flight of worn steps leading down, but they turn so quick that the flashlight don't show nothing more.

I don't like it a-tall. I ain't none too cautious, nor nothing like that; but this idea of poking into a rat hole where you don't know what's at the other end of it, and with the certainty that this Cortez is coming back before long to catch you between two fires as it were, ain't exactly appealing.

I sort of hesitates a second like a feller will before taking a dive into ice-cold water, although knowing he's got to do it, and puts my foot slow on the first step.

Then I jumps back, like I'd got a electric shock; for out of that hole came pealing the same blood-curdling screech I'd heard twicet before—the yell of a woman in awful agony.

CHAPTER XIII

GRUESOME DISCOVERY

"**S**ANTA MARIA!" gasps Pedro, starting to beat it.

"Come back here!" I snapped, throwing a spotlight after him with my flash lamp.

When I want to, I can slip a forty-five-caliber authority into my voice; and him being used to taking orders, it stopped him.

He came edging back, his teeth rattling like the dice in a alley crap game.

"What is it?" he squeaks, crossing himself with both hands at once—a sort of double cross. "Is it a ghost, señor? One of the dead Vorezas?"

"Ghost your grandmother!" I sneered, with what Milt Leffingwell used to call a touch of sang-fraud; only this was more fraud than sang. I was feeling a little shook up myself.

"That, Pedro," I says, "is an old garlic fiend of a nurse having a nightmare from smelling her own breath."

If Greta could stuff that explanation down my throat, why shouldn't it get by with a ignorant yokel like him? Living off in the pigsties like he did, he wasn't likely to know much about the habits of the folks in the big house nohow.

"It is the hag, Dolores," I told him, "dreaming that she has fell out of a garlic tree."

"But the garlic does not grow on trees, señor," he argues. "It is a plant." He held his hand out to show the height, about two feet off the ground.

"Granted," I says. "I merely put that in to make it harder. But nobody can't slip anything over on you, can they, you old fox?"

"I bet you, no!" He pounds himself on the chest, all swelled up.

I was jollying him along, you see, to get him over his scare. When he started to puff up like that and dispute with me, I felt I had him. A single-track, jerk-water mind like hisn couldn't possibly run two ideas at one time.

"Still, one might dream of garlic plants as tall as redwoods," I urged. "Eh, amigo?"

I was aiming to make the point that the reality of things wasn't usually such-a-much, 'twas only our own fancies that made 'em seem big or horrifying; and that, therefore, him and me might as well go ahead and find out what was the straight dope on this screech we'd heard.

But he didn't have no more imagination'n one of his hogs. He just keeps insisting that he's a very smart man, and no one could make him believe garlic growed on trees. 'Tis a small, low plant with a thin stalk and a flower at the top, he says; very good for soups, and in chile con carne, or goat stew. So I give it up; no use wasting precious moments trying to drill philosophy or Bell's letters into that low-brow.

"All right," I says. "Have it your own way; garlic is garlic. But what I want to known now is, since I am planning to take a little trip into this interesting hole in the ground, are you game to accompany me?"

"No?" as he backs away, and commences crossing himself again. "Well, I can't say I'm disappointed, 'cause I didn't hardly expect you would. Yet one last boon I crave, dainty page, ere our ways part." This last was cribbed from a title in that old-time picture I was telling about, although I admit 'twas a dead loss of nice language, using it on a tramp like him.

"I may have to make a quick get-away," I lapses back into English again. "So you saddle up Henry Ford and that pinto pony of the señorita's, and take 'em up into the patio where they'll be handy for me. Pronto!" To show that I meant it, I give him a kick that landed him clean up at Henry Ford's stall. Well played; what?

Also, to make sure that he didn't sneak out on me, I waited until I seen him leading the two cayuses up the ramp. Then I turned and dived down into the rabbit hole. Oh, I don't know that, strictly speaking, you could exactly call it, diving; that is, unless you was implying slow-motion camera stuff, if you get what I mean.

As a matter of fact, I wasn't much more anxious for the job than Pedro. Not that I was leery of ghosts, or nothing like that. I suspicioned pretty well what I was going to find; and I thought I knew, too, what was the *cause celebre* of that screeching.

There wasn't no real danger as I figured it, 'lessn I might happen to collide with one of the greasers in the dark, and he should slip a knife into me before I could apologize. They're a bit abrupt that way.

No; what bothered me was the fear of being caught at it. That'd muddle up things considerable; for I'd not only fail in what I was planning to do, but it'd put me in dutch with Gerta. She'd never believe the real reason for me snooping around down there. She'd think I was spying for Esteban. Nothing I could say or do would ever square that with her. She'd have more respect for a bedbug.

Still, for her sake, I had to take the risk. If I wavered any, I had only to think of what would happen in the morning if Tyrell came and found his daughter still there; and that would nerve me up again. There was hardly a doubt but what the gal was somewhere at the other end of this secret passage. Nothing for it, but to go ahead and locate her, and then stage a rescue.

So I inches down into the hole, hugging close to the wall, and feeling my way with my foot 'cause I didn't dare use the flashlight; and yet not moving so dern slow neither, on account of not knowing how soon that Peruvian lieutenant'd come hot-footing it back.

The steps, as I said, went down a little way and then turned;

and then went down a little way more and turned again. But
when they turned this second time, they started to go up, as
I discovered by stumbling over the first step and barking my
shin. It was painful, but it gave me the combination as you
might say; for I see now that this stairway is just like them at a
subway station where you go from a express to a local platform
by passing under the tracks. In other words, when I got to the
top, I'd be just opposite where I started from, only behind the
wall instead of in front of it.

With this knowledge, I took back the rude remarks I'd been
making about that step and its female relatives, and pushes
cheerily ahead. A bit too cheerily, as it turned out; for as I
rounded the last turn, spang, I butts right into a big greaser
who growls, "Halt!"

It took me plumb by surprise, although I ought to have
knowed there'd be a sentinel on this side same as on the other;
but I'm one of them that carries my wits around with me.

"Mariposa!" I sings out the password that Cortez had given.

'Twas lucky, too, that I didn't hesitate none, I guess, 'cause
when he pushed back the slide of a old-fashioned dark lantern
what he'd shut off when he heard me coming, I seen that he
didn't have no rifle, but a *machete*, which in the hands of these
spiggotty races is considerable more effective.

Also he had the darn thing raised; so the chances is, that if I
hadn't spoke out snappy I'd 'a' been halved same's a grapefruit.

When I seen it, and the threatening way he was holding it, I
shoots three more "Mariposas!" at him real quick, to make sure
that he ain't hard of hearing.

But bless his dear heart, he wasn't inclined to be fussy. I had
gave the password all right, and he knew I belonged in the
household; that was enough for him to figure me a brother in
good standing.

He lowers his old corn cutter, and with a grunt to signify that
he hadn't no further interest in me, eases himself back on the box
where he'd been setting, and starts to roll a cigarette.

Some folks'd have lost their poise over a incident like that; but not me. I give a bored salute like I was a major general full of business, and hustles along. By the time I got around the next corner and leaned up against the wall to kind of pull myself together, my hair was laying down natural again, and the cold sweat on my spine had almost dried.

Also, I took advantage of the opportunity to give some study to my surroundings. Remember that fillum somebody screened—kind of a trick thing—of a kid who got through the looking-glass? Being only a reflection, you'd think that what she found was just the same as t'other side, only turned around. But not so.

Well, this here layout reminded me of that fool story. On t'other side of the wall was just a big, open cellar, with horse stalls in it, and a ramp leading down, but over here, it was different.

There was the same dobe walls, and the same irregular tiles to walk on, and the same underground smell; but the whole place seemed to be made up of twisting, branching passageways, with hollowed-out chambers offn 'em, like in the cataclysms of Rome or Paris. If you didn't watch your step mighty close, you'd be lost afore you knowed it.

Three of them passageways run off from where I stood; but although I took a chance and flashed my light along 'em, t'wasn't better'n a toss-up which one of 'em to take. They altered off at right angles almost right away, and they all looked practically alike.

"Best thing I can do," I says to myself, "is to shut my eyes, turn around three times, and then follow my nose whichever one of 'em it's pointing to."

But just then the question was decided for me by another of them terrifying screeches. It came plainly from the right-hand burrow, and before the echoes of it had died away, I had cork-screwed around three turns of the narrow passage, caroming from one wall to another in the darkness, and saw a dull, red light ahead of me.

It seemed to come from a sort of chink or hole in the wall, and after halting and reconnoitering to make sure that there wasn't no guards about, I snuck cautious up to it, and took a peep.

Did I get a eyeful? I'll say I did.

What I seen was a big cave or vault, which as near as I could locate it, must have been dug out beyond the foundations of the house.

Down at the end where I was peeping through was a bunch of prisoners, all heavily ironed—two or three greasers that looked like fairly well-to-do small ranchers, the proprietor of the El Toro Cafe at Yavisa, and a couple of Esteban's troopers—with about twenty of Cosette's soldiers around 'em as guards.

They didn't look none too happy, them captives. Tony, the big gink from El Toro, appeared just about ready to cash in. He was trembling like a shaved dog in a snow storm, and his yellow, wicked face had changed to a sort of sickly green.

But I didn't give much more than a glance to that part of the show. My eye was drawn to the upper end of the vault, where there was a kind of old-time judgement seat, and on it was setting— Who do you think?

You guessed it. Gerta! Yet it wasn't Gerta, neither. Not the girl that had sat with me in the moonlight, anyhow. Nor yet the one that had rode with me on her little pinto, slim as a boy in her khaki shirt and canvas breeches. Nor the one tricked out in lace and diamonds, with a rose in her hair, and all that princess stuff, like she was that first night I pulled in. Nor the one that had read poetry to me in the library.

This was a different Gerta—miles away, especially from that girl in the moonlight. Here was something no man on earth'd want to kiss and cuddle, not no more'n he would want to kiss a granite block out of the walls of Sing Sing.

She had changed her commencement-day dress for a robe of dull, black silk like what a judge wears, and she wore a black cap on her head. But it wasn't the clothes that counted, grim and somber though they was. 'Twas her face, white and stony as if she was carved out of marble, and kind of the way she was setting, too; not no more give to her'n if her backbone was made outn this now—azimuth. Reinforced concrete, that's what she was.

Only her eyes moved, and they was cold and dead looking as points of icicles. Just to look at her, you knowed you couldn't assay a ounce of pity or womanly softness out of her, not by no process. 'Twasn't there to be got.

Seeing her put me wise, too, to what this was all about. This here vault was prob'ly the judgement hall of the Vorezas in the old days when they had the power of life and death over their peons, all fixed up gloomy and underground so as to throw the fear of the Lord into offenders. Now that she had taken over the property, she had dusted it out, and was using it in the same way. She was holding court; that's what she was doing.

On the right of her a barred door was standing open, and through it I could see a line of rusty cells, which I judged was the hoosegow where her interesting collection of birds was kept until it was their turn to say, "Good morning, judge." Over on the other side was a solid iron door which, although it was closed, seemed to attract a whole lot more notice, just why, I couldn't make out at the moment.

It wasn't long, though, before I seen the reason; for I had hardly took in these various details, before Gerta gave a nod toward one of the prisoners—a small-time rancher—and he was grabbed by a couple of the guards and hustled up in front of her.

"Joe Miguel," she says, "under orders from Esteban, you poisoned twenty head of my cattle, and maliciously destroyed a thousand dollars' worth of my crops. Useless to deny it; I have positive proof of your guilt. It is just that you should pay. There-fore, write me an order to your wife for five thousand pesos, so that I may send my agent with it to get the money."

"Five thousand pesos!" He acted like he thought she'd gone looney. "Santa Maria, señorita! There is not so much money in the whole world. Strip me to the bare bones, and you could not get more than three hundred pesos all put together, and even that it would take weeks to assemble."

He might just as well have saved his breath, for all it got him.

"Five thousand pesos," she said. "Do you write the order?"

"Señorita, it is impossible," he insisted. "Let me tell you how—"

But there he stopped. I, for one, didn't blame him. For just then that iron door to one side opened, and out from behind it came that same devilish shriek. You couldn't help looking, and what you seen made your blood run colder still. There was a room there, lit up with a flickering red glow like from a fire, and by it you could see old-fashioned instruments of torture like what you've seen in pictures of the Spanish Imposition. Nor that wasn't all. You could hear the strokes of a whip and a sort of sobbing, whimpering moan after each stroke, like somebody was just about all in.

"Another man," says Gerta, "who told us that we must strip him to the bare bones to get our just payment for damages rendered. We are doing it—with the lash."

But the rancher still held out.

"I cannot, señorita!" he pleaded. "I cannot. All that I have I will give, my land, my crops, my cattle. But—"

A masked figure in a long, black robe came to the door of the torture room, and made a sign to Gerta.

"So?" she said, with no more feeling than a cake of ice. "One ransom we will not collect, eh? He cared more for his money than his life. Very well; throw his carrion into the slack lime, and get the rack ready for this one."

At a nod from her, the guards started with the half-fainting ranchero for the door of that room; but just as they reached it, out came a stretcher with the body of the dead man on it, and the ranchero after one shuddering look at it chucked the sponge.

"No! No, señorita!" he howled, throwing himself on the floor and groveling. "I yield. You shall have the order. Give me ink and paper, and I will write."

I ain't weak-stomached or nothing like that; but I'm here to tell you that the whole Atlantic Ocean couldn't make me no more seasick. That there scene was ghastly. The worst of it was Gerta. That frozen face of hers, and her voice indifferent as the wind at the north pole! Talk about them janes of antiquity, Lucreezia Borgia and Helen of Troy and such, sitting in their box at the amphitheater, a-munching chocolates while the lions chased a bunch of Christians over the gridiron, and stopping now and then to applaud prettily: "Well bit, captain, isn't he a darling?" or, "Judy seems a bit off in her game to-day; she's only got three so far." Believe me, they didn't have nothing on Gerta. Inexorable! That's the word I've been trying to think of, and that was her.

Was this the girl that had tinkled her guitar up there on the roof, and sang old ballads in the moonlight? No wonder she told me she had something to tell me before she let me kiss her. You'd no more think of kissing the woman up there on the judge's bench'n you would a refrigerator full of snakes.

Somehow, it didn't seem real to me. 'Twas just like that fillum, "Through the Looking Glass," I was telling you about. Everything on this side of the hall was topsy turvy and wrong and upside down.

But it was real enough, all right—pretty damn real, I guess, to that poor wretch she'd had whipped to death without even the quiver of a eyelash.

I was sickened, disgusted, revolted. Yet I couldn't get out of my mind that girl with her hair hanging down her back what had reminded me of apple blossoms and spring.

God help me! As Shakespeare says, with all her faults, I loved her still!

CHAPTER XIV

EXCITING CHASE

NEXT UP was the genial mine host of the El Toro; and
believe me, folks, if it'd been a barber shop, they wouldn't
had to waste no time getting that guy fixed for the razor. He
was all lathered up a'ready.

But Gerta was like one of the small-town tonsorial artists
when there ain't no other customers around; she kept rubbing
it in on him. Only difference was, she didn't advance no line of
conversation about prohibition, or Philadelphia's chances for
the pennant, or was Smithers going to get the nomination for
mayor, or what did he think of this here now Arbutus in the
fourth at Pimlico.

She just set and looked at him; and the stiller she set, the
more the sweat pumped out of that big greaser. I'll bet he was
sloshing in his shoes.

"Antonio Moreno," she said at last; and for all she spoke low,
the sound of her voice made him jump like a cannon firecracker
had gone off behind him. "Antonio Moreno," she says, "no need
to tell you that your life is forfeit. You know how treacherously
you have played the spy for Esteban, and how you plotted to
betray me to him."

She paused, and a couple of them boys in the black masks
come edging out of the torture room toward him. Gosh! It
gives me the creeps myself to see 'em. The genial mine host, he
flopped down on the floor, and began jabbering for mercy in six
different languages.

"Stand up!" she says, but she might as well have addressed her remarks to a soft-boiled egg. So two of the guards yanked him up on his feet and held him.

"Richly as you deserve punishment, I am going to spare you this time, Moreno," she said. "You shall be released, furnished with a horse, and allowed to return to Yavisa unharmed—on one condition."

"Anything. Anything, señorita!" he groveled.

"It is not, as you probably suppose," she went on indifferent-like, "that you promise good behavior for the future. In the first place your word is of no value; and in the second, if you do not behave, I will get you just as I did this time, and that will be the end of you.

"No," she said, "my condition is simply that you deliver without delay a message from me to Jeff Tyrell. Tell him that I want the one hundred thousand dollars he stole from his daughter's estate. Tell him that, since he evidently does not care what becomes of his daughter, I propose to find out just how highly he values his own skin. Report to him what you have seen here, and tell him that unless the money is paid over before to-morrow night neither he nor his daughter will ever leave Mexico alive. If he thinks he can escape me, let him try it."

I read her like a book. It was a bluff she was pulling, 'cause she'd found out Tyrell wasn't aiming to come across with no ransom money, and it had turned her plumb desperate. Just bluffing she was; but you'd never have guessed it from her face or her manner. She sure played her hand like she had 'em.

To anybody like me, that was in on the know, it was almost pitiful; 'cause I seen just how hard that bluff of hern was going to be called in the morning, when Papa Jeff showed up with a fist full of French seventy-fives.

Game! I'll say she was. Cool as if it didn't mean nothing more to her than a extry chop for breakfast, she waved her hand to the guards that had Moreno.

"Blindfold this man, and take him to the gate," she said. "Then furnish him a horse, and let him go free."

But at this, the old bean, which had been sort of clogged up in the last ten minutes, begins to hit regular again.

"Whoa, there!" says I to myself. "That ain't never going to do. To turn this guy loose and send him with a message like that to Tyrell is leading right into Jeff's hand. It gives him proof that his daughter is a prisoner here, and justifies him in this habeas corpus he's starting. I'm afraid," I says, "that both the wise, young judge and the prisoner at the bar is going to find themselves disappointed. Decision is overruled."

Just how I was going to manage it, I wasn't at the minute entirely clear. But as things turned out, it was easy. I've generally noticed, when somep'n simply has to be did, the way to do it shows up.

This was the modest operandi, as Milt Leffingwell used to say. As them two guards, obedient to Gerta's orders, blindfolded Moreno and started to pilot him out of the entrance, they naturally had to pass down the corridor where I was standing. So when they went by, I just crouched back in the dark of my little niche; and them not being on the look-out, remained happily unseen.

Then I slips softly after them a piece down the passageway and drawing my automatic, whispers them well-known words, "Hands up!"

The response, as is usual, was prompt and satisfactory.

"Keep 'em aloft," I growls. "Eyes front, all three of you. Also, not a sound. If any one of you lets out a peep, starts to turn around, or makes a funny move of any kind, he'll finish it in hell.

"Now you on the right, lead off," I continues, addressing the guard on that side, "and head straight for that empty dungeon along the passageway here."

I didn't rightly know that there was any such thing, but I figured that there ought to be; and my figuring was correct. We hadn't gone more'n twenty steps, before the big hick marches us up to a low, iron-sheathed door with a heavy, old-fashioned bolt on the outside of it.

I made the three of 'em stand beyond it; warning 'em not to forget for a second that I still had the drop on them. Then I drew the bolt, pushed open the door with my foot, and flashed my lamp over the interior.

By heck, it might have been made to order for what I wanted—solid walls and ceiling, tight as a bank vault, practically sound-proof, and just about big enough for the three of them with a little crowding.

"In you go!" I says. So completely did I have 'em overawed that they shambled in like so many sheep. With a quick jerk, I pulled the door shut on 'em and shot home the bolt.

So that was that. Not a chance of 'em busting the door down, and they could pound and holler all they wanted to. All you could hear out in the corridor was just a weak sort of tapping, and you had to be right by the door to get even that.

Yet somehow, I couldn't feel comfortable over it. Everything had worked out too smooth and easy; there must be a hitch somewhere. Also, I wasn't no closer to my main objective, which was to locate the Tyrell girl and get her away from there. I wasn't no closer to it, and time was passing.

I left the dungeon and my three captive song birds—twittering bravely but vainly in the effort to make 'emselves heard—and I snuck back along the corridor toward the judgement hall.

But hey nonny nonny, I hadn't hardly reached my old listening post, before I heard someone coming, Sister Anne. Oh, my prophetic soul, my Uncle Ebenezer; as Milt was wont to remark when tearing his hair. I sure had suspicioned right, when I felt that this program of mine wasn't going to run along without a hitch in it somewheres.

For now, to judge by the sounds that assailed my ears, there was not one but three hitches approaching—Wong, the chink, breathing fire and fury in pidgin English; Cortez, the Peruvian, breathing ditto in Español; and that there sentinel what I'd tied up in the horse stall following suit with a patter all his own. Three full-voiced hitches, r'aring like tigers, and a pack of lesser hitches behind 'em! On your way, Red. On your way!

Listen. 'Dj'ever get into one of them alleged side-splitting comedies where the star is chased around and around the set by all the rest of the cast and maybe a couple of trick lions? It's supposed to be sure-fire stuff, although I have yet to see the audience that gives it even a snicker.

But that was just the moldy, old, moth-eaten scenario that I drawed in this instance. Up and down these underground passageways they raced me like a rat with a bunch of ferets after him. And mind you, 'twas all in the dark, too; for I didn't dare use my flashlight. Dodging, twisting, turning, doubling, so mixed up in my bearings that I couldn't find my way out no more'n if I was in one of the mystic mazes at Coney's Island. They fair run me ragged.

I'd dive into an opening, thinking that it led straight to the exit, and first thing you know I'd bang smack into one of them babies, and have to backtrack to where I started from. All the time, the gang was closing in on me.

Finally, when I was just about all in, and could see their lights and hear them yapping on all sides of me, I stumbled into a sort of narrow opening, and found myself on a winding stairs.

I hadn't no idea where they led to, if anywhere; but it was what you might call a Hobnail's choice. Not ten feet away from me on one side, I could hear a squealing, "Mokahai!" and not ten feet away on the other side, a growling, "Gringo peeg;" while in the middle distance, so to speak, the Peruvian was indulging in equally uncomplimentary dialogue. Believe me, Reginald, 'twas a small-time Tower of Babel.

So up I sprints lightsomely and encounters a door. It was not where I expected a door to be, and consequently I added a few stanzas to that international cussing chorus. But every cloud has a silver lining; and it is chiefly owing to said door that this fillum of mine runs on continuous, instead of breaking off at this point in a bowl of chop-suey and paprika.

When I recover from my surprise, which is in about a split second, being that the chink is only about four steps behind me with a knife a foot long, I dodges through the door, and shoots home another of them old-fashioned bolts which is fortunately on the inside.

"I guess that'll hold you for awhile!" I mutters, pausing to draw my breath; for this here friendly door is made of planks a full two-inch thick, and bolted and braced like a battleship. Even if they got axes, 'twould take 'em at least a half hour to chop through it.

Still 'twasn't no place to linger. Not knowing where them stairs run to, for they continued up on the other side of the door, how could I tell but that them coyotes might come around to get me some other way.

Nevertheless, before plunging ahead, I took a chance and unlimbered the old flashlight so as to see where I was going; but can't say as I gained much by it. All I could make out was that the stairs wound on up a piece further to another door.

Another door! Do you get that? Suppose the durn thing was locked? Somep'n seemed to tell me that it was. Then and in that case, I was neatly trapped. All I could do was to wait on that stretch of stairs until they come and got me.

So never doubting what the result was going to be, I trudged up to this next door, and gave it a sort of hopeless push with my foot. Then I got the jolt of my young career, 'cause the fool door swung open without the slightest trouble in the world, and looking down a short passageway, I seen a glimmer of moonlight and the railing of the balcony over the patio that run by Gerta's private quarters.

This here stairs I'd just come up was evidently her own secret passage to the crypt, winding down to it inside one of the thick adobe walls of the old hacienda. If I'd had any doubt on that score, it was settled as I stepped through and pushed the door

shut behind me; for it closed with the click of a spring, and looking back, I could see it was all covered with stucco on the outside,
and fit so closely that you couldn't tell it from the rest of the wall.

I didn't stop to investigate, but I'm satisfied that I'd have had
to fool around quite a while before I got wise to the combination that'd open her up again. 'Twas sure lucky for me that it'd
been only on the latch, else I'd been mewed up there 'tween the
two doors just as I thought I was.

Howsoever, I ain't one that crosses bridges before I come to
'em, or after I'm over 'em, either. I was out. No need to bother
about might-have-beens. The chief consideration now was what
to do next.

Get the lay of the land, please. Right down that passageway
ahead of me was the balcony. A swing over the railing, and a
short drop, and I'd be in the patio. Then all I had to do was hop
on Henry Ford, right out to the gap in the stockade that Pedro
had fixed for me, and beat it gay to the border.

That's what anybody but a damn fool would have done. But
I was the hero of this piece, remember—everybody's a hero to
himself, even if his valet and the rest of the world regards him
as a hunk of cheese—and heroes, as Milt Leffingwell once told
me, has to be damn fools, else they wouldn't be heroes.

To put it plain, I just couldn't go off and leave things in the
mess they was. Gerta might have some little ways that I didn't
altogether approve of—the thought of that dead greaser still
turned me a little sick—but that wasn't no excuse for leaving
her to the tender mercies of a couple of buzzards like Tyrell and
Esteban.

Also, I had to know how it all come out. Across the border
I'd be safe, but I'd be itching so with curiosity wondering what
was happening, that I'd be apt to run a temperature. Think I was
going to take any chances of maybe having to go to a hospital
with fever? Not me. Safety first's my motto.

So, instead of leaving P.P.C. cards for all inquiring friends
and acquaintances, as was sane and sensible, I decides to creep

down to the office, and pretend to have been asleep there, while all the skullduggery was going on. Then when Wong and Cortez and the sentinel made their charges agin' me, I'd swear they was either lying, or else they'd been imposed on by some enemy passing himself off as me.

Maybe it would have worked, maybe not. Maybe, too, 'twould have given me the chance for a private interview with Gerta—which was what I was really after—so's I could give her the low-down, as I now saw I should have done in the first place, on what it all meant, telling her straight that she had to get the Tyrell girl off her hands, or else lose everything. And maybe, then, she'd have listened to reason.

Maybe, I say. But the trouble was I didn't carry none of that strategy into effect. For as I tiptoed down the passageway toward the balcony, a door suddenly opens on one side of it, and standing there in the glow of the lamplighted room behind her is a pretty fair-looking female, a blonde in a pink kimono.

She was an absolute stranger to me, hadn't never set eyes on her before; but that didn't prevent me from identifying her right off the reel.

"Oh, here you are Miss Tyrell," I says, swinging off my hat. "I've been looking all over the place for you."

CHAPTER XV

LOCHINVAR

THE GIRL grabs at her chest, and jumps back.

"Who are you?" she stammers. Plain to be seen, she's just as much surprised as I am, only she don't carry it so well.

"Don't be alarmed, ma'am." Old G.W. Chesterfield himself didn't have nothing on me. "I'm Red Conners, at your service. Here to rescue you, ma'am."

"To rescue me?" She looks kind of uncertain, wondering of course if it wasn't some kind of a trap.

But as she paused to give me a frightened once over, there come a hell of a thumping and pounding from down the stairs where them three Siberian bloodhounds is trying to bust open the door.

"There is trouble in the house?" she squeals, all of a twitter.

"You're dead right, there is," says I; "and going to be more. No time to argue, ma'am," I says. "This is your chance to get away but to do it, we'll have to step lively. You've just got to take me on trust as a friend, and come."

Now there's a subtitle that I've never seen fail yet to convince the Tessies of the silver screen that everything was all jake; but this mutt don't even give it a tumble.

"Oh, I don't know what to do!" she whimpers.

She sizes me up with another doubtful look, and I guess I don't appear so good, 'cause she half shakes her head. But just then a fresh burst of hammering comes up from below, and she changes it to a scared nod.

"I'll go! I'll go!" she says. "J-j-just wait. I'll dress and be with you right away."

"Dress?" I snaps at her. "This ain't no garden party; it's a escape."

I looks beyond her into the room, and sees a sort of a dark cloak hanging over the back of a chair. In two strides I got to it, and picking it up, wraps it around her.

"Come on," I says, catching her by the hand.

But she hangs back, and starts to hedge again, meowing like a sick kitten that she didn't know, and she wasn't sure, and how awful it was. By gad, she made me sick with her white face, and her china-blue eyes, and her whining. She didn't have no more guts than a lump of putty.

I couldn't help but think how Gerta would have acted in the same fix. With her, it would have been "Yes," or "No," just like that and what she said, you couldn't have budged her from it. But this frail, she didn't know her mind—if any she had—two minutes in succession.

There's only way to deal with that kind, and I done it. I didn't stop to argue with her no more, but just scoops her up in my arms, and starts with her for the balcony.

She let's out a screech, and begins kicking me with her heels.

I shuts off the music by clapping my hand over her mouth, and addresses her stern.

"Keep quiet," I growls, "or if you don't, I'll give you a poke in the jaw. Now, behave!"

Cave-man stuff. That's what gets this fluffy-ruffles type every time. Red blood is their natural food and drink, same as it is to a tiger cat. Not a yelp out of her after that; nor a kick. She just snuggles down to enjoy being carried off by the great, rough brute.

Lugging her out to the balcony, I took a quick survey of the situation. All the excitement that was visible to the naked eye you could have crowded into a burial vault and never raised a ripple. The house was dark and silent; the patio deserted, except for the two horses standing over to one side of it agreeable to my orders, and Pedro in the sleep of gentle innocence beside 'em.

But hark! "Is it a car rattling o'er the stony street?" as Milt was fond of asking if something was dropped in striking a set.

In this case, it was not. It sounded more to me like that door on the stairs had gone down under the infurious battering of the alley forces. Not a second to lose. Two minutes more, and they'd be on top of me.

I whistled shrill and sharp, and at the call Henry Ford jerked loose his lead rope from the relaxed fingers of Pedro, and came cantering across the patio, the pinto pony trailing him.

Then, grasping my fair burden firmly, I started for the steps running down to him. But at that moment, up the ramp came pouring a mob of Cosette's soldiers, with Gerta at the head of 'em, waving torches and completely shutting off my exit; while at the same instant I could hear the snarling of the three musketeers and their henchmen as they dashed from the secret stairway along the passage to the balcony.

Cannon to right of me, cannon to left of me. I couldn't go back, and I couldn't go forward. Looked like I was ketched, eh, what?

But it takes more than a squeeze of that sort to decompose Red Conners.

"Hold fast!" I barked like a Amsterdam Avenue conductor to this pillowsham I was loaded with.

Then I flings myself with her over the balcony railing, and hangs by one hand. Henry Ford is just underneath me, his back about two inches from my dangling toes.

"Whoa, Henry," I says, and he stands like a rock.

Then I let go, and lands pretty as you please square in the saddle, with the lady jolted but unhurt still in the hollow of my arm. Another second, and we was streaking it for the archway and the great open spaces.

Bang! A red-hot stripe flicks along the side of my neck, and I hears another bullet go zipping past my ear. But the archway was already looming above us. One more plunge, and we was through, incidentally knocking over the sentinel that tried to stop us.

I turned my head, and shot one glance back, just as we cleared the danger zone. It was Gerta who nicked me; for the whole thing had been so quick that the others didn't have no chance to get into action. That come a minute later with a cracking and sputtering that sounded like a Chinese Fourth of July—a wild fusillade that didn't hurt nothing but the 'dobe walls of the patio.

But she had drawed as quick as she saw what I was up to, and had blazed away at us as we went thundering out through the archway. In that look I flung back over my shoulder, I seen her guns still flashing and smoking. Believe me, them two spitting canisters wasn't no more hostile nor deadly than her eyes—gleaming sort of green in the torchlight, and out of a face that was white as chalk.

She hadn't been exactly no Dotty Dimple, when she was setting down in the judgement hall, but, gee, boy, that was a cream puff beside the pan she had on her now. I'd seen her mad before, but never nothing like this, nor in just the same way. She was rabid, I tell you. And there wasn't no doubt what she was aiming to do neither: she was trying to kill me.

Get that, will you? Two hours before she'd been singing with me in the moonlight, and begging me to hold off from kissing her, same as any other normal girl; and here she was, doing her best to murder me. Some temper'ment, I'll tell the world.

But the most surprising part was that she'd missed me, 'cause you couldn't rightly call that little scrape on my neck a hit. She's missed me, and Gerta didn't know how to miss. I remembered how she'd stepped through the screen doors at the El Toro, and without even bothering to take aim, had bored Esteban through his two wrists.

I'd like to have thought that she missed a-purpose, not really wishing to get me. But that didn't reconcile with the green fire in her eyes, nor yet with the fact that she'd actually drawed blood on me. No; it was over-eagerness to get me that made her miss, and not under-eagerness. Why she should have turned so vicious all for a sudden, blamed if I could figure. I hadn't done nothing that really justified it, so far's I could see. Suppose I had snooped a bit? Well, after us being so clubby and all, wouldn't you've expected her to ask for a explanation, 'sted of starting right in to blow my head off?

But these was later thoughts. At the moment, I was concerned chiefly in getting away from there. Down the road toward the gate I galloped for about a quarter of a mile, so as to throw 'em off on my intentions; then swinging sharply around behind some low sheds, I beats it for the northeast corner of the grounds, keeping my eye peeled for the clump of yuccas that was to serve me as a guide post.

Presently I spied it. All now depended on Pedro's brother. If he was true to his trust and the two smackers that'd been promised him, we'd have clear sailing through the fence. If not, I might as well make my peace with Heaven.

My heart was in my mouth as we raced toward the fateful spot. That line of stockade certainly looked solid as the United States treasury. Not a gap nor a break in it. Then slowly two of the posts swung out, and a narrow opening showed itself.

"Go to it, Henry!" I said, and through it we tore.

Free at last. A shadowy figure beside the fence growled, "Gracias," as I flung back the two iron men. Then came the pounding of hoofs behind us. I half turned in my saddle to see whether the gap was closed or not. It wasn't yet; and as I looked back, I seen a equine head and shoulders come busting through.

"Right on our heels, ain't they?" I says to myself, and I drops the bridle to reach for my automatic.

But there wasn't no rider on this horse. How oft does the— something or other—that we most fear turn out to be a blessing in disguise, as was said by a piece in my school reader. Instead of being bestrode by an enemy, the cayuse that come through the fence was none other than my old companion of many a joyous canter, Gerta's pinto pony. Being loose in the patio, he had naturally followed his stablemate, Henry, although with all the twisting and turning we'd done, I hadn't sighted him before.

It was a big relief to me in more ways than one. "Here," says I, "is where I shake my fair burden," which I'm free to admit I was quite ready to do, she not being no flyweight, and in addition laying absolutely dead in my arms like a sack of mush.

Besides, although we had a good start, I knew that, if they gave us any kind of a chase, Henry Ford was practically anchored, carrying double weight like that.

So I reined up, and letting the pinto range in alongside of me, I catches him by the bridle.

"Can you ride?" I says to the girl, sliding down out of the saddle with her, and dumping her on her own two feet.

"Not as I am," she beefs. "To do that, I'd require proper riding togs. I was just getting ready to—to retire," she minces, "when you carried me off. And I'd dropped one of the bedroom slippers I had on."

She lisped it out in a sort of injured way, and she held up one bare foot, expecting me no doubt to throw a fit over the poor little tootsie.

But for once I couldn't rise to the occasion. That crack about riding togs had just about floored me.

"Say!" I let loose, when I finally caught my breath. "What do you think this is? A little jog around the bridlepath in Central Park, with me grooming along behind? You'll ride," I tells her, "if you've got to do it in the costume of this here Lady Go-dive-her; for otherwise, you're very apt to be getting measured for a wooden overcoat. Don't think, girlie," I says, "that these folks don't mean business. An inch to the right, and that bullet I got would have fricasseed my brains, 'stead of only scoring me along the neck like it did."

She took a high C on that.

"Oh, were you hit back there?" she squealed. "I thought I felt you swerve, and then gather me closer as if to shield me. You were really struck by a bullet. Really and truly?"

"How many times you want me to tell you?" I growls, getting a little sore at that "Really and truly?" she kept repeating. "If you doubt it, just put your hand on my left shoulder there, and you'll get the proof."

I twisted my shoulder around to her as I spoke, and she leaned over and touched it.

"Blood!" she yelped. "Your shirt is soaked with it. You are wounded! Wounded for me!"

She rolled up her eyes like a duck in a thunderstorm and flopped over on me, clutching me in a stranglehold around the neck.

"Oh, I believe I am going to faint," she says.

I was helpless, with my two hands full of bridles, which I didn't dare let go for fear the horse'd bolt. I could only stand there and let her clinch.

Just at that minute, a long pencil of light came sweeping around from the searchlight at the gate, and picked us out. Full on us they held it, showing to all who might be looking an affecting tableau of us apparently clasped in each other's arms.

CHAPTER XVI

A BAD JOB

THEY SAY every actor craves the spotlight. But there is a time for all things; and this was once where I could very comfortably have passed it up. Picked out as we was by it, I knew the gang would be down on us in about a couple of minutes.

"Gee whiz!" I jerks loose from the clinch the jane has fastened on me. "Can't you see what we're up against? Climb onto that pony, I tell you; and don't lose no time doing it, neither. You've got to ride now, whether you know how or not."

"But first let me bind up your wound," she quavers, grabbing at me again, and holding up a little trick han'k'cher that wouldn't have made patch for a katydid's trousers.

She probably meant well; but I was foaming to get started.

"Hell's bells!" I roars. "I ain't got nothing but a mere scratch; keep that first-aid of yourn for somebody that's lost both legs and mebbe a arm. Will you get onto that horse?"

To avoid further argument, I lets go of Henry Ford's bridle, and heaves her up into the pony's saddle.

"You might at least be a gentleman," she sniffs as the damn pinto jerks back and tromps all over my foot. "I was only trying to do a kindness. And if the handkerchief wasn't big enough, I could have torn a bandage from—from elsewhere."

"Humph!" say I. "Strikes me, that one good bandage offn elsewhere'd turn you into a Lady Go-dive-her for fair. The part must appeal to you.

"Enough of that, though," I continues, for by this time I

had ketched Henry Ford and was once more aboard him. "It's riding and not repartee that's our long suit in this juncture. Hit her up, sister."

I slapped the pinto a belt cross the rump, that jolted him into almost unseating his fair rider; and away we fanned.

Unnecessary to describe that ride. We kept going; that's about all there is to tell. 'Twasn't more'n a hour before I was satisfied that we'd shook off whatever pursuit there was; I could run rings around that bunch with my eyes shut. But I didn't tell the Tyrell girl so.

Course I eased up on her, soon's I was sure we was really shut of 'em. Even for myself, I don't know as I'd care to do a long stretch on horseback in nothing much 'cept a silk kimono and one bedroom slipper; and after we'd gone through a patch or two of chaparral she had still less protection agin' the elements. Not that t'was a bad night a-tall; but 'twould be idle to deny that there's a certain chill in the air down there after the sun sets, which makes you hanker for something more'n just bathing-girl costume.

Furthermore, it didn't take the pinto long to discover that he had a greenhorn on his back, and start to have fun with her; and a horse's sense of humor is what Milt Leffingwell would call sardonic. With Gerta, that ornery little runt'd skim along as smooth and easy as a swallow; but now, to watch him, you'd think he was geared solely on eccentrics. Of all the stiff-legged, rabbit-jumping, hard-gaited exhibitions I ever seen, that was about the limit.

'Twixt shivering with the cold and hitting the saddle unexpected-like every second or so, Rosie must have been pretty well unhinged. I took off my coat and gave it to her, and I tried to make the going as smooth and easy as possible; but you can't always pick and choose on a chase like that.

I'd have felt a whole lot more sympathy for her, if she hadn't been so damn yellow. Gerta would have stuck her chin up, and grinned, and took it as the fortunes of war; but this dishrag kept squawking and blubbering and vowing she was going to die even when the traveling was nice and the pinto behaving hisself. 'Twas the kind of baby-doll stuff that a sody-fountain lizzard might have fell for; but me—I wanted to break her neck.

As I tell you, I slowed down on the pace when I reckoned it was safe to do so; but I never let on to the dame. If I'd have wised her up that there wasn't no more danger, she'd have flopped on me completely. So I still acted like I was terrible worried, and every now and then I'd stop and pretend to be listening like I'd heard something. Then I'd give a order in a quick, gruff voice, and start off in a different direction.

Just stalling I was; follering round and round in a circle. Anybody with goose sense would have tumbled to that; for the night was clear, and after the first time or two I didn't take no trouble to avoid familiar landmarks. But this Rose girl was so took up with her own sufferings, that she wouldn't have knew if a circus parade had gone by, with a steam calliope at the tail of it.

That might have been a occasion that was worth while, just us two together out there on the wide, rolling range, with a couple of good horses under us, and the dark, velvety night wrapping us around, and just a hint of real danger to give a zip to it—it might have been if the right sort of girl had been along. But not with no squalling fraid-cat like this here Rosie. I'd have sold out at any stage of the game, and been glad of the chance.

But all things have to end sometime. Finally the stars wheeled off down the west, and the hills began to take shape as the blackness faded into gray. And after a while, the dawn came up like thunder, as the poet says, from over back of the Voreza ranch.

In the red and yellow of it, I seen what I'd been keeping my eyes peeled forever since it was light enough to make out your hand before your face—a party of Esteban's men what was only about three miles off.

I pulled up short.

"Well, be good to yourself, Miss Tyrell," I says. "Here is where I quit you."

"Where you quit me?" She forgot to groan for a second, and just set staring at me. Then as I pointed to the crew ahead, she gave a despairing gasp.

"You are going to desert me?" she yowled. "You are going to run away, and let me be taken by the enemy?"

"Them ain't enemy," I told her. "Leastways, not to you. Them is some of Colonel Esteban's fellows, and if you tell 'em who you are, they'll take you straight to your pa."

"To my father?" She let out a shriek. "To Jeff Tyrell!" She whirled the pony around and grabbed at my bridle. "Oh, anything but that!" she begs. "If you have any pity, get me away from here. Hurry! Hurry! Why, don't you know," she says, "that stepfather of mine is the worst enemy I have?"

Well, I ain't like the feller that had to have a brick house tumble on him before he could get anything through his head. It was plain I had made some sort of a mistake in my calculations; but I didn't stop just then to see where my figures were wrong.

"Come on," I says. And we slid.

You've got to remember, though, that it was now broad daylight, and also that us and our horses had been out all night, whereas this Esteban outfit was, so to speak, fresh.

Naturally they took after us, and losing them wasn't nowhere so easy as shaking the ranch bunch the night before. But there ain't no fox that's got anything on Henry Ford. He seemed to know just what was expected of him; and if I ain't mistaken, he also give a word or two of earnest exhortation to the pinto, 'cause that little skeezicks cut out all them playful stunts that he'd been indulging in and settled down to his old, swallow-like gait.

Lickety split we went but lickety-split, too, them Esteban roughnecks come after us. And as I tell you, they was fresh. I knew we could only hold them off for a little while. On a straight race, they was bound to wear us down, and finally overhaul us.

I knowed it, and so did Henry Ford. Already he is beginning to breathe pretty hard. He turns his head around to the little pinto nosing along at his saddle, and commences working his ears.

"Hey, Jack!" he signals. "We can't keep this up much longer; I'm about all in now. You know the layout round here better'n I do. Ain't there some way we can hide out on 'em?"

The pinto wigwags back with something which evidently don't look so good to Henry, and for a time they held quite a argument, a-flourishing them four ears of theirs like a passel of boy scouts out on signal-flag practice. But finally Henry was convinced.

You think I'm kidding, don't you? Anyhow, here's what happened. As soon as they'd quit their semaphoring, Henry laid back and let the pinto take the lead; and the little yaller jack rabbit bends off in a wide circle toward the hills in the East.

"Let him have his head!" I hollers to the fool dame, who was sawing on him, trying to hold him in. "He's got the brains in your combination."

She flashes me a kind of indignant look at that; but it must have percolated even through the ivory under them fair tresses of hern, that we didn't have much show as the cards lay, and so most any sort of a chance was worth taking. She minded me, that was the main point; and the pinto, left free to himself, began to do his stuff.

Ever see a rabbit doubling on a pack of hounds? Well, that was him. Zigzag, turn and twist, he went; but always edging closer and closer in toward the hills. Henry kept pounding along behind him stride for stride, never losing an inch even on the quickest shifts the little feller made.

Finally, when they'd maneuvered the Esteban crowd on one side of a low rise, and us on the other, and we was for the minute out of sight, the pinto gave a quick cock of his ears forward, and dived for a patch of mesquite just ahead of us. Lord, he went so fast that all you could make out was just a streak of yaller in the sunshine.

That sudden lunge took me unexpected all right. But not so,

Henry. He' caught the signal, "Full steam ahead!" and believe me, he didn't waste no time following it. One yelp was all I had a chance to give, telling my fair companion to lay flat on the pinto's neck and hold on; and then me and Henry was into them thorn bushes ourselves.

As they rustled to behind me, I caught a glimpse back under my arm, from where I was low-bridging along Henry's mane, of them Esteban fellows just topping the rise; and from the way they checked up, kind of all at sea, I judged they was some surprised at not seeing us anywheres about.

"But you can't throw 'em off as easy as that," I says to myself; "not leaving a trail like we done that a blind baby could follow."

Or, rather, that's what I started to say. But before I finished, I found I needed all my language for cussing. That patch of mesquite we'd sailed into was probably the orneriest specimen of its kind in all Mexico. A thousand hands seemed to be grabbing at me; I was gored from head to heel with thorns and stickers. Barbed wire would have been child's play in comparison.

A dozen foot more of it and me and Henry would have been prime Hamburger steak. As it was, he emerged about twenty pound lighter, and me with the neckband of my shirt still intack. Modesty prevented me from looking to see what had happened to that there lingerie of Rosie's; but from the low, heart-rendering moans what reached my ears, I was inclined to believe that both she and it was some shy.

Still there wasn't no need for her to beef like she was doing. That pinto, as I have mentioned previous, was a regular chaparral hound; and 'twas odds, she wasn't scratched up nowhere within fifty percent as bad as I was. I'll bet Gerta wouldn't have put up no such fuss, not if she'd been run through a meat chopper.

As we come through on the other side of the mesquite, I riz up in the saddle and sort of shook my head to clear my eyes. What I seen made me realize that the dern little pinto knowed his business all right.

Ahead of us, wound away into the hills a hidden arroyo—just

a mere crack in the ground, with high, steep walls—which, with the mouth of it screened by those mesquite bushes like it was, nobody would ever guess was there.

Up it the pony was racing, unheeding the bundle of groans on his back, and Henry was clinging hard at his heels.

By gum, we had a chance after all! Sooner'n negotiate them thorn bushes, the greasers would probably circle around, figuring to catch us on the other side of the hill; and from the lay of the land, they was almost certain to be drawed away from us.

"Don't you care for a few scratches, sister!" I sings out to hearten up the dame. "Our heads is bloody but unbowed, and this is where we make a get-away."

But I'd forgot that the national bird of Mexico is the machete. The words wasn't hardly out of my mouth, before I heard a hacking and chopping behind us which told me that the mesquite was going to serve as no protection. With twenty of them keen-edged corn cutters working on it, a passageway'd be mowed out in no time; and where we'd sacrificed everything but honor, them lucky stiffs would come through without neither blood or pain.

The one hope now was to find a narrow spot in the arroyo, with maybe a big rock advantageous which I could crouch behind with my automatic and pull a Verdun. Then, if perchance there was a spring handy, and the ravens'd bring us some chow, we could hold out until night and slip away under cover of darkness.

But, instead, and against all the prerogatives of scenario-writing—not to mention Holy Writ—the damn ravine suddenly widened out into a sort of circus ring with straight up-and-down sides, and come to a stop.

The respect I'd been entertaining for that pinto pony dropped from fever heat to zero in just about the bat of an eye. There we was, stuck in a natural pit, with no way out except the arroyo along which the foemen was already coming.

On top of that, as if to show his utter heartlessness, the flea-bitten little brute bucks Rosie nearly off his back into the sand, and before I can head him off, claws up the perpendicular bank like a cat and is gone.

No use trying to follow him. Henry Ford is a horse, not no mountain goat; and neither am I. I gave one look at the path he had took, and shook my head. Possibly I could have made it alone, but not with a helpless encumbrance like the Tyrell girl; and for Henry, it was simply out of the question. And what good would it do us to get up there, and be without no horse.

No; all that was left us was just to set quiet, and wait for Esteban's merry men to come along and scoop us in.

CHAPTER XVII

ROSE

I STARTED TO bawl out Henry Ford for the fix we was in.

"Curses on you, Jack Dalton," I says, or words to that effect. "Now see what you have got us into by blindly trusting to that low-life pinto friend of yourn. The dirty, little double-crossing gnat!" I says, "A giraffe, which is all neck and no brains, would have had more intelligence than to follow his lead."

But Henry, as it were, turned the other cheek to my harsh words. He gave a soft, little whinny as if to draw my attention, and then turning his head, looks off fixedly to the other side of the hollow where a lone, stunted tree stuck out over the top of the bank.

I'm not asking you to believe that he meant anything by it. I'm simply telling you what happened. But I couldn't have got a plainer hint if he'd handed me a diagram drawn to scale, with lines A-A and B-B onto it.

Quick as a flash, I had my lariat offn the saddle, and tearing across the hollow, flung it up and by a lucky cast roped the tree with it on the very first try.

No time to test it and see whether it would hold or not. Clatter, clatter, them cutthroats was coming up the arroyo at a gallup. Seconds counted now.

I rushed back to where Rosie was still setting kind of dazed-like on the sand right where she'd lit. She'd been jolted so hard that she didn't have no breath left to caterwaul with; that was one thing to be thankful for.

I didn't stop to give her no explanations. Experience had taught me 'twas useless with that dumbbell. I just caught her up in my arms, and run back to where the lariat was dangling from the tree.

Some climb it would have been, 'specially with that dead weight of plumb uselessness hung onto me; but again Henry got credited with a assist.

Just as I reached the lariat, he trotted up and took his stand directly beneath it.

Not hard to catch the idea in that, was it? I dumped Rosie onto him, swung myself up ahead of her, and then telling her to hold on to me pick-a-pack, I grabbed the rope to steady myself, and stood up on the saddle.

In that way, I had only to go a few foot hand-over-hand, until I reached the tree, and was able to work back along it and clamber over the edge of the bank.

True, my heart was in my mouth while I was about it, 'cause the little, old tree—'twas a sort of twisted cedar—bent almost double under the weight, and its roots began to pull out of the sandy soil. Course I'd done dozens of stunts on location that was harder and more ticklish; but in them cases I knowed if anything went wrong all that could happen was for Milt to tear his hair a bit and say "We'll have to try that over again." Here, it had to go right, first dash out of the box. Otherwise— Well, you can probably guess the answer as well as I can.

So I don't make no apologies because, when Rosie was safely dumped into a patch of bushes back from the bank, and having retrieved my lariat, I tumbled down beside her, I was weak as a rag and in a cold sweat that soaked my few remaining garments like I'd been doused in the river.

Maybe I'd have fainted, I was so all in, if I hadn't kind of forgot myself in watching the capers of Henry Ford. My first thought was that the darn fool had been nibbling some of this here loco weed and was off his nut, the way he was carrying on.

No sooner was we off his back and shinning up the rope than he commenced caracoling around down there on the sand like a calico circus horse doing the "Hi, hi!" finish to his act. Then when he'd circled the hollow about twice that way, and had mussed up all our tracks, he started making short, crazy rushes at the bank over acrost from us, where the pinto had gone up.

Not being a jack rabbit like the pinto, he only fell back each time he tried it; but he was still gamely persevering when Esteban's bullies with a yell came sweeping onto the scene, and discovered him.

Then for the first time it struck me that there might be a method in his madness for naturally they didn't pay no attention to the side where we was hid, but concentrated what minds they had on the spot where Henry was performing.

Their reaction to that, as Milt used to say, was, not unlogically, that me and the girl had managed to scramble up the bank and then tried to get the horses to follow us, succeeding so far as the pony was concerned, but failing with Henry 'count of him being bigger and clumsier. Really, you couldn't blame 'em. We wasn't nowhere around. We must have climbed out somewhere, and the pinto's plain trail and Henry's frenzied efforts to follow sure seemed to point to that one place.

Now far be it from me to claim that them two cayuses doped out all that there strategy in advance. Horse sense is one thing and man cunning is another; and, as the line goes, never the two shall meet. But you've got to remember that Henry, being so much with me, had more'n ordinary equine intelligence; while the pinto was trickier than an Injun.

All I know is, that when things looked hopeless for us out there on the range, them two went to wigwagging with their ears, and then the pinto guided us up the hidden arroyo, dumped Rosie, and beat it up the bank, while Henry, after showing us another way out, did his level best to make the greasers think

we'd took the same route as the pony. Mebbe 'twas all the long
arm of coincidences what the scenario writers is always talking
about; but it sure had every earmark of a plan that them two
knowing beasts had settled between 'em. I ain't expressing no
opinion. You can write your own ticket.

Yet, if so, it only goes to prove how easy the best-laid schemes
of horses as well as mice and men can go into the gluepot; for
that whole clever frame-up come nigh being ditched by one
little brown-and-yellow lizard.

'Twas this way. The greasers, completely took in by Henry's
camelflaggin', was part of 'em turning their horses and riding
down the arroyo to head us off, while the rest was dismounting
and swarming up the bank on the chance that we couldn't have
got very far away. Just then, as I was eagerly watching 'em, and
beginning to congratulate myself on giving 'em the hinky-dink,
this Rosie person lets out a whoop from behind me that sounds
like the siren on a fire engine.

"Oh! Oh! Oh!" she shrieks, grabbing me in another of them
"Save me! Save me!" clutches of hern.

I clapped one hand over her mouth, and grabbed her by the
throat with the other to shut off her wind.

"You hadn't ought to do nothing like that, Miss Tyrell," I says
reprovingly. Some people would have pasted her; but I always
try to remember that I'm a gentleman.

Her eyes was popping out of her head, and she was making
kind of smothering sounds where I had her by the windpipe; but
she kept on pointing into the bushes and registering terror just
the same. Then I seen what 'twas, that had got her so goofy—
nothing, so help me, but that little, harmless lizard.

I waggled my foot at it, and it whisked off about its business.
Then I eased up a mite the pressure on her throat.

"Was that what you was kicking up the fuss about?" I says
disgusted-like. "Anybody that's acclimated to Fifth Avenue
ought to recognize the breed."

"I—I thought it was a snake," she shivers.

"S'posin' you did," I snaps, "is that any excuse for raising the roof? Let me tell you, sister, there ain't no fauna in Mexico more poisonous than them tarantulas of Esteban's. You start anything like this again, and I'll smear you right. Get me?"

She quieted down at that, merely sniffling and rubbing her throat, and, as it happened, there wasn't no real harm done, 'cause the enemy was making such a hullabaloo they couldn't hear nothing but theirselves. I actually felt kind of sorry for the poor mutt; but 'twasn't no time to show weakness. Discipline had to be preserved.

Luckily I didn't neither; for, first thing I knowed, she was sort of edging up to me, and had a-hold of my hand, stroking at it. Treating 'em rough sure does get 'em. I reckon, if I'd knocked her for a goal, 'stead of merely choking her, I couldn't have fought off her endearments. But I wasn't in no humor for a petting party just then, and coldly withdrew my hand.

By this time, too, the highbinders had all cleared out—them what hadn't climbed up over the cliff taking the horses and riding around the other way, so that they could all meet and follow the trail left by the pinto pony.

Naturally, they had took Henry Ford with em; and it sure brought a lump to my throat to realize that I was bidding farewell forever to the partner of my joys and sorrows, although it was some slight satisfaction to see him sling three of 'em and kick half a dozen others good and proper, before they finally got away with him.

I mastered my emotions, though, as the thieving crew swept off with him down the arroyo, and turned to Rosie.

"Well," I says to her, "we are alone at last, eh?"

She switched around, mad-like, and hunched up one shoulder at me. Miffed, I guess, 'cause I wouldn't respond to her advances.

"All right," says I. "If that's the way you feel, suit yourself. We're sixty miles from no place, and we're shy on food, water, and horses, along with other things too numerous to mention. Strikes me, if we don't want to put on a revival of the well known

Babes in the Wood, and have the dear, little birdies cover our still forms with leaves, we'd better be getting our heads together, and figure what we're going to do next."

But you couldn't beat no sense into her. Might as well have tried to go into conference with a doll. Just like some of them can say,"Pa-pa," and "Ma-ma," and open and shut their eyes, she had her little bag of mechanical tricks. She could get upstage like she'd been with me just now and say,"Sir-r-r!" or she could coo and snuggle up to you or she could act abused and shed real tears. But there wasn't no meaning to it, no more'n when the doll says "Pa-pa." All the cubic space in her above the eyebrows was just attic.

The only time she struck what Milt calls the sincere note was when she panned me for the fix we was in; `and she sure done that vicious and fairly continuous. 'Twas all my fault, she kept harping. Which in a way was true, but it didn't help none to solve the problem we was facing.

"I'm a sight, she says; and believe me, what with her red nose and her bunged-up eyes and her streaked face, that wasn't the half of it, dearie. "And I'm hungry and thirsty and scratched and sore from head to foot." She goes to blubbering again. "Like a fool, I trusted myself to you, and see where it's brought me. I'll die here in the wilderness; I know I will."

"There, there!" I went to patting her on the shoulder, which is all a man knows how to do under such circumstances. " 'Tain't quite so bad as that. The luck has broke agin' us, 'twould be idle to deny; but we'll pull through all right yet. Course," I says, "with Esteban's outfit cluttering up the great open spaces like they is, we'll probably have to hide out where we are until evening; but, come nightfall, we'll strike out and go someplace."

"How can I go any place?" she sniffs, sticking out the hoof from which she'd cast the bedroom slipper. "Barefooted, and all in tatters."

"Rags is royal raiment, when worn for virtue's sake," says I.

Now, I leave it to you, if that ain't a noble line. But does it make a hit with her? Not no more'n if I'd said, "The cat is on the mat." She just switched away from me peevish, and spit like a cat. I hurried to put on another record.

"Howsomever," I says, "that, as you imply, is properly a subject for later discussion." You can always get a nitwit like that by pretending you're letting them do the thinking. "William-nil-liam," I says, "us two is anchored in these sylvan shades for several hours yet; and as you so justly remark, our present most pressing need is a commissary department. Permit me, there-fore, lady, to absent myself for a brief time until I can locate the dining car. In other words," I tells her, "I am going out to try and rustle us up a breakfast."

I was luckier than I had any license to be, seeing that she called me back every two seconds to spill some fresh scare on me, or else to make sure that I wasn't deserting her, and also seeing that it wasn't exactly a land of milk and honey. But by sheer chance I managed to stumble on a little old crab-apple tree, with a half dozen or so shriveled nubbins on it which, if they wasn't food, was at least a harmless imitation of it, and also served to quench your thirst.

Gerta in the same fix would have been tickled to death with a find like that but this spoiled darling merely turns up her nose. Guess she expected me to come back with a platter of ham and eggs from the way she acted. I notice, though, that she munched down them crab-apples so quick, that before I hardly set tooth in one the rest was all gone. Still I let that pass. *Place aux dames,* is always my motto.

"Now, sister," says I, "the next number on the program is a snore specialty; and since one of us has got to watch while the other snoozes, we'll toss up to see which hits the hay first. We'll spell it two hours on and two off."

So I flipped a peso and won, if you want to call it a win when I was woke up every four minutes for some fool reason or other. Really, it was a relief to me when it come around my turn to watch. For two hours at least I'd be free from her eternal pestering.

Soon as she was off to dreamland, I stretched myself out with my back agin' a convenient rock, and began to think.

There was a lot of things I needed to have explained to me by my fair companion but she was so scratched and jolted and out of temper, that I hadn't judged it wise to take 'em up as yet. She was one of the kind that can't make no allowances; and it sure looked like, with all the best intentions in the world, I'd made a misnomer, or whatever the dictionary word is for pulling a boner.

What I'd been aiming to do was to get Gerta out of a hole by restoring this she-Charlie Ross to her more or less distracted parent; and, lo and behold, the victim of the outrage objects. Not only that, but she claims Jeff Tyrell ain't her parent 'cept in name only, and is her worst enemy. Likewise, several times on our ride when things was going bad, she'd asked me hysterical what I wanted to take her away from Gerta for.

With that, it strikes me that where I found her wasn't in no dungeon cell nor bare attic chamber like you'd expect, but right in Gerta's private quarters, with powder puffs and hair curlers and all the comforts of home, and nary a lock or bar to keep her from roaming wherever she chose.

It certainly was one hell of a abduction—more like a set-up, it appeared to me, cooked up between them two girls.

But a set-up on who? And wherefore? And to what end? I puzzle over this for some time in vain; and then I suddenly tumbles to the whole game.

You'd probably never guess how; but, if so, that's cause you ain't got a analytical mind, nor trained yourself to putting two and two together. Hadn't Rosie said that Jeff Tyrell was her step daddy and at the same time her worst enemy? Now what is it that makes trouble in families as well as most every place else? Correct; it's the old long green ten times out of nine.

The odds was, as I seen it, that this kid had been left a legacy or something of the kind, which Papa Jeff had managed to switch to himself, and which she couldn't pry him loose from. Then Gerta, being already in the holdup business, had proposed this kidnaping scheme, figuring that Tyrell couldn't afford to have 'em saying over in Texas that he wouldn't unbelt to save his daughter from the clutches of a pack of bloodthirsty Mexican ruffians.

The more I thought it over, the surer I was that I had it right. Wasn't no doubt but what Jeff would short-change anybody he had a chance to, even to the third and fourth generation. It was just like Gerta, too, to try and help out a old schoolmate in distress, never counting on the risk to herself.

Yet, if so, you'd 'a' supposed that Gerta'd have been tickled to death to have me rid her of such a liability, instead of trying to blow my head off my shoulders for it. There wasn't nothing in the deal for her personally, and she must have knowed she was laying up worries for herself in bucking Tyrell, even if she didn't rate him as dangerous as he was. Why, then, in Heaven's name, should she get so fussed up at me, when all I'd did was to lighten her burdens for her. Fussed up? Gee! Her eyes was glinting green fire when she banged away at me there in the patio, and—

Eyes glinting green fire! By gum, that gave me a clew. She was jealous; that's what it was. And why not? Here was a bozo, that'd been making desprit love to her only a hour before, apparently eloping with her best friend. Small wonder that she took a crack at me. How was she to guess at my real motives? Men has been hanged on less evidence than what she had.

Well, do you know, that explanation chirked me up a whole lot. There ain't nothing else so heartwarming and soul-satisfying to a man as to have his girl believe him one of these, now, Don Juans. Being hungry and thirsty and up against it forty ways from the ace didn't count nothing with me any more. I just laid there, and purred.

"Them little misunderstandings is what gives a kick to the near-beer of true love," I says to myself. I fell to picturing a grand reconciliation scene, after I'd got Rosie safe across the border and off my hands, and had come back again to the ranch.

Ain't no director on earth ever doped out a prettier finish than I had, with the heroine icy and aloof at first, but gradually melting as the manly hero squares hisself. Subtitle: "How could I ever doubt you, Red?" And then the "clinch" up there on the roof of the old hacienda in the moonlight with the oleanders screening us in.

While I was entertaining myself in this way, the sun kept mounting higher and higher and in there under the bushes it was warm and quiet and sort of drowsyish—getting on toward the siesta hour as the Spaniards call it. I closed my eyes a minute-like to run that final reel over again, and see if maybe I couldn't put a bit more stuff into the wind-up.

Then I didn't know anything more until I woke up with a start by hearing somebody yell like a Comanche Indian, and I opened my eyes to see this Rosie person waving her arms and capering on the edge of the cliff.

"Hey, here!" I barks at her. "What's eating you now?"

"Oh, we're saved! We're saved!" she hollers. "Gerta and a whole party of her men have just come up the arroyo. This way!" she screeches down to 'em. "We're both here. If somebody throws a rope over that cedar tree, you can come up."

Could you beat it? That reconciliation scene with its moonlight and oleanders faded out so quick it'd make your head swim. Instead, I had a swift flash of Gerta's underground judgment hall, with yours truly officiating as chief mourner. Fat chance for a guy to square hisself, with the beans spilled all over the kitchen that a way, and him ketched red-handed, so to speak.

Hell hath no fury like a woman scorned, eh? You said it, Reginald.

CHAPTER XVIII

BACK AGAIN

I GAVE ONE peep over the bank to make sure that the Tyrell squab wasn't delirious or nothing like that. Then I dived for the bushes.

No mistake. Gerta was down there—herself, personally—and with her about forty of her greasers. And it didn't need no more than a single slant at her to convince me that this wasn't no place to linger. New Hampshire granite'd have looked like sponge cake 'side of her.

But don't' get me wrong here, either. I didn't desert Rosie—which ain't saying what I might have done, only happily the choice didn't come to me. However, facts is facts. It was her that shook me. Before I could stop her, the cuckoo, gathering the remains of her blue kimono around her and in that one bedroom slipper, had went scrambling and slipping down the bank right into the midst of them. After that, I could feel sorry for her, but I couldn't help her. My cue was to be moving.

Maybe a chipmunk or a black beetle or something like that could have whisked through the underbrush faster'n what I did; but I doubt it. I was scared—no use trying to pretend I wasn't—but it wasn't no fear of being captured, nor of what might be done to me. Not a-tall. Even the thought of the merry, old torture chamber wasn't what sent me scurrying. It was the idea of facing Gerta O'Beirne, with no better defense to offer than this wishy-washy story of mine. Every word of it true as gospel, of course; but so might there be a good excuse for a man caught kissing the cook. It'd be hard work, though, persuading his wife to swallow it. I could see the cold, scornful curl of Gerta's lip at this romance of mine, as plain as if it was happening.

A blunder is worse than a crime, as William Jennings Bryan has so aptly said; and before Gerta and me got down to matching explanations, I wanted a considerable higher showing in my batting average.

So believe me, I dusted—in and out through briars and cactus and every sort of twisted, thorny, poison plant that grows—wriggling on my belly like a snake, burrowing like a mole, rooting like a hog—making the personal acquaintance of a million different kinds of stinging insects—a companion to horned toads, and a brother to varmints. Dodging, turning, sopping to listen, eeling on again—east side, west side, all around the town—careful to cover my trail every foot I moved, not daring to let a tuft of grass rustle or a twig snap as I passed.

It was probably a half or three quarters of an hour that I was playing hide-and-seek in that devil's garden; but it seemed considerable longer—like the Paleozootic Age, or something like that. I know now just how a fox feels when a pack of hounds has got him cornered. All around me, I could hear them greasers tramping and cussing and swinging their machetes. Once, there was a couple of em within less'n a foot of me, and how they missed hearing the beating of my heart is sure a mystery. To me, it sounded like the pounding of the bass drum in front of a side show, when they're starting up the ballyhoo.

At last, though, I throwed my pursuers off, and wormed myself clear to a little runnel in the sand, a sort of furrow overgrown with creepers both vegetable and animal, that wound out of the thicket and gave me a chance to get away. And what happened after that, I can't rightly say.

You see, I was pretty well played out; not being in the habit of using my feet for anything much 'cept to stick in stirrups and kick greasers with, and still less to jogging crab-fashion on my hunkers like I'd done in that durned jungle. In addition, the sun was glaring in my eyes and beating down on my head until my brain felt like a fried egg, and I went blind from the dazzle.

I remember stumping and stumbling over a lot of country. How many miles, or in what direction, I'll never tell you. Maybe most of it was just round and round in a circle. The sweat poured offn me in a fog, but my tongue was so dry you could 'a' druv it through a board. Hot? Why the hinges of hell were icicles in comparison. The dust in my nose and throat was like burning fire, and I choked at every breath like a flivver without gas on a steep hill.

I'd reel along five or six steps, and then go down and want to stay there. Must of been out of my head part of the time I guess, 'cause I kept imagining I was in the ring with a big, red giant what was smashing me at will but couldn't put me out. I was groggy with punishment, weaving, all in; but I wouldn't give up. Just one idea stuck in the old poached bean. Gerta O'Beirne shouldn't have the satisfaction of sneering at me as a lying half-wit. That'd be just a shade worse hell'n what I was going through. I had to get away from her.

Maybe it was a hour, maybe all day, that this kept up. Don't ask me. All I know is, that I finally staggered into a little gully, and found myself beside a spring. Blind, bull-headed luck; nothing else to it. God sure does look out for the Irish.

I couldn't hardly believe I wasn't dreaming until I'd tumbled into it and felt it splash on me; and then I was sure I'd died and gone to heaven.

I wallered in it, clothes and all; and, if you'll believe me, I was so baked that the water sizzled when it touched me same's if I was a red-hot stove. I drank the spring most dry, and what was left I soaked up like a sponge. Then I crawled off into a thicket a little piece away and went to sleep.

What woke me up was a horse cropping grass close beside my head. It was dark by this time, and not desiring to have him make a mistake in the darkness and bite my ear off. I naturally jumped over, which made him throw up his head with a snort, and pull back to the length of his picket rope. And that started some more horses to stepping around.

"Hasta!" says a bird with a frog in his throat, like a greaser talks, from over by the spring.

"It may be a snake that disturbs them, Señor Capitan," says another voice, also speaking in Spanish "Shall I investigate?"

"No," says the first one. "They are quiet now."

After that, the horses could have lunched off my hair before I'd have made a sound, especially as I gathered from the number of 'em and from the other voices I heard, that there must be about thirty men in the party. Discretion is the better part of valor, as the old woman said when she kissed the pig. I just shrunk up as small as I could, and stopped breathing.

Course I didn't know yet who the gang was; but it was a hundred-to-one shot they was enemies. In that neck of the woods, enemies was what I didn't have anything but.

And I win. By listening in on their jabber, I succeeded before long in locating 'em. They belonged to Esteban's outfit and from what I could make out they was starting on considerable of a *pasear*, which is greaser for hike.

A lot of what they passed back and forth was lost on me, being mostly grunts and hog-Spanish, which you can't find in them books that fits you in six easy lessons to travel unaided through all countries of Latin America. It may surprise you, but not a single mention did these ignorant louts make about the gardener's grandmother or the little sister of Maria's aunt, or any of them other charming characters of Mr. Ollendorf's.

Still, by picking up a stray word here and there and owing to a fair knowledge of international profanity, I managed to piece out of their chatter some information that interests me strangely.

Their gallant leader, it appears, has been double crossed by a certain party unidentified except under names which is unfit to print, and as a consequence has been compelled to call off the attack on Voreza ranch scheduled for that morning. Not only that, but he was bidding farewell for a season to the old home town, and with his army split up into small bands, was streaking it for the mountains.

Just why or wherefore old Crooked Mouth has decided to take this unexpected vacation, I don't quite get; but the news certainly didn't arouse no undue regrets in my bosom. On the contrary, only the presence of company restrained me from giving three rousing cheers. Yavisa, I felt, would be a happier and better place for his absence.

But wait! Whilst I was still digesting the glad news, and wondering how come a constellation so devoutly to be wished, I got what you might call a socker on the nose.

Listen. This here bunch that I'd fallen in with was, it seemed, a sort of a rear guard; and like wasps and scorpions and other pernicious vertebrates, Esteban's retreating organization carried its sting in its tail. These fellows had been left behind to clean up a little job of work which their boss, owing to his hurried departure, had been unable to finish, to wit, nothing less than the raiding and burning of Voreza ranch, and a general massacre of its inhabitants.

They had a friend on the inside, their captain explained to 'em, Marengo, the foreman, who after the moon had set and everybody was wrapped in sleep, would open the secret gate in the stockade to 'em. Then they was to scatter out and knife as many as possible before being discovered. The garrison knowing that Esteban had pulled his freight would probably be too pickled to notice anything; but even if an alarm was raised, there'd be so much surprise and confusion it ought to be easy.

"But give no quarter," says this playful Rollo, "even if they surrender—that is, for the men. The women we will take with us. And especially see that no harm comes to the Yankee señorita. The colonel counts on the money he can raise on her to reestablish himself once more at Yavisa and be in a position to take vengeance on the lying dog who has dared defy him."

Now what would you make of that? The only guy I could figure out, that fitted to them invidious specifications, was

myself, and it must have been my misleading tip carried by
Marengo that had skewgeed Esteban's program. Expecting me
to show up with Gerta on an early morning ride and give 'em
the chance to kidnap her, him and Tyrell had doubtless decided
that it'd be a waste of good ammunition to storm the defenses
at the ranch. Why needlessly muss up the property, when with
Gerta in their power they could force her to turn it over to 'em?

True, that didn't make altogether clear the reason for Esteban scooting to the tall timbers; but I had too much else on my
mind just then to puzzle over what Milt would call a nonessen-
tial detail. 'Twas a situation and not a theory that confronted me.

Here, in a coupla hours or so, that gang of wolves, aided by
Marengo, 'd be on the inside of the stockade, and Gerta'd be
carried off to the tender mercies of Esteban. And the only person
that could stop it was Red Conners.

Gee! What a comeback! The discredited outcast appearing
in the nick of time to save the girl and the old homestead. Do
you wonder that I thrilled at the possibilities of the layout?
Maybe, that reconciliation scene among the oleanders wasn't
out, after all.

Still, 'twould be idle to deny that there was technical diffi-
culties in the way. For one thing, I hadn't no more idea where
I was than Adam's off ox. If I started off for the ranch, I might
go roaming all over the range. Stars wouldn't help none, 'cause
I didn't know whether to travel north, south, east, or west. Also
there was my feet to be considered. The old dogs was so swol-
len and sore, that for traveling purposes they was useless. I'd be
lucky to hobble as far as a mile on 'em. And yet somehow I had
to get to Voreza ranch ahead of these burglars, and warn Gerta
of her danger.

'Twas the captain of their outfit what really eased me out of
the perplexity which I was bogged down in.

"Now, little pigeons," says he to his gang, "we have had a wearing day, you and I, and it will be an hour or more before we can
set out. Let us rest until then."

He couldn't have gave an order that would appeal more to them greasers; and that made it unanimous, 'cause it was all I could do to keep from kissing him. Like a flash, I seen my way clear.

Only one guy was out of luck, a heavy-set little *cholo* what the captain picked on to play sentinel.

"Pancho, you will watch," he says. "Rouse us up, when the moon drops behind the hills yonder."

Then he lays down, wrapping his head in his blanket, and the others follow suit. In two minutes, the whole bunch was snoring, "Sweet Adeline"—that is, all except the sentinel, who, kind of sulky at being left out of the harmony, sets down on a rock with his back to me, and starts to rolling cigarettes.

I waited till it was a certainty they was all bye-bye; then I commenced to move. Very cautiously I crawled around the horses, and inched up toward the sentinel from behind. There was a open space of about ten feet I had to cross to get to him, where if he'd turned around he couldn't have missed seeing me. But he never made a move until I was right back of him, and then it was too late.

"Put 'em up!" I whispered, jabbing my gun into his ribs, and up they went.

Holding folks up has got to be such a habit with me by this time, that I was practically letter-perfect in it.

Spinning the old rigmarole, that if he made a sound or a funny move of any kind I'd blow him off the map, I marched him over into the bushes and, relieving him of his hat and serape, gagged him and tied him up.

All this don't take so long to tell, but to act it out is different. By the time I finished with him and come back to the circle of sleeping comrades, the moon was well down behind the hills. Not that I fretted over that; dark stage was what I wanted for my next turn, and the darker the better.

Howsomever, I couldn't delay much more without arousing questions, which was the one thing I wanted to avoid. So muffling myself up in the sentinel's serape, and pulling his bell-crowned hat over my face, whilst crouching down to make myself as near his size as nature permitted, I steps over to where the captain was hitting on all six.

The next few seconds was going to tell the story. Do you wonder that I waited to draw a long breath, like a fellow will before he does a high dive. If I was recognized for a imposter—good night! I had to pass one hundred percent greaser, or else pass out.

Twicet I leaned down to shake el capitan into consciousness, and twicet I drawed back. Other ways of accomplishing my purpose flitted across my mind. There was plenty of machetes laying around. Suppose I started in on a hog-killing bee? Or suppose I treated 'em all like I had the sentinel? Or else, suppose I druv off their horses. But you can't kill nor tie up even thirty Mexicans, without a strong chance of having a light sleeper among 'em that'll wake up on you and crab the game. And to make off with their cattle, maybe wouldn't help much, since, with them knowing their way, they might reach the ranch afoot whilst I was still scouting around the range trying to locate it.

Besides, them methods savored of crudeness, as Milt would say, and didn't have none of the dramatic finesse of the plan I was aiming to follow.

So I screwed up my courage, and on the third try grabbed the captain by the shoulder, and jerked him into wakefulness.

"Diablo!" He sets up quick, and reaches for his gun. Then he sees the sentinel's hat looming over him in the darkness. "Oh is it you, Pancho? So soon? But truly; the moon is down." He yawns and rubs his eyes. "You had a quiet watch, eh?"

I didn't answer him for fear of giving myself away, but slipped over among the horses, leaving him to kick the others out of their dreams. Then while they was mounting, I crouched over and pretended to be fixing a spur, so as not to make a mistake and pick on the wrong horse. When the rest was all in the saddle, though, and only one cayuse was left, I swung aboard quick.

"Forward!" says the captain, and away we raced helter-skelter.

Once or twice, the buddy that rode beside of me tried to draw me into conversation, but each time I'd start my pony up with a dig of the spur, and act like I was too busy managing him to indulge in repartee.

'Meanwhile I was keeping my eye peeled for familiar landmarks, and finally when we'd covered a mile or so, I got my bearings. The ranch laid off to the south about a good hour's ride away.

Immediately I went to the bat with the ruse I'd schemed out back there at the spring, and for a starter jammed under my saddle a handful of burrs I'd brung along with me.

Zowie! It worked almost too well. I thought them buckers of Idaho's at Fort Lee had showed me all the stiff-legged, back-arching meanness what a horse can perpetrate; but this here bronc I'm telling you about had variations what put them right back in the merino class. Talk about riding the earthquake and the storm. He tried a rear-back, a back-throw, and a pin-wheel on me all at once, it seemed like. I never yet got dumped by anything what I was fairly settled on; but, believe me, I'd 'a' gone that time, if, in a flash between spasms, I hadn't reached back and pawed out them burrs.

With that, he'd have quieted down again, but by a trick what old Idaho learned me, I forced him into a thrilling imitation of a runaway.

Off to the night we sailed, me seemingly powerless to hold him until I'd crossed a rise that hid me from the rest of the party. As the brute went lunging off with me, hell bent apparent for the north star, I could hear the derisive cackling of them greasers over my predicament.

But I guess they wouldn't have been so amused, if they could of saw me swing him around as soon as they was out of hearing, and then chase him for all he was worth in the direction of the ranch.

The night was so dark that I could likely have rode right up to the stockade without anyone spying me; but to be on the safe side, I turned the bronc loose, and sneaked in the last hundred yards or so afoot.

"Hey, there!" I called, expecting to be immediately challenged. But not a twitter did I get in response. Again, I sung out, considerably louder, and still got no answer. Was I too late? Had the massacre already been pulled off?

Then I tumbled. As the bandit captain had surmised, the whole garrison, with the news of Esteban's leaving, had gone and filled up on *pulque,* and was now laying down on their job. Probably I could holler my head off, and nobody would pay any attention to me.

I stood there and cussed a minute, uncertain just what to do. There was always the chance, you see, that some guard might be up there with a rifle, only waiting to get a fair bead on me before he plugged away. But at that instant, the breeze wafted to me the sound of drumming hoofbeats. My late associates was coming, and coming fast. You know what Brodie did. Well, that was me. I couldn't just stand there and scratch my dome.

Running along the fence until I struck a likely place, I shinned up and over. Believe me, that old saying about a fellow's heart getting into his mouth ain't no lie. Every second I expected to be drilled, and when my knee ketched for a breathing space, and sort of held me, I nigh passed out. But it was all waste emotion. I dropped over safe and unharmed on the inside, and started off for the officers' quarters.

On my way over, I encountered quite a few of our men in doorways and stretched out on the ground; but they was all dead to the world. The place reminded me of that old fairy story where the princess and the whole damn shebang went to sleep for a hundred years. But from the looks of 'em it would take more'n a kiss to wake up these geezers—about a dozen sticks of dynamite, I figured.

Even the commandant's sentinel was nodding. He kind of

half came to, as I raced up; but I brushed by so fast that he couldn't get his senses together in time to stop me.

I busted right into Cosete's room. Him and some of his officers was setting in a poker game. They all had their coats off, and as lit up like Luna Park. As I came in, one of 'em was just opening a fresh bottle of wine.

"*Nom d'un chien!*" says Cosette, staring at me kind of stupid. "Eet is M'Sieu Red. Ze prodigal 'ave return." He let out a high, silly laugh. "Geev him a glass of wine, Emil. Zen we take him out and shoot him."

"Not for me." I waved the stuff aside. "And not for you guys neither, if you know what's good for you. Listen, Cosette—"

"Een a minute. Een a minute, M'Sieu Volstead." He picks up his cards. "I 'ave a good 'and 'ere. I zink I open—*Nom d'un chien!*" He lurched to his feet, for I'd reached over and jerked the paste—boards out of his hand.

"Name of twenty dogs!" says I. "And then some. Minutes count right now, let me tell you. Leave that pair of deuces lay, and pay attention to me. Do you saps know"—I swung around to the rest of 'em—"that a picked crew of Esteban's murderers is practically right on top of you?"

Well, that sobered 'em for a second. Then this Cortez, the Peruvian what Sancho had butted in the stomach with his musket, staggered around the table. He was the worst pickled of the lot.

"Yah!" he jeered. "It is a pack of lie. Do we not know that Esteban is in flight? Why waste time with this American cur? He is a traitor, and this is but a ruse to save his neck. Take him out for his insolence, I say, and string him up."

Several others promptly seconded the motion, and I'll have to admit that for a second or two things began to look squally.

Wonderful how a habit grows on you. Almost before I knew what I was doing, I had backed into a corner and whipped out the old automatic.

"Put 'em up!" I says, facing the crowd. They weren't so drunk

but what they got me. Them paws went up faster than if it was
a primary school with the teacher asking if anybody could tell
who was the Father of his Country.

Holding 'em steady—or as steady as a lot of souses could be
held—I started to talk turkey to 'em. But—

"Put them up, yourself!" says a voice low but sharp from the
doorway.

And out of the corner of my eye, I seen Gerta standing there
with her two guns bent on me.

CHAPTER XIX

PRISONER

"**IN TROUBLE** as usual, I see, Mr. Conners?"

It was hot there in the stuffy room; but, take it from me, that voice of hers made you want a fur-lined ulster. I had a edge on it like the Adirondacks in January. And t'wasn't no colder, neither, than the gray of her eyes looking at me over the muzzles of them two guns.

I sort of choked up at the injustice of it, when I'd never done nothing more than sackerfice myself for her own good.

"Trouble?" I bust out. "Not in half so much trouble, ma'am, as some other folks will be, if I ain't listened to. I was just trying to tell these hopheads that—"

"I will hear you later," she cut in sharp. "Just now my business is with Captain Cosette. Captain, will you tell me why the ranch is left unguarded to-night? I have just made the rounds, and found not half a dozen sentinels on post.

Cosette didn't say nothing, just stands there hanging his head like a kid 't's been caught playing hooky; but this pest of a Peruvian, he tries to excuse it.

"What is there to guard against, señorita?" he hiccups. "Grasshoppers and crickets? Esteban is miles away, and—"

"On the contrary, lieutenant," she says pretty icy. "Esteban seems to be extremely close at hand. I have just captured a detachment of his men who were attempting a surprise attack upon us."

That held 'em for a minute all right. You never seen a cheap-er-looking lot of guys in your life. Even the drunken Peruvian wilted. But Gerta didn't show no mercy.

"Small thanks to you gentlemen that the attack did not succeed," she went on, and the way she said it was like the flick of a whip across their faces. "Unable to sleep, and apprehensive on account of the general carousing that the guard might be negligent, I decided an hour ago to make a tour of the defenses myself, and by sheer luck happened to be at the spot when these raiders came creeping through a gap up near the northeast corner of the stockade.

"Fortunately, it was too dark for them to see that I was alone. They thought I was at the head of a party that had the drop on them; and throwing down their weapons, began begging for mercy. I marched them up to the house—thirty of them—and with the aid of old Ursula locked them up. The I came over here to learn what my gallant defenders were doing."

I couldn't help feeling sorry for Cosette. He couldn't even look at her, and turned his face away, he was so mortified. But his eye happened to fall on me, and he gave a sort of a gasp.

"Mon Dieu!" he stuttered. "A surprise sortie? A raid by Esteban's men? Ze nor'east corner of ze stockade? Zen zis one must have been telling ze truth, mademoiselle, when he tried to warn us."

"Tried to warn you?" She stared at him, and then at me like it was hard for her to believe. "This man?"

"Assuredly, mademoiselle. He came bursting in here, claiming to have overheard zese brigands plotting to surprise and massacre ze garrison. But naturally, considering ze source, we regarded his story as a mere canard."

She frowned and bit her lip; then her head went up proud-like, and she stuck her guns back in her belt.

"I seem to owe you an apology, Mr. Conners," she said stiffly. "My impression, when I came into the room and found you holding up my officers at the point of your revolver, was that you were acting in concert with the band I had just settled with."

"How do we know that he was not?" butts in this nuisance of a Cortez again; I began to suspect that the fellow didn't like me. "Consider, señorita. Perhaps, this pretended friendship was just a ruse to decoy your brave officers into ambush?"

"Why bother to do that?" I shrugs airily. "Old John B. Aguardiente already had you helpless."

But this pinhead had ketched a tailhold on a idee, and with drunken obstinacy he hung onto it.

"Do you not see the cunning of him, señorita?" he sputters. "Ah, he is one crafty devil! Out on the range he falls in with these stragglers from Esteban's command. Perhaps they are strangers to him; more likely he has had previous dealings with them. *Quien sabe?* Who knows anything of the fellow's past? At any rate, he sees how he can use them. He is furious over the escape of the lady whom in his mad infatuation he sought to abduct; and he guides them to the gap in the stockade of which he knows.

" 'But first,' he says, 'let me see what the official staff is doing.' And he comes to us with his Judas warning. He expects to be doubted, but he reasons that while we are occupied with him, his rabble companions can safely get inside. Or, if on the other hand, his story is accepted and the bandits repulsed, he will be the savior of the ranch and his past misdeeds forgotten. Either way the coin falls, he will win. If the bandits are victorious, the lady—the object of his reckless passion—becomes his prize. If they lose, he will offer some plausible explanation for what he has done—the smooth-tongued monster of duplicity—and await another opportunity to carry her off."

Not so bad for a Peruvian souse, eh? But he had it in for me, and I guess malice can put a bite even in a mushy pickle. And he sure made a hit with the other officers; you see it gave them a sort of alibi. But what annoyed me was that Gerta seemed more'n half took in by his fool argument. Her face got dark and set again, and the look she gave me was anything but cordial.

Course I could have shot them fool charges full of holes in a dozen places; but I centered on what seemed the silliest of 'em.

"Reg'lar district attorney, ain't you?" I sneers at this Cortez. "Where do you get that stuff about mad infatuation which I am supposed to have abducted her on account of? The object of my reckless passion? Huh! Who says so?"

I put the question kind of general, r'aring back on my heels and facing 'em all. But it was Gerta who answered me.

"Who says?" she repeated with a sort of contemptuous quirk to her lip. "Why, the lady herself. You told her, she says, that catching sight of her one day on the balcony while talking to me, you had fallen instantly in love with her, and had then and there made up your mind to win her at any hazard. You boasted, she says, of how you managed to—to deceive me"—her voice caught for a second—"while you were laying your plans.

"Then when the opportunity came and you were sure I was out of the way, you rushed in upon her with vows of passionate devotion. Frightened, she tried to run away, to resist you; but you seized her forcibly and bore her off, swearing you would have her if you had to fight the whole garrison. Your intention, she says, was to fly with her to the camp of Esteban, with whom you had been carrying on a clandestine correspondence for some time."

Well, sir, I was roodled. I just couldn't seem to get my breath for a minute. The nerve of that Flossie coming back and passing out such a line of blah—making me out a sheik—when I'd steadily turned down all her bold advances.

"Rose Tyrell said that about me?" I finally gulped.

"Much more." Gerta's lips tightened. "But why repeat what you already know. Surely you'll not deny it. Even your ingenuity would find it hard to frame any other explanation for what happened. Why, we ourselves saw her struggling in your embrace when the searchlight picked the two of you out just outside the stockade."

What was the use? I felt like giving up. Every move I'd made was misconstrued, twisted into evidence against me. And then—I ain't no mind-reader, but I sensed it somehow that Gerta wanted to believe in me, if she only could. I bucked up to fighting trim.

"No, I ain't denying it," I snaps. "I ain't denying nothing—not here, and not to a audience of chimpanzee extrys. But, if you'll give me the chance, Miss O'Beirne, I'd like to face this victim of my hellish designs in your presence, and make her admit that she's the damndest liar—which is some pinnacle for a blonde— that ever stood on French heels."

Maybe it wasn't so much what I said as the way I said it— the honest punch to it—but it got her. The steel went out of her eyes; the hard, straight line of her lips softened just a mite. Still I don't believe anybody except myself noticed it. Her manner stayed just as formal and cold as ever.

"It is the right of every person, I suppose," she says, "to face his accuser. You shall have your wish, Mr. Conners. But you will have to wait. There are other matters more pressing at the moment. We have given up too much time to this, as it is. The immediate demand is the safety of the ranch. How do we know but that other marauding bands may be threatening us?

"Captain Cosette"—she turns to her right bower—"put a guard over this man, and have him held here until our return. I want you and the other officers—such of them as are able," she says—"to accompany me on a tour of the stockade, and see to the posting of an efficient line of sentinels."

Well, at that, they all stiffened up. Even Cortez, the Lima bean, tried to act like he'd only been affected a little by the heat and was all right now. After Cosette had called in a couple of his troopers and told 'em to see that I didn't escape, the bunch trailed out after Gerta, each of 'em aiming to walk a chalk line. It just goes to show how a once proud and haughty sex has deteriorated. If a man had come in there and tried to interrupt their revels, they'd have chucked him out on his ear; but this two-by-four squaw had only to crack her whip, and they followed her like a pack of trained poodles. Still, I didn't have no right to say nothing. In their fix, I'd have been as bad as any of the rest of 'em.

I turned from the degrading spectacle to give my brutal jailers the once over; and as I did so, I was struck by a certain vague familiarity in the look of one of 'em—something about the eyes.

"Surely," I says to myself, "nature even in her wildest mood never cut two pairs of lamps so tee-totally on the bias."

And with that for a clew, I finally recognizes under the disguise of a clean face and a uniform 'stead of picturesque tatters, my recent chief of staff, Pedro, the hog-tender.

"Greetings, little fairy," I hails him affectionate. "How come all the military pomp and power?"

But he's as stiff on duty as a police force rookie, and pretends not to know me. If I don't keep back where I belong, he growls, he'll jab me with his bayonet. A little brief authority has gone to his head, I reckon. How was I to know that them villainous contortions of his mug was intended for a wink.

Later, however, when his companion had sunk into the coma which is a greaser's normal habitat, he sidles over to me and opens up pour-parlers.

"Ver' nice *serape,*" he says, referring to the one I'd lifted from the bandit sentinel. "Ver nice *sombrero.* Señor no want, eh?"

"A fair exchange gathers no moss," I whispers back. "Tell me what took place after my more or less hasty hiatus last night, Pedro, and said baubles are thine."

"But we mus' spik Ingleez," he cautions, with a jerk of the head toward his somnolent buddy. "So him no understan'."

"All right," I agreed. "Go ahead in your own way, as the lawyers say. What happened just after I left?"

He crossed and uncrossed his eyes a dozen times and gave an imitation of a rattlesnake having a fit, thus signifying, I gathered, that there had jolly well been hell to pay.

But thence forward his words and music was mainly concerned with his own adventures, which though ambiguous, was not wholly unedifying.

He tells me—partly by pantomime which I could follow after a fashion, and partly by language which I couldn't—that when he seen what a hullabaloo my unadvertised departure was creating, he began to consider his own situation. Undoubtedly, if the facts came out, he would be blamed for assisting me, and judging from Gerta's evident displeasure—here he pictured with his hands a volcano in full eruption—the least he could expect was boiling in oil.

Then a dazzling stratagem occurs to him. Didn't I tell you that 'twas a greaser what put the poke in hocus pocus? The only person that knew for certain of his being hooked up with me, he reasons, is this sentinel that we'd tied up and left in the horse stall. So what does cute, little Pedro do but chase down there and set up a yelping like the house was afire. Then when the crowd came running to see what all the racket was about, he is apparently struggling with the sentinel.

"Thees ees the traitor who was in cahoots weeth the dam' Yankee," he announces proudly. "E was just preparing to take one of the horses and skip, when I capture heem weeth my bare 'ands."

As it happened, Cortez was in the crowd, and believing that this was the sentinel what had prodded him in the bread basket and given him the wrong steer, he won't listen to a word from the unfortunate guy, but orders him into irons, while, clapping Pedro on the shoulder and telling him he is a brave fellow, he takes him into his own command.

"Ver' smart man, me." The clown grins, all swelled up over his low cunning. "I bet you, I be a general yet, someday."

He was one of the party, he tells me, that goes out the next morning after me, and was in the hollow when Rosie came fluttering down from the cliff in hysterics and her one bedroom slipper.

The Señorita Gerta, he remarks, don't seem none too gracious toward her old boarding-school pal; but what passed between them, he wasn't near enough to overhear. All he knew was, that the yellow-haired doll was weeping wildly and flinging her arms around. He gathered, however, from her gestures and the way she kept pointing to the top of the cliff, that she was panning me fairly vicious.

Then, he says, Gerta had her wrapped up in the cloak and sent off to the ranch under escort, while she herself and the men began beating through the jungle at the top of the bank in search of me. The orders was to catch me at any cost.

"Two times I see the señor wreegle through the mesquite, and I could easy capture 'im," lies Pedro pounding himself on the chest; "but the señor ees my fren'. So I shout, 'Ho! Over 'ere! Over ere!' And each time, I lead the pursuit away from heem."

Finally along toward afternoon, he tells me, they gave up the hunt and started back toward home. On the way they sighted a small company of Esteban's men off over the range. These latter promptly beat it for the far horizon—all except one, a single horseman, what turned and headed straight toward the ranch crowd, same as a homing pigeon.

They thought at first it was a deserter, or, maybe, a escaping prisoner. Some believed it might possibly be me; I had nerve enough for anything, they said. But when the horseman got nearer, they seen he wasn't coming of his own free will; 'twas his mount that was bringing him in. He was pulling for all he was worth and sawing on the bridle, trying his best to stop or turn that runaway brute. But he might as well have tried to turn or check the Twentieth Century Limited.

Right up to Gerta, the intelligent animal galloped and stood and then under his caked dust and sweat, they recognized him.

"El Flivver!" Them greasers shouted. "El Hennery Ford!" The devil *caballo!*"

Say, you could have pasted me with a sledge hammer, and I wouldn't have felt it, I was that flumbusticated.

"What?" I grabbed Pedro by the arm. "Do you mean to tell me that old Henry got away from them dog stealers, and come back all of his lonesome?"

"Not of hees lonesome," says Pedro. "As I tell you, he breeng a prisoner on heem."

"Precisian," I rails. That's a nifty I picked up once from Milt. "But no matter. He is back. That is all that counts. Sound the loud timbrel, exultingly s-i-i-ng! Gee, comrade! I feel so happy, I could almost cry."

"Santa Maria! Eet was the same way weeth the Señorita Gerta," says Pedro, as if just truck by a recollection. "She order thees 'orse fed and watered, and later she come down where he is. She not theenk nobody ees around. But me, I am in then next stall enjoying my siesta; so I see her. She pat and caress thees Hennery Ford; then she lay her cheek against his neck and cry very quiet, very pitiful. You theenk she ees happy, too, señor."

I don't answer this, cause I'm so puzzled myself. And anyway Pedro, it strikes me, ain't one to shed no light on feminine idiot-syncrasies. Consequently, I moves the previous question.

"Go on," I says, "and tell me what else happened. Shoot the whole roll."

So, resuming his narration, he informs me that this bandit prisoner what Henry Ford brung in has under due encouragement spilled some surprising news.

The Mex national government, it seems, after months of what Milt used to call *dollchy far nienty,* has suddenly woke up to the fact that Esteban is a brigand and a outlaw, and has announced its intention of reestablishing law and order at Yavisa. In other words, what I surmise is, that somebody up at the capital thinks he ain't been getting his proper cut out of the graft, and is kicking over the old apple cart.

Anyhow, the government's out after Esteban—no matter of doubt about that—and a Federal army is already close at hand, with instructions to nail his pelt to the barn door, and chase all his rat-eyed followers out of the district.

But Esteban, the old fox, averse to having any bounty collected on his ears or nose tip, ain't caught napping, so this prisoner says. Tipped off on this projected raid just in time, and realizing that he ain't no match for the forces coming against him, he has gathered his gang together and is hot-footing it to the mountains to hide out and wait till the clouds roll by.

Sure enough, says Pedro, when they got back to the ranch they found the news confirmed by reports from Gerta's own scouts that it was moving day with the Esteban outfit. And after that, there wasn't no holding the garrison. Them for a *pulque* party, and discipline be damned.

"All except me," boasts this runt with his shirttail on the outside of his pants. "I am a soldier, always ready. I theenk, señor, I will join the Federal troops when they arrive. Soon you will be calling me el capitan, then colonel, then general—maybe, someday, el presidente of Mexico. *Quien sabe?*

Who knows, indeed? Stranger things than that has happened. But I had other matters to think over of more importance than Pedro's ambitious dreams.

What he'd told me in regard to Esteban coincides so closely with what I heard the bandits themselves talking about back there at the spring, that I size it up as pretty near the truth. I seen now of course that I wasn't the guy they was razzing so for double-crossing their leader. That must have been somebody with considerable of a drag on the government. But outside of this one point, my conjections tallied up pretty near to the facts.

Also, another thought came to me. With Esteban out of the way, and Federal troops controlling the district, there wasn't no reason why the Voreza Ranch couldn't be made to pay in a normal fashion, and without running any sidelines of blackmail and extortion.

My heart leaped at the suggestion of what I could do with that big, splendid property, if only the costly military establishment was cut out, and all its energies turned to production. It kind of stirred my ambition, don't you know, same's Pedro and his martial career. But of course it was only a dream. I couldn't stay there at Yavisa unless—unless I could manage to square myself with Gerta.

You see, I wasn't banking heavy on getting anything out of my forthcoming interview with the Tyrell girl. Demanding to face her was the one card in my hand at the time, and I'd played it; but the chances was that she'd stick to her lies, spite of all I could do to shake her. Probably she'd even made it worse. Them brainless fluffs is often cute as the devil at putting a man in the hole, and so stubborn in their deceitfulness that TNT wouldn't budge 'em. No; the more I considered getting her to recant, the less hopeful I felt.

And still—even when the prospects seemed blackest—I couldn't forget that idea I'd gathered—a sort of telephysic flash like—that Gerta wanted to believe in me. Nor yet I couldn't forget what Pedro had told me about her crying on the neck of my horse.

He was still babbling on and kind of disturbing me with his visions of empire when I wanted to think; so I hangs up on him.

"That will do, *amigo*," I said. "You have given me much food for reflection, and I want to chaw on it for a spell."

"But there is one thing more, señor," he persists, "which should be set straight. Since the señor left, I have talked to a number of people, and none of them has ever seen garlic growing on trees. They all say as I do, that it is a small, low plant which—"

"Hist!" the other sentinel interrupts, suddenly coming out of his trance and jumping to his feet. "Be quiet, you!" he growls at Pedro in Spanish. "The officers are coming."

A minute later, Cosette and the bunch came trooping in at the door. The captain looked around.

"Where is Mademoiselle Gerta?" he frowned. "She left me up at ze far end of ze stockade, and told me to meet her here."

"How long ago was that?" I asks.

"Long enough for her to have reached here twice over."

Cortez, the Peruvian, breaks in with his high, silly laugh.

"Who ever expects a lady to be on time?" he says, giving a

twirl to his mustaches like he was the last word on all pertaining to the fair sect. "Don't you know—"

But just then a soldier busted in at the door, pale and panting from hard running.

"Señor Capitan," he gasps to Cosette, his words all jumbled up, "Marengo, whom you ordered us to search for and place under arrest, has just escaped through the main gate. The guards fired, but missed him in the darkness. He has taken the fastest horse in the corral, and has carried off a woman with him. Who she is, we do not know, for he held her muffled in a *serape;* but we heard her scream as she passed."

Marengo! Esteban's scheme to capture Gerta, and hold her to ransom! So that was why she hadn't showed up!

CHAPTER XX

TO THE RESCUE AGAIN

"*SACRE BLEU*" says Cosette.

I'd often seen them words in print and on the screen, but this was the first time I'd ever heard 'em spoke. Generally, in subtitles, they is used to give a comedy flavor. But take it from me, the way Cosette rolled 'em out, they had all the genuine, milled-edge ring of a "Hell's bells!"

But that was as far as he went. He didn't have nothing to offer; and his officers just stood there gawping like a flock of google-eyed sheep. As usual, it required the hair-trigger style of brains made in U.S.A. to rise to the situation.

"Pedro!" I lands a kick on the future president of Mexico where it would best serve to stir him into action. "Get Henry Ford here. Pronto!" And Pedro prontoed.

"Name of a name! But what would you? Cosette begins waving his arms, when he sees me ordering one of his men around that way. "You are a prisonair, M'sieu Red. Eet ees ze command of Mademoiselle Gerta zat you be held here until she return."

"That's a life sentence, the way things stand," I says. "Behave yourself, cap. You know damn well that unless me and Henry go after her, there won't be any return; 'cause we're the only two on the ranch that can overtake this lousy foreman or save her from falling into the hands of Esteban."

Cosette knows it's the truth. He gives a uncertain shrug of the shoulders, and turns to the others.

"What do you say, gentlemen?"

This naturally was a cue for the Peruvian to start broadcasting, and he swings off into a bedtime story about how it's a soldier's place to obey orders no matter what he thinks himself, and that since Gerta had directed me to be held, it'd be plumb irregular to turn me loose.

But I'd been fed up on this bird a sufficiency for one evening.

"For cat's sake!" I cuts in. "Won't somebody take this wise-cracking Willie Woodchunk out and drown him? A soldier's place is to obey orders, is it?" I says to him "Then obey this one. Shut your trap, and hand me that canteen on the table there and them two sandwiches what's left on the platter."

I must have put a Milt Leffingwell voltage into my tone, I guess 'cause he don't try no comeback, just sort of acts hypnotized and done like he was told. I hitched the canteen onto my belt, and stuffed the sandwiches in my pocket.

"Now," I says, for I heard Pedro clattering up to the door with Henry Ford, "if anybody thinks they are going to stop me, let 'em try it." But nobody raised a finger.

"Signal the main gate to let me pass, cap," I called to Cosette as I swung into the saddle. "So long, boys!" And away me and Henry galloped into the night.

Gee! It was a relief to be up on that old rascal's back again after all I'd been through and he acted almost as tickled as I was. Spite of being on the go all the night before, and routed out again at this ungodly hour, he was playful as a colt and tried all sorts of affectionate little tricks on me. But soon's we was outside the stockade I steadied him down.

"Cut the comedy, old-timer," I says. "This is serious business. Not knowing how fur we've got to go, nor what we may not be up against; so save the energies that you're putting into them crowhops and kitten stuff for the hour of need. Might be just that extry gallon of gas you're wasting that'll be required to pull us under the wire, Mr. Shean."

As I've said before, Henry is a sensible horse, sensibler than most humans; and it didn't take more'n that one word of mild reproof, coupled with a cut or two of the quirt, to make him understand.

"Now," I says when he had settled down to his regular gait, "let's discuss this job orderly and unemotional. Gerta is gone— abducted by this slimy Marengo and toted off to Esteban—to be held for ransom. But we know, as Esteban probably don't, that ransom is out of the question. You can't get blood out of a turnip; and with the ranch already mortgaged up to the gun'nels, and her merely subsisting on the little contributions she levies from the neighbors, where is the money coming from? So, when old Crooked Mouth finds she can't come across what's going to happen then? You know as well as I do, Henry. As the screen says, and never was a truer word flashed in this case: 'A fate worse'n death.' He'll make her the fifth or sixth Mrs. Esteban, either with or without the benefit of clergy."

I'd said I was going to go into this thing unemotional; but it took somebody harder-boiled'n what I am to think of Gerta, with all her pride and her thoroughbred fineness, in the power of that loose-lipped, cold-eyed devil. My hands went to shaking so that I could hardly hold the bridle, and big beads of sweat popped out all across my forehead.

"By God, Henry Ford," I blubbers, "it's up to us to save her, and how are we going to do it? We put up a awful front back there at the ranch, but we're only false pretenses and we know it—four-flushing greenhorns that's butted into a regular profes-sional game.

I was clean submerged; no mistake about it. All the diffi-culties and the craziness of our attempt swept down on me like a big, black cloud, through which I couldn't even see a ray of light. Here was me and Henry, strangers in the country, out chasing a guy who'd been born and brought up on the range, and knew all its shortcuts and bypaths like you know the lay of your bedroom—chasing him in the dark, moreover, without an idee of what direction he'd took, and handicapped further by the start he had on us of at least twenty minutes.

A real, bonafide buckaroo might have picked up Marengo's trail, and follered him like a Injun, although I'm of the opinion that most of that trailing stuff you hear about is bunk. But I was only a counterfeit anyhow, and just about as fit to play blood-hound as a frankfurter.

Face to face with the facts, I realized what a total loss I was. Me and Henry had just about as much show of overtaking that tricky greaser and rescuing Gerta as we had to being chose to do a tableau of Little Eva and her lamb.

Yet us two was Gerta's one hope. As I said, it was up to us to save her; and we had to manage it some way. But how, how, how? That was the question that boiled in my brain, and by the very hopelessness of finding an answer to it made me feel limp and worthless as a dishrag.

Out there on the wide range, in the stillness and blackness of the night, I seemed so little and cheap and no account, and the odds against me so tremendous, that I fair give way. The thought of Gerta in such a fix and with only a trifling ham like me to depend on choked me up; and—would you believe it?'—the tears streamed down my face and I went to rocking back and forth in the saddle, boohooing like a baby.

Then Henry began talking to me. You think a horse can't talk, eh? Well, that's 'cause you ain't never pulled up with one and learned his language. Believe me, this skate of mine could sling oratory around worse 'n Henry Cabot Borah—not in words maybe, but in a dozen other ways which is even more expressive.

"Buck up there, you big stiff," he snorts at me disdainful. "What's all the bellyaching about? Ain't you a American, male, white, red-headed, and of Irish descent? Where in fact or fiction did you ever know that combination to be beat? Furthermore," he says, "ain't you got the best horse, bar none, 'twixt here and Jersey City?"

"Such being the case," says he, "are we going to let ourselves be whipsawed by a mud-colored greaser and his miserable, blue-roan bronc? Perish the thought," he says. "We've got four hoofs, a coupla fists, and two heads between us, even if one is a pump-kin head. And we're going to rescue Gerta and bring her back in triumph. Hold to that idea," he says. "don't let no other sugges-tion get into that alleged brain of yours; and you'll find it comes true. Where there's a will, there's always a contest. Every day in every way, we are getting better and better."

He perked me up considerable with that confidence talk of his, even if there wasn't no foundation for it; and first thing you know, the old bean which had been stalled for the last half hour began catching her spark.

All of a sudden I recollected some conversation I'd overheard the bandits back at the spring getting off, but to which I hadn't paid no particular attention at the time.

They'd spoke of carrying the Yankee señorita back in the mountains where they expected to meet Esteban and turn her over to him and, luckily for me, they'd got into a dispute about the best way of reaching this hangout, which their leader had decided by telling 'em it was up a narrow gap marked by a lone pine tree, and describing to 'em the trail they'd have to follow to reach this gap.

Now, it struck me that Marengo would undoubtedly head for this same place; and, since he was traveling double, he'd natu-rally go slower 'n what me and Henry did. We ought to arrive at the gap before he did, and to give him the surprise of his life, when, thinking all his troubles over, he started to go up it and join Esteban.

At once I began running over in my mind the directions I'd heard how to reach the gap. Did I have 'em right? Yes, I was sure I did. I must bear to the west of Voreza ranch for about twenty miles, until I came to a low range of foothills on the other side of which I would sight three peaks. I must set my course to the south by the tallest of these, and head directly toward it until I saw another tall peak to the east. Aiming toward this, I would presently strike a rough trail which would lead me to the gap.

"Henry," I says, "you're right, old sox. It's believing does the trick. Faith ain't exactly moved mountains in this case, but it's certainly made 'em serve our purpose. Heretofore, we was hunting for a needle in a haystack, but now it's like a needle on the floor when you're barefooted. You simply can't miss it."

"Well, it's good you've got somebody along who's got a little horse sense," says Henry in the superior way that members of your family has of talking to you. "If you didn't, you'd still be sunk in that gulf of deep despair what you was wallering in so helpless until I hooked up to you and drug you out. It's me Gerta ought to thank when she's rescued," he grumbles; "but, instead, you'll go strutting around, playing hero and taking all the credit. Well, such is the way of the world," he says; "the cheesier the cheese, the louder it proclaims itself. Modest worth always get lost in the shuffle. Where do we go from here?" he asks kind of snappy.

By this time dawn had broke, and it was getting light enough for you to gain some idea of your surroundings. As it happened, not by no forethought, but maybe guided by subconscious suggestion or something—we had struck off in a westerly direction when we left Voreza ranch; and as we had been pushing right along, 'spite of my qualms and misgivings, we had covered considerable ground.

So now, as I peered ahead into the dim grayness of the early morning, I spied off a little to the left that low range of foothills what was set as my first landmark.

"Cheerio, Hank!" I says. "We're on the right track, all right. Step on her a bit." And heading around to the hills, we hit such a lively clip that by sunup we had crossed 'em; and there, sure enough, away to the south loomed them three tall peaks, gleaming like gold in the yellow sunlight.

"Plain sailing ahead!" I carols exultantly. "It's all over but the shouting." I felt so good that I started to sing that fav'rite ballad of old Idaho's, "I Buried My Love on the Lone Pra'ree."

"Humph!" interrupts Henry captiouslike. "Pretty jubilant ain't you? Only a bit ago, you was sniveling and squealing like a hairless poodle in a snowstorm; but the minute the sun starts shining and the road gets smooth, bang goes your chest-measure. 'Look what I done!' you say. 'Ain't I the curly wolf?' No cause for celebration yet, what I can see," he says. "There's many a pebble 'twixt here and that gap, which might work into the frog of my hoof and lame me up. And then where would you be?"

Could you beat it? Here, he'd been pitching into me unmerciful for my downheartedness, and telling me not to think nothing but success; yet now—out of mere petty jealousy, as near as I could figure—he himself was trying to spread gloom over everything in sight, same's a sprinkling cart. He ain't the first of these optometers I've knowed, that practiced considerably different from what they preached.

Still and all, it would have took a whole lot more than his grouching to damp my spirits just then, especially as not long after this we come upon the cabin of an old Mexican woman, and I stowed away a hearty breakfast of frijoles and coffee, for, as may be imagined, them two sandwiches hadn't done much more than whet my appetite. You must remember, I'd been running completely shy on food since that crab-apple banquet of the morning before. Maybe, that was the reason I'd given way to fears and discouragement so easy back there in the night.

Anyhow, them frijoles inside of me, together with a sack of extry ones to serve as sustenance on my journey, did give a sense of solidity that before was sadly lacking. I noticed, too, that Henry with a feed of oats inside of him, and a bag of ditto hitched onto the saddle, was far less morose in his observations. And for all this provender, including tip, we paid—read it and weep, you Broadway suckers—the magnificent sum of three cents in American money. Wasn't that enough to drive dull care away of itself?

Still, as we took to the road again, we didn't indulge in no spirit of leverage. This wasn't a picnic, we both realized, but, as I'd said previous, a serious business. Things had gone along jake so far; but we was still a long way from accomplishing our mission and lots of detriments besides pebbles in Henry's hoofs was on the road just aching to put a crimp in us.

As I pointed this out to Henry, both of us sobered down, and
he lunged off into a gallop, shaking his head and trying to take
the bit in his teeth when I pulled him in. I could understand
that. Whenever I thought of Gerta in the clutches of that half-
breed viper Marengo, a sort of a wave of sickness'd go over me,
and 'twas all I could do to keep from racing my fool head off.
Every fibroid in me seemed to be urging, "Hurry! Hurry!" and
before I thought I'd be jabbing my spurs into Henry for a sprint.

Yet I knew, and so did he, that that wasn't no way to turn the
trick. It was steady plugging that was going to win out for us, if
we won at all, with a lot of energies held in reserve to overcome
unforeseen delays and obstacles on the way, and especially for
the supreme dash we'd have to do if, when we secured Gerta, we
was pushed to make our get-away.

Oh, no; we wasn't in no holiday mood. There was too much at
stake for that; too much responsibility resting on us two—too
much chance that some trifling mistake or accident would ditch
the whole enterprise.

Not that we didn't run into a raft of 'em; accidents and
mistakes, I mean. You could hardly expect it to be otherwise, with us follering an absolutely unknown trail. Twice we
got hopelessly lost, and sweated ourselves to shads before we
managed to get our bearings again. And once, in trying to take
a short cut, I run us into a swamp, and we had to make a detour
of almost fifteen mile before we was once more on terry firma.

We had rough going most of the time; and some, that to
just call rough, would be like saying that hell was running a
temperature.

Howsoever, all things considered, we didn't do bad. By
sundown, we had sighted the single peak to the east, which,
according to directions, was the guidepost that'd point us along
the trail leading to the gap; and I still figured that we was well
ahead of what Marengo could have made, burdened like he was
with a female prisoner. Naturally, he'd have picked up another
animal somewhere for Gerta; he wouldn't try to travel all that

distance, carrying double; but even so, and in spite of his knowing the road, he'd have been hard put to make the time we had.
Horses like Henry Ford ain't to be picked off of every black-
berry bush.

Here, the old rascal had been pounding away for nearly
seventeen hours—fighting through jungles and deserts and
swamps and what not—and yet he was fresh as paint, r'aring
to go on. I'd planned to lay up where we was for the night; but
he kept arguing with me that it was silly to lose so much of our
lead on Marengo and that, whatever risk there was, we owed it
to Gerta to push ahead.

So, finally, against my better judgement, I yielded to his
persuasions; and so soon as the moon came up, we was once
more on the move.

Some moon she was, too, bigger and brighter even than the
one what Gerta and me had sung to on the roof. No trouble
picking out the trail with it shining down on us. A blind man
could almost have done that.

Up, up, up we climbed, winding through deep defiles and
ravines; yet, no matter how thick the timber, or how steep-
walled the bullies and hollows, there was always light enough
to see your way.

So moon! As I looked at her, big and round and silvery up
there in the heavens, I kept wondering if Gerta was watching
it, too, and if it brought any comfort to her.

Surely, she must know that after that hour of ours together—
that unforgettable evening only two nights ago—I'd never lay
quiet, and let her be carried off by a dirty greaser. She must
know that I'd be out to rescue her, if I broke my neck doing it,
or—But no. She believed, or at any rate had been made by this
lying Rosie to suspicion that, when I took her in my arms there
in the moonlight and tried to tell her she was the one girl of all
the world, I'd only been faking.

Faking, eh? Well I'd soon nail that slander. She'd see things very different, when she found me saving her from Esteban, and heard of all I'd done and dared in her behalf.

By heck—my jaw set and I stiffened into steel—I had to pull this job off clean, not only for her sake but my own. If I didn't—if I failed—

"Here! Here!" snaps Henry Ford. "What the hell you trying to do, you big ignoramus?"

Would you believe it, I was so busy thinking, that, quite obstetrical to my surroundings, I was trying to force him over a precipice what we was skirting, and which was more 'n a hundred feet high.

Lucky, also, for another reason, that he called me just then; for as I yanked him back from the brink, and stared around kind of dazed-like to get hold of myself, I seen just ahead of us a lone pine tree standing like a sentinel above a narrow crevice in the rocks.

The gap! We'd reached it. And I'd been so lost in my reveries, that if it hadn't been for Henry, I might have passed right by and never noticed it!

However, here we was at journey's end. And now, the next thing was to arrange a proper reception for Mr. Marengo.

Dismounting from Henry, I led him back into a thicket of saplings where he'd be easy to get at, and yet was concealed from the view of anybody coming along the trail. Then I scouted around to get a idea of the place, and plan out my campaign.

Couldn't have been a handier arrangement of the landscape, if I'd ordered it direct from the factory. The gap through which Marengo would have to pass was just a fissure in the mountainside—not more 'n wide enough for two horses to travel abreast—and on either side of the mouth of it was a upstanding crag.

One of these was too steep for anybody to climb; but the other, on the side where the lone pine tree was, had a easy ascent up it from the back, and a sort of cup-like hollow on top, where you could lie as snug as behind breastworks, and pick off anyone that come moseying along the trail below.

It kind of puzzled me that Esteban, with his camp so near, didn't have guards out to protect what was, so to speak, his front door; but greasers is a shiftless lot, often careless about such things, and I merely supposed he felt so safe off up there in the wilderness that he didn't think it worth the trouble.

Still, you'll understand I wasn't peeved none at his oversight. If any of his men 'd been hanging around there at the gap, I'd have been put to the bother of bumping 'em off, or else have had to go further down the mountain, where there was a chance that Marengo might slip by me on a side trail.

As it was, all I had to do was to boost myself up to the top of the crag, stretch out comfortably on my stomach so as to look down the road, and wait for developments.

Developments was some time in arriving, I must admit. The moon circled down behind the range and set. The night wore slowly on. And try as I would to keep 'em open, I'd find my eyelids blinking down. I was short, you must remember, more'n a few hours in my slumber account; and nature seemed hell-bent on making up the deficit. For just a cat nap I'd have cheerfully bartered a month's salary. But I was determined that I wouldn't get caught drowsing again, like I had with Rosie back at the hollow, and by sheer force of will I held myself awake.

I'd visualize myself diving into pools of ice-cold water, and listening to brass bands, and fighting with hungry tigers—everything that was lively or exciting. But it was some battle, believe me. First thing I'd know, that ice water'd get like a summer sea, and the tigers'd snuggle up to me soft and friendly-like, and the band'd start playing lullabies.

Yet I clenched my nails, and chawed my lip, and pinched myself till I was sore; and so managed to make out. And so another dawn finally flushed up from the east, and found me keeping a vigil what was bent maybe, but still unbroken.

"Ain't that kidnaping coyote ever going to show up?" I now

began to worry. "Or is it possible, he's worked some greaser trick on me, and got here first?"

But while I was pondering these contingencies, my ears suddenly caught the faint clop-clop of horses' hoofs off down the trail, and peering out from my watch tower, I seen the skunk crossing a little clearing about a mile off. He was belaboring his jaded bronc up the slope, in the pitiless way that a Mexican treats animals, and was dragging behind him by a lead rope a mule on which was huddled a bowed figure wrapped in a kind of dark shawl.

At that sight, all my sleepiness vanished. I tingled with a sort of murderous rage. For Gerta to look so forlorn and crushed and cowed—Gerta that always sat so light and jaunty in the saddle, no mater how long or hard the ride—he must have abused her brutal. My fingers clutched around the grip of my automatic; I seen every shade of red, from pink to deep crimson. If a bullet would have carried that far, I'd have dropped him in his tracks then and there.

But 'twas senseless to warn him by futile shooting, or even to let him out so easy. Better to play it safe and sure like I'd planned. So I clamped down on my emotions, and wormed out to the edge of the crag. There was some young trees and a mess of undergrowth at the foot of the cliff, kind of masking the approach to the gap. But just below me and inside the entrance was a open space; and 'twas there I was aiming to halt him.

And then, as I waited tense and on edge for him to come up, I heard a dry chuckle behind me that rasped along my spine like the whirr of a rattler.

"Don't move, Señor Red, or attempt to use that gun," said a mocking voice. "You will realize, I am sure, that I have the drop on you."

I shot a glance out of the tail of my eye back over my shoulder, and seen the scarred, yellow face of Esteban grinning down at me.

CHAPTER XXI

FOOLED

"AH, WHAT a gringo fool you are!" says Crooked Mouth, generously rubbing the fact in on me. "Did you believe, you long-eared donkey, that I would leave a spot like this unguarded? Why, you rooting swine, a sentinel up in the branches of yonder pine tree has had you under surveillance every moment of the night. The instant you approached, it was signaled to my headquarters; but I ordered that you be left unhindered, given free rein, so that I might see what you were up to.

"And now, you dog," he says, giving me a kick in the ribs, "toss that gun back to me, and get up. I want some information out of you."

Wasn't nothing to do but obey. But as I shuffled sheepish to my feet, a kind of a idea came to me; that kick in the ribs sort of jolted up my wits as well as my entrails.

"Just a minute, colonel." I eyes him haughty. "Let us understand each other. I don't relish your style of cross-examination, nor yet your way of addressing me like a barnyard catalog. You've got me covered, it's true, but you can't make me talk, 'less I want to. So, if your aim is to find out anything from me, I'd advise you to take a milder and politer tack. Granted," I says, "that you can pull my tongue out by the roots but you nor nobody else can make it wag, not without my own consent."

He was cunning enough to see that I had it on him in a way, and that he'd best concede the point. Probably he figured that he'd make up for his self-restraint later on. Far as I was concerned, I was merely sparring for wind, of course. I didn't have nothing on my chest, even including my under-shirt, which I wasn't willing to reveal to all the world; but, as long as he thought I had, can you blame me for taking advantage of his heterodoxy? I ain't just sure of that last word, but you'll understand what I mean.

Well, he studied me for a minute; then he gives a shrug of the shoulders.

"Bueno," he says more oily-like. "A bargain, eh? Have it your own way then, even though I see that I shall be the loser; for I am satisfied that I know already all that you can tell me."

I was satisfied of that, too; but I slanted my eyes sly-like, and tried to look mysterious and diplomatic.

"Suppose," he says, "to confirm this, señor, you tell me who it was sent you on your unfortunate mission?"

"Who do *you* think?" I parries.

"Who?" He belched out a blast of Spanish fire and brimstone. "No one but that treacherous, double-dealing hound, Jeff Tyrell."

Say, did you ever groping around in a dark room and then all of a sudden stumble on a button that flooded the place with light, and made everything as clear as day to you? Well, that was just the way I felt.

So it was Tyrell that the bandits back there at the spring had been cussing as the source of all their troubles. Him and Crooked Mouth must have fell out, probably over a division of the loot; and Jeff, to get even, had snitched to the Mexican government and had his old pal set out on the sidewalk.

"But look here, colonel," I stalls, while I am digesting this disclosure and trying to figure how I can profit by it; "don't you know that me and Tyrell ain't exactly what you might call buddies?"

"Rot!" he says, or rather, some greaser word I ain't never heard before, but of which the meaning is plain. "He always claimed that he could buy you, if he ever needed you. You are here. That proves you have been bought."

"But not that I've got to stay bought," I suggests brightly. "Suppose I was guaranteed safe-conduct away from here, there's a good deal I could spill about Jeff's plans, colonel, that you ain't hep to."

I could read him like a book. He believed I had some inside dope and he'd promise the earth to get me to talk; but as for really letting me out of his clutches—not a chance. He had that old grudge against me from the first day I landed in Yavisa to settle, and now that he had me, he intended to collect with interest. Meanwhile, though, I could likely play him along by peddling out to him supposed tips on what Tyrell was up to— most any line of skullduggery would do—and to gain time.

"Yes, sir," I repeated impressively; "There's quite a few things about Jeff that I could put you wise to, colonel."

He was hooked all right; but he tried to act like he wasn't.

"Humph!" He puts up a sneer. "Tyrell's purpose is plain enough to me. He wants the Voreza ranch. Originally he planned to seize it; but now he has adopted another idea. He has bought up some dubious claims against Miss O'Beirne, and on them intends to oust her and take possession. Through the Federal authority she has brought in, he expects to secure a valid title. That was his quarrel with me. He knew I would never countenance such barefaced robbery."

As to this last, I held a little different reading. More likely, I thought, Jeff had been afraid that Esteban was going to hog the ranch himself.

However, that was a detail. The main point was that I had picked up another piece of valuable information—if I ever got a chance to use it.

"So," I nodded, "that was your reason for raiding the ranch house as a parting token of regard, was it? You thought you'd make it pleasant for Jeff to move in, eh, by burning all the buildings and killing off the livestock?

"Also," I adds, "I suppose it was to put some sort of spoke in his wheel—by making it impossible to serve papers, or something of the sort—that you carried off Gerta?"

"Gerta?" He stared at me. "Carried off Gerta?"

Wasn't no question of his surprise. He kept scowling at me puzzled-like, as if he couldn't make it at all.

"Why, sure," I said. "Wasn't that on the program, or did the boys decide to pull it off as an added number? Anyhow, she was carried off. That's her, Marengo is bringing up the trail."

"Gerta?" he sputtered. "Car-r-ramba!" And impulsive like, he half turned toward the edge of the cliff, as if to confirm it for himself.

It was the opportunity I had been waiting for. Esteban's wrists were still bandaged where Gerta had plugged him; but even so, I'd known better than to tempt his gunmanship at that close range—at least, while his eyes was on me.

But when he turned, his glance shifted half a point, the barrel of his gun wavered away from me. I took one quick backward step to the edge of the crag, and—jumped.

Anybody else 'd killed hisself, doing that; but I'm still here, ain't I? You want to remember that I'd had two years' experience dare-deviling for the films under Milt Leffingwell. As a matter of fact, I'd worked almost the same stunt in one of my "Reckless Rudolph" pictures, as you'll recall if you've ever saw "The Pit of Perdition."

The idea had come to me, you see, when I was laying there on the ground and Esteban first made known his presence. And before I got up, I took careful note of distances and all the conditions both above and below, so as to be prepared for the trick if he ever gave me half a chance.

Just underneath the point where I jumped, you must understand, there was a good-sized tree; and I landed nicely in it, as per calculation, allowing the light upper branches to break my fall, and then about halfway down gripping a stouter bough, and then swinging from limb to limb toward the ground.

Lucky for me that Esteban's game wrists made him a shade awkward in handling his weapon; for even with his attention diverted, he came within an ace of getting me. Just as I cleared the edge of the crag, his revolver barked out; and I don't believe that bullet missed my head a half a inch. Also, as I went down through the tree, his shots kept cutting off leaves and twigs all around me, although of course he was then firing wild.

Still them shots didn't serve as no impediment to me getting out from under them. Monkey-like, I shifted to another tree whose branches interlocked with the one I was in; and from there, into still another tree with boughs that overhung the trail.

Looking down, I could see Marengo halted almost directly under me. Startled by the shooting, he'd stopped to try and make out what it was all about, and whether to go forward or back. So busy was he, too, in staring up at the top of the crag, that he'd never noticed me parachuting around in the foliage.

The sight of him there gave me an inspiration. Seizing a supple branch, I took a long swing, and letting go at just the proper moment, landed behind him on his horse, and gripped him around the arms.

Naturally the bronc started up and done a pinwheel or so; and struggling like we were, we both went off. But I lit on my feet, and managed to still keep Marengo pinioned.

We had been carried away by these various gyrations from the cover of the trees out into that open spot at the mouth of the gap, where I made a easy target for Esteban. Looking up, I saw his crooked mouth twist into a grin of triumph, as he leveled his gun and took deliberate aim.

But with a lunge, I threw Marengo in front of me and ducked behind him just as the report rang out.

Bang! Esteban wasn't one to miss often. I felt Marengo stiffen and then sag in my arms. Also, I must have loosened my hold on him, I guess; for one of his hands reached over and jerked out his gun.

I doubt if he understood. Like a broken-backed wolf, he just snapped at the first thing in sight.

"Dog!" he gurgled through the blood pouring out of his mouth; and, as he died, fired at the top of the crag.

A single shot, mind you; and from the wavering hand of a man that was, so to speak, already moribund. But it was Esteban's time.

Where it hit him, I don't know—knee, shoulder, heart or stomach. But he was standing right on the edge of the cliff. He flung out an arm, lurched, tried to recover himself, and then with a sort of strangled yell went over. And there wasn't no trees where he dropped; nor yet was he a Reckless Rudolph. I didn't go over to see whether he was breathing yet or not; I *knew*.

Neither did I stop to close Marengo's eyes, and say a prayer over his remains. Them things is proper in the fillums all right; but I was mindful of what Esteban had told me about a sentinel perched in that lone pine tree, and I didn't lose no time beating it to cover.

Also, I didn't know how many other bandits might be in the immediate environment, nor how quick they would be down on me like a swarm of hornets. Luck had psychoanalyzed two bad dreams for me at oncet, but you couldn't expect a elimination contest like that to continue. On the whole, it seemed wise for me to seek pastures new, while, as the saying goes, I still retained my health.

The mule on which Gerta was tied, mulelike was grazing indifferent to the turmoil a little piece away. I grabbed his lead-rope, and without stopping to cut her loose, or receive her grateful thanks or anything, larruped him into a run down the trail.

Meanwhile I kept whistling for Henry, and after a minute or two he came dashing up to me. Running alongside him, I made a clean vault into the saddle, still keeping my hold on the lead-rope, and away we all went lickety-split down the mountainside.

Whether we was chased or not, I can't say. I only know that we wasn't caught up with. It couldn't be done, not at the pace we set, and over such going. Rough? You said it, brother. Why, we just the same as committed suicide every step we covered. And don't never tell me that a mule ain't a steeplechaser. That there thistle-fed hybrid went over jumps—crisscrosses or fallen logs, hurdles of solid rock, river pools in deep-worn gullies—that 'd have made a English hunter turn tail and run at the sight of 'em. Not that he done it from choice, you understand. He had to. Henry and I seen to that.

But at last we came to a spot, where it seemed reasonably safe, and where I reckoned we could stop and sort of take stock of ourselves. A kind of a knoll, it was, where you could watch out from all sides, and where there was a spring of fresh water bubbling out from among the rocks.

I leaped down from Henry, and ran over to the mule, full of compassion for Gerta. A mule ain't no single-footer at the best; and after such a breezer as we'd took, I realized that the poor girl'd just about be jolted loose from her back teeth.

Quickly I slashed the ropes that fastened her, and gently started to lift her down to the ground. She didn't answer me when I spoke to her, nor didn't seem rightly to understand what I was doing; just kept up a kind of weak whimpering like a sick kitten.

But as I hefted her, she let out a screech that'd have done credit to a locomotive, and grabbed me around the neck in a throttling half-nelson. What I figured at first was that maybe some of her bones was broke from all that bouncing, but I soon seen it was only the high-strikes.

"My hero!" she whooped, laughing and crying at the same time. "I might have known that you would come to rescue me."

Say, that voice sent a kind of cold chill running all though me. If I hadn't already set her down, I'd have dropped her sure; for the dark shawl in which she was muffled, head and all like a greaser woman, fell back and showed me the yellow hair and doll-baby face of Rose Tyrell.

Hero? I felt like thirty cents' worth of curdled Welsh rabbit.

Could anything on earth now make Gerta believe that I was on the level? No man alive would have took the chance that I had, or have did what I've done, except for the woman he loved.

CHAPTER XXII

UNDERSTANDING

FIGURE IT out for yourself. What would *you* think? Under every appearance of guilt, and with the evidence of the victim herself dead against me, I'd already made off once with this queen, and had been balked.

What's the next move of a infatuated moron, such as I was supposed to be? Why, to try again, of course. That kind never gets tired of trying until they either marry the unfortunate dame, or else happily bump 'emselves off.

So who would believe I hadn't known that girl I was after, when me and Henry sallied forth in the night on our errand of rescue? Try to tell 'em that I thought all the time it was Gerta, and they'd smile superior and wink the other eye.

"Pretty good bluff you put up, old man," they'd say; "but, really, don't you know, I wasn't born yesterday."

That's what I'd got for listening to the chatter of some dirty bandits, and quite forgetting that there was more than one Yankee señorita at the ranch; for, as I saw plain enough now, it was Rose Tyrell that Esteban had been planning to abduct. That was the reason of his surprise when I told him Marengo was bringing Gerta up the trail.

But who could you get to believe that I'd been mistaken? Why, they'd doubtless claim that I was in cahoots with Marengo—just as that Peruvian cutey had twisted my gallant effort to save the ranch into a trick, and had found ready listeners for his theory.

By gum, it seemed like everything I done or didn't do only acted to put me worse in Dutch.

So far as Gerta was concerned, I was out. That was a cinch. A woman might forgive you one elopement with her best friend; but she'd rightly draw the line, when you got to making it a habit.

All them tender words and meaning glances I'd gave her in the moonlight would only be regarded as dust throwed in her eyes to blind her to my true purpose, and the memory of 'em would rankle in her breast until it turned all her thoughts of me into poisonous hate.

Golly! I felt like murdering this yellow-headed pest that had wished herself on me—it'd have been justifiable homicide, if anything ever was—but, hell, what was the use? The wise crackers then would have said, "Jealous Suitor Slays Sweetheart," or maybe called it a "Death Pact." So I restrained my reasonable impulses, and didn't look no more at a handy-sized boulder what was tempting me.

"It's you, is it?" I says pretty sour, as I unclasped the hammerlock of them white, clinging arms and backed away from her.

"Of course, it's me, Red," she coos. "Who else did you expect it to be?" Then her eyes began to widen, and her lower lip dropped. "Why, I believe—" she gasped. "Red, you don't mean to tell me that you didn't know—that you did all this for—"

Can you equal 'em? Here, this jackrabbit had been slandering me to a fare-you-well, giving me the worst of it every way she knew how; and yet she really thought she was so irresistible that it was for her I'd dared the perils of mountain and desert and the claws of Esteban. Well—maybe I would at that; her or any other woman. But just then, I told myself I'd have seen her in hell first.

"You didn't know—" She stared at me.

"You're dead right, I didn't," I growled. "I never dreamed until a minute ago, that you was anyone but Gerta O'Beirne."

"Oh!" She let out a yip, and rolling her eyes up, keeled over in a dead faint—or, if it wasn't quite as dead as it appeared to be, it was a mighty good imitation.

Well, you know how it is yourself. I more'n half suspicioned she was playing possum; but when I seen her laying there still and white like a broken lily, I got kind of scared and soft and remorseful.

"Poor, little thing," I thinks. "She sure has had one rough deal."

I gets some water from the spring and sprinkles it on her; and then, as she began to come to, I lifted her head on my arm, and started to chafe her hands. I'd have cut her corset strings, I suppose, if she'd had any; but they don't wear 'em no more.

"There, there!" I crooned. "It's all right. Don't you worry."

First thing you know, she had snuggled her cheek over, and was sobbing up against my shirt.

I didn't want her there, God knows; but could I push her away? I ask you.

Here she was, all worn out and forlorn and broken-hearted; and if she got any comfort out of sniffling into my shirt, I wasn't the man to deny it to her. I'd have done the same for a lost pup.

So I sat there, rocking her in my arms and trying to soothe her; and after a while her sobs quieted down, and she was breathing, soft and regular. Clean tuckered out, poor kid, she'd dropped off to sleep.

I didn't like to disturb her; she needed the rest all right. So I just let her stay where she is. But that old bye-bye stuff is mighty contagious, let me tell you, especially when you've been fighting it off all night.

Next thing I knowed, I opened my eyes to find it was late afternoon, and all around me was a lot of greasers in uniform and an almost equal number of civilians, which long experience with the films led me easily to identify as newspapermen and press photographers.

I'd just been dreaming that I was right in the way of an old-time buffalo stampede, and was pinned down by a log across my legs so that I couldn't move—all worked up, probably, from the sound of this troop coming up, and from the weight of Rosie on me, laying like she was.

But the reality didn't seem no less fantastic than the nightmare. Where these folks had come from or what they wanted was beyond me. They was grinning friendly, and trying to shake hands, and even cheering some; so it was plain they wasn't no enemies. But beyond that, their appearance was a complete puzzle. All that me and Rosie could do was to blink and rub our eyes and yammer, until one of the newspaper guys enlightened us what 'twas all about.

The news of Rosie's abduction, it seems, had kicked up considerable excitement over in E. Pluribus Unum, the alleged land of the free. You know how it is; sometimes wholesale murder can be pulled off and nobody gives a damn, and then again some little thing'll start the American eagle to screeching his head off.

Well, this was one of them occasions. Old Vox Populi read about "Beauteous Texan Maid in Hands of Bloodthirsty Mexican Brigands," and let out a holler all the way from Maine to Californy. Washington promptly got busy, and Charlie Hughes or somebody sent a telegram demanding Rose Tyrell safe and unharmed or Esteban's head on a charger, or some similar nifty of the sort in such cases made and provided.

As this charger idea happened just then to chime in with Mexico's national aspirations, there had been immediate and gratifying acquiescence on the part of our sister republic to the south.

The commander at Yavisa had at once been notified to get Crooked Mouth at any cost, so here he was, on the warpath, and with a body guard of corespondents and camera men representing both big press associations and all the leading papers of the country.

When I explained to him that Esteban himself wasn't, so to speak, no more, he bristled his mustache and swore like a regular trooper; but there was a look in his eye that told me he was just as well satisfied. Say what you please, that half-breed wild cat wasn't the most pleasing customer in the world to tackle.

Still, said the Federal general, he must push on and round up the rest of the bunch, and when I'd tipped him off about the gap and how to get to their hangout and all, he ordered an immediate advance and intimated that in about twenty-four hours the Esteban gang would be as much ancient history as the ones that used to follow Monk Eastman.

He was compelled to go ahead, though, without the assistance of the reporters and camera men. They all headed back for the border claiming that public interest in the expedition ended with the recovery of Miss Tyrell.

One of 'em offered Rosie a seat in his car, as she said she'd had all of Mexico she wanted, and if she was once back in God's country, she'd never come within smelling distance of the place again.

But that was after her and me, managing to shake off the pesting of the crowd for a few minutes, had a heart-to-heart talk together.

There was a difference in her. She felt that she wasn't in any danger no more, and besides she was all puffed up at the thought of being a international figure.

"Red," she says, sharp and masterful, "we must decide at once what we are going to do. If we return to the border with the newspaper men, it means an inevitable encounter with my father; yet on the other hand, if we accept the commander's offer of an escort back to Yavisa, we shall—"

Kind of matrimonial, eh, what? I backed away from her, same's a free horse at the sight of a bridle.

"Say, where do you get that 'we' stuff?" I broke in. "You're of age, ain't you? And anyhow, I ain't never been appointed your guardian. Far as I'm concerned, I ain't going with no newspapermen, nor no escort neither. Me and Henry Ford is capable of—"

"Oh, you mean that you want me to go with you alone?" She cast down her eyes and kind of pinked up. "Of course you have saved my life and all that, Red, and we have been together unchaperoned. Still—"

"I don't mean nothing of the kind." I was getting exasperative. "You're in safe hands. You don't need no more. So the sooner you and me head our separate ways, the better I'll be satisfied."

But you couldn't dent that bullet-proof vanity of hers. Like this here guy, Narcissus, in Holy Writ, she was so in love with herself, that she couldn't believe everybody else wasn't the same way.

"I understand, Red." She bathed me in a indulgent smile like a Sunday-schoolteacher's. "With the coming of these newspaper men, you have grown conscious again of society's artificial standards. But my cowboy wants to remember that faint heart never won fair lady." She shook her finger at me in a arch way that made my flesh creep. "What has become of the dashing wooer who carried me off the other night, swearing that he would have me if he had to fight the whole garrison?"

She spoke so sincere, that I stared at her kind of aghast. And then it broke on me. By heck, she'd told that lie so often that she'd finished by believing it herself. She'd hoped herself into figuring me as a great lover and her as the object of my storm passion, a second Romeo and Julia.

"But why," I asked sarcastic, "spill them sacred confidences to Gerta O'Beirne?"

"Who said I did anything of the sort?" The smile left her lips, and her blue eyes narrowed. "So she's been talking about me, has she? The cat. I knew she was jealous. She could hardly treat me decently after I got back. And what if I did tell her?" she snapped. "It was the truth."

"No," says I; "it was not the truth, Rosie."

"Why!" she kind of gasps. "How can you stand up there and deny it? Didn't you come bursting in on me and tell me there was trouble in the house, and you had come to rescue me and—"

"Sure," I admits. "But if you'll cast your mind back, you'll remember. I asked you to trust me as a friend—not as no sweetheart. I never said nothing about being nuts over you, or fighting the whole garrison for your sweet sake, nor none of the rest of that mush. That was embroidery you added to the story yourself, and it wasn't a square deal. You showed me up in a false light. Gerta wouldn't have done that to a fellow, what only tried to help her."

"Well, I don't care." She started to cry. "You dragged me around all night, and put me in an awful position. Gerta kept demanding the reason for what you'd done, and I had to give her some sort of an explanation. And—and you needn't set her up as any model, either," she spit out. "She's tricky and deceitful and—"

"You're like the lawyers," I says. "When they ain't got no case, they call the attorney on the other side a horse thief and liar."

"But it's the truth," she insisted excitedly; "and I can prove it. Why, she pretends to have a torture chamber there at the ranch, and—"

"Pretends?" I couldn't help breaking in.

"Just that. It's nothing but stage-setting and illusion to frighten the ignorant *peons*, and get the impression abroad that she is absolutely ruthless. She told me all about it. There was no law in the community, she said; and when Esteban's supporters stole her cattle or burned her crops, she'd scare them into making redress. But it was all pure bluff—just some red lights and some old torture devices that had been at the ranch since the early days of the Vorezas. And she'd have gruesome sounds made in an adjoining room, and get old Ursula to give that terrifying speech of hers. And then at the appropriate moment, she'd have a wax figure carried out like a corpse, and—"

" 'Twasn't no wax figure I saw." I shook my head.

"Ah? Then that must have been the night you made off with me. She told me while she was putting on her judgement robe, that she was going to use a real dead man that evening—one of Esteban's followers that had been killed in a skirmish with a party out under Captain Cosette. She said the idea revolted

her, but she was going through with it, because she had Tony
Moreno, the proprietor of the Cafe del Toro, as a prisoner, and
she was afraid the wax figure might not impose on him.

"You see," Rosie branched off, "she expected Moreno to carry
a harrowing description of his experience to my stepfather. She
was always planning schemes like that," sneeringly. "When I
first came to visit her, I naturally told her about my troubles.
Mr. Tyrell had converted a lot of my money to himself, and I'd
found there was nothing I could do about it; so, of course, I was
very low in my mind. But she said there were more ways than
one of skinning a fox; and then she told me about this fake
torture chamber of hers, and said jokingly that since she was
already in the extortion business, she might as well extend her
operations. She proposed that I should stay hidden in the house,
while she sent messages to my stepfather purporting to come
from Mexican brigands that were supposed to have captured
me. He'd have to pay the ransom demanded, she said, in order
to save his face in Texas.

"Well, it sounded plausible"—the frail sort of squinted up
her eyes and I thought at the time she was disinterested, just a
good friend, although I'm not so sure of that now. I've found
out that she is practically bankrupt with her old ranch, and it's
struck me that maybe she was planning to borrow the money if
I got it, or perhaps try to have me marry Ted. Or, possibly," she
suggests meaningly, "she was merely keeping me under cover,
so as to prevent my meeting you."

Did you ever notice how quick a dishonest person is to impute
scabby motives to other people? But I didn't say nothing. Let
this bimbo take all the rope she wants, was my idea, and see how
quick she hangs herself.

"But Gerta O'Beirne would have been fooled, if she ever
expected to get a cent of my money." She cocked her head to
one side, a regular Miss Smarty. "My stepfather was too shrewd
for her, and I'd have been, too. If he ever got that message of
Tony Moreno's threatening him with the horrors of the torture

chamber, I'll bet he only laughed at it. He knows as well as I do, that she hasn't the nerve to torture a fly."

Say! I never appreciated how heavy the memory had laid on my stomach of what I'd seen down in that underground judgement hall, until I realized the blessed relief of knowing it wasn't true.

I'd tried to frame all sorts of excuses for Gerta of course; but I couldn't make 'em stick. That there torture business, when considered on the level, was too damn prejudicial. 'Twas in a way like picking out a beautiful peach, and finding on the underside of it a great, spreading spot of corruption.

But if it'd been only play-acting and strategy, that was a different matter. It was all of a piece with her swagger there at the Cafe el Toro, when she'd called for whiskey and dumped it in the cuspidor. You couldn't help but admire the bluffs she'd put over on the greasers, when so far as cold-bloodedness went, all she had was a fistful of chicken livers.

In my enthusiasm, I grabbed Rosie and hugged her.

"You're a wonder, kiddo," I said. "I take back all the hard things I've ever said about you, and the even worse ones I've thought."

"Oh, Red," she snuggles up to me, "I knew everything would be all right as soon as you understood. And now, dear, we must really decide what we are going to do. Of course, if you insist, I'll go with you alone, although it is so unconventional and I don't know much about the Mexican marriage laws."

But at that, I came out of my trance.

"Look here," I switches away from her. "Are you proposing to me? Because if you are, lay off. My affections is otherwise engaged."

It was after that, that she accepted the seat in the newspaper boys' car, and started for the border. I waved to her as she drove away, but she was so busy vamping them hard-boiled journalists that she never seen me.

"So that," I says to myself, without no especial tug of the heart strings, "is the last of you."

If it only had been!

CHAPTER XXIII

ANGER

AND NOW whither away, gentle Annie?

You called it. Straight for Voreza ranch and another interview with Miss O'Beirne; for the disclosures of her little playmate had stiffened up my spine something wonderful. Bamboozler, was she? Well, by Godfrey, she couldn't play nothing on me any more. We was going to have a showdown.

So young Lochinvar, he rode out of the West; through all the wide border his steed was the best. He stopped not for brake, and he stayed not for stone—

Only in this case he did.

I hadn't gone more 'n ten mile, until that pebble Henry had been talking so much about worked into his hoof, and lamed him so that he couldn't scarcely hobble.

"Now, see what you've went and done," I bawled him out, as I realized it'd be a day or two anyhow before we could travel again. "By stubbornly holding to your prognostications of evil, you visualized that stone right into your damned old frog. The thing you greatly feared has come upon you. When'll you learn that you mustn't never see anything in the universe but the good and beautiful?"

In spite of his pain, he gave a jeering horse laugh.

"Fat chance," he rails, "when I've got you always bobbing around for me to look at." Henry, I will say, could sling a mean repartee.

However, there was no use bandying recriminations. There

we was; and there we'd have to stay until the disability subsided. We might as well make the best of it.

Fortunately, Henry's *betise*—which is French for damfoolishness—had hit us at a spot where we could lay up very comfortably. There was water and shade; and, as the Federal general had stocked us up with fodder for man and beast to cover a two-day ride, we wasn't going to suffer none for grub.

I first busied myself in getting the pebble that had caused all the trouble, and then when I'd patched up poor old Henry's inner tube and bandaged it with a bunch of cooling grasses, and had fed and watered him, I set about making camp for myself.

It'd been getting along toward sundown when we started out, and by the time I'd done all this and had b'iled myself some coffee, and had toasted some bacon, it was plumb dark.

I'd been through a pretty strenuous time for some days now— on a steady stretch, you might say—and this was the first chance I'd had to take a real, undisturbed rest. You'd 'a' thought I'd curled right up and gone to sawing wood, wouldn't you?

But not so. Sleep was never farther from my thoughts. I set there, with my back agin' a tree, smoking and watching the firelight flicker across the leaves overhead, whilst I ran over in my mind all the things that had happened, and dreamed them dreams that only comes to a man once in his lifetime.

I was all on edge to be on my way of course—cussin' the delay—impatient to see Gerta, and get the necessary explanations over, and stage the grand reconciliation scene, that I'd pictured so often.

Yet it was kind of pleasant to put it off, if you know what I mean—like a kid that's got a penny in his hand and keeps turning it over, and thinking of all he's going to get with it, and yet holds off from spending it. And it sure was restful and soothing, just to lay off after all I'd been through, and to loaf and think. The breeze rustled soft through the trees, and the night wrapped me around, and once in a while Henry'd give a light stamp or whinny drowsily to let me know I had companionship.

Then presently the moon came up, and off in the woods a nightingale started singing. Leastways, it ought to have been a nightingale if it wasn't, although it might have been a screech owl and I'd never have knowed the difference, I was that torpid and serene.

I was thinking of Gerta and of what a wonderful girl she was, and of that little quirk at the corner of her lips when she smiled, and of her cuteness and sassiness and unexpectedness, and of how she'd doubled up that big burglar of a Moreno, same as if he had stomach-cramps, with her red lights and her wax figures. I was planning how I'd make that old ranch hum to grind out profits for her. And then just about when I'd cleaned up more millions than Rockefeller, and we was celebrating our golden wedding with all our children and grandchildren present—I drops off to sleep.

Well, the next morning, I was quite ready to go on. The pleasures of anticipation was all exhausted by this time, and I was hankering for the reality. But Henry informs me that, although the game hoof was considerable better, it'd still be a day before he was able to take the road. And he goes into a exhaustive description of how tender a horse's frog is, and how a foreign substance getting in there is apt to play hell with his whole system. By heck, from the fuss he made over that there pebble you'd have thought it was the Kohinoor diamond he'd picked up, 'stead of just a ornery bit of flint.

Still he was undoubtedly lame yet, or else, if he was malingering, playing it so well that I couldn't detect it. So there was nothing to do but curb my impatience, and try to be philosophical.

But being philosophical ain't so easy, let me tell you, when you're all on fire to get to the girl you love, and all that stands in your way is a darned old skate's mollycoddling of himself. Him and his sore hoof! This was a case where froggie wouldn't a-wooing go.

By nightfall, I'd fretted myself so over the delay that I was almost in a fever; and Henry and me was no longer on speaking terms.

On the second morning, though, after some stalling he finally consented to make a try at it.

"But you gotta go easy with me," he grumbled. "I want a chance to pick my road. That frog's still pretty sensitive, and if I get another pebble jammed up in there, Lord knows what the results would be. We'll just amble along."

"Sure," says I. Leaping into the saddle, I gave him a dig with the spurs and a cut of the whip that ambled him a mile in about one thirty-seven flat.

He didn't do no choosing of the road. Make no mistakes about that. He went via every shortcut that I could find—pebble or no pebbles; and he went with the throttle wide open, too.

I knew he was fairly aching for a accident to happen; but, as I've said before, the Irish is special favorites of the Creator, and 'spite of the malicious animal magnetism he was throwing out, we got through without mishap or affliction of no kind.

'Twas about noon next day, that I came loping down into the hills back of Yavisa; and who should I run into but Captain Cosette on his way back from town.

"Name of a name!" says he. "But you have been cutting ze wide swath since you have been gone, M'sieu Red. Getting your name in the papers, and making all kinds of *esclandres.*"

"Getting my name in the papers, eh?" I says, kind of puffed up at the idea. "Sho! They didn't go and print a story about that Esteban business, did they? And mentioned my name, you say?"

"Mais oui! Not only your name, but your picture as well. Here, I have it wiz me."

He took a El Paso paper two days old out of his pocket and handed it over to me. I was grinning kind of sheepish as I unfolded it, tickled to death at my importance, and yet ashamed of showing it. But I guess that grin died the quickest death on record.

Wow! There on the front page and a-covering four colyums was my picture right enough. But my picture, how?

Them sneaking camera men had snapped me when they first come up, and while I was still asleep. There I was holding Rosie in my arms, and I reckon I must have been dreaming at that moment of the buffalo stampede, cause I was clutching her tight like I'd never let her go. One of her arms was 'round my neck, and our faces was so close together that, if I hadn't known different, I'd have swore myself that I was kissing her.

I've seen lots of mushy posing for the screen; but never nothing that was so oozing, dripping with sentimentality. It was like a schoolgirl's dream. Positively sickening.

And below it, the damn newspaper had printed a line what read:

> Recovered Heiress Claims She Is Not Going to Marry Her Infatuated Cowboy Rescuer. What Do You Think?

Say, I couldn't think, I couldn't reason for a minute. I just sat there, clutching that libelous sheet between my two hands, and staring at that outrageous picture. No need to read the article that went along with it. Rosie had had all the way to the border to fill the newspaper boys up with her own special line of guff. Easy enough to know what a blah she'd made out of me.

"Has Gerta seen this?" I gasped hoarsely.

Cosette nodded.

"And what did she say?"

"Not much." He shrugged his shoulders. "But if I were you, M'sieu Red, I would not go on to ze ranch. I would turn and ride for ze bordair as fast as my horse could carry me."

Well, I ain't saying but what his advice appealed to me for a second. Then I set my jaw, and notched up my belt. By golly, I'd come for a show-down with this girl, and I was going to have it. If she could look me in the eyes, and tell me she believed that, after our night on the roof, I could be such a rotter as this picture made me out, I was willing to take my punishment. I'd go away.

But she had to tell me so with her own lips. I wasn't going to turn tail and run before I knew what was biting me.

"Not me," I says to Cosette. "And not Henry Ford, neither. As George Washington said: 'The Old Guard dies, but never surrenders.' We've started for Voreza ranch, cap, and we're going there, if hell cracks open on the road."

"As you will." He shrugs again. "But in order that you may not get into trouble, perhaps I had better give you a pass." He pulls a little pad out of his pocket and commenced writing. "Zere is a report that a detachment of Esteban's troops have broken through the cordon of Federal troops up in ze mountains, and may be headed zis way. Ze Federal vice commander in zis district has parties of his men out reconnoitering, and if you should happen to encounter one of zese, it might be unpleasant for you unless you were identified."

I thanked him, and taking the paper he handed me, stuck it in my hat. Then, after a little further palaver, he waved his hand to me and rode on. He was following the trail, but I knew a shorter if rougher way over the hills, and I took that. The sooner I knowed my fate the better, was how I felt. No use lingering under a sword of Democritus. If it was going to fall, make it snappy. Also, I was afraid that if I fooled around overlong, the courage to face her that I'd pumped up might trickle away.

So prodding old Henry up, I cantered along at a pretty smart gait, and about twenty minutes after I left Cosette I came to a cleft in the hills, where the ground on my side sloped down gradual to a sort of overgrown ravine, but on the other side rose in a sharp bluff, with only one steep path up it to the level plateau on top.

I was speeding toward this ravine and the path up the bluff, all sail set, when I seen some horsemen come racing out on the plateau.

I made 'em out as Federal troopers; and was glad I'd happened to run into Cosette and get that pass, since otherwise they might have nailed me as a suspect and hauled me off to the hoosegow.

With the paper though, I felt perfectly easy, and so drilled right along toward the ravine, 'spite of the arm-waving and threatening gestures they kept treating me to.

They were traveling pretty fast; and I realized that I had better put on extra speed so as to reach the ravine and get up to the top of the bluff before they intercepted me. If I didn't, and they stated coming down that narrow path first, they'd probably clutter it up to such a extent that I'd be delayed quite a while in getting through.

So I gave Henry the office, and we swept over the sloping ground at pretty near a racing clip. The troopers, too, were going to the bat with their horses, driving 'em for all they were worth.

And then out from behind them, like they was standing still, flashed the little pinto pony; and on his back, riding hell-for-leather, was Gerta O'Beirne.

She didn't head for the path like the soldiers were doing, but for a much nearer point, where the bluff sheered down in a straight wall; and she didn't check the pinto until she was right on the edge of it.

Then, jerking him in so sharp that he went up on his two hind feet, she hollered down at me something that I couldn't understand.

At that same time, she flung out her hand, and there wasn't no trouble understanding what she meant by that. It said, "You get the hell out of here!" as plain as if it was wrote in smoke letters across the sky. And that undoubtedly, or words to the same effect, was what she was hollering at me.

But I hadn't come this far to turn back at her mere say-so. She was first going to hear my side of the story, whether she wanted to or not; and I didn't pay no attention to her, nor to her waving and gesticulating, than if it had been a fly up there on the bank fluttering its wings at me.

I was within about two hundred yards of the ravine now, and to show her how indifferent I was to her orders, I waved my hat, and let Henry out to his top speed.

She seemed took back for a second by my audaciousness; then she pulled two guns and leveled 'em full at me.

Honestly, I had to laugh. It was too ridiculous. At that distance, there wasn't one chance in a thousand that she could hit me with them popguns of hers. Besides, I knew from what Rosie had told me about her, that she wouldn't shoot. I never felt safer in my life.

"Here, young lady, is where you get one of your bluffs called," I grins to myself.

And then—Crack!

As the revolver spoke, Henry Ford stopped short in full stride, and went down like a stone, plowing up the ground with his shoulder as his momentum carried him on.

I felt him recoil as the shot struck him, felt him collapse under me, felt myself pitched over his head as he went down. And then—I passed out of the picture.

CHAPTER XXIV

RESOLUTION

WHEN I opened my eyes again, I was in my own bed at the ranch, and I wondered hazily for a minute or two if all these adventures I've been telling you about might not be merely a touch of bad stomach from something I'd eaten.

But the time of day didn't hit in with that. If nightmares was all that was the matter with me. I wouldn't be laying in bed at noon. The merry clatter of the alarm clock would long since have put to route them phantasms of darkness.

Furthermore, there was a strong aroma of arnica in the room, and also of something else—garlic. Yes, a sidelong glance showed me old Ursula dozing at my bedside. She wouldn't be there, unless I was sick or injured.

Lastly, when I lifted my hand to my head, I found a bandage encircling my brows.

It was all true then. And since I couldn't locate any other damage, it didn't take me long to figure that what had happened to me was a cracked nut I'd got when Henry pitched me.

Henry? At the thought of him, a pang went through me like somebody had stuck a knife to my heart.

Good old Henry Ford! The best horse, the truest pal that a man could ask to own. And Gerta O'Beirne had killed him. Shot him on account of her jealous anger against me.

By God, I told myself, I'd have thought more of her if, instead of Henry, she'd have put that bullet into me. She had welshed on that; she didn't have the nerve. But she hadn't stopped in her hate and rancor from butchering a poor, dumb beast that hadn't never done no harm to nobody, 'cept maybe kicking a few greasers.

My throat got dry and my heart seemed on fire when I thought of it. A woman who could do such a thing—well, there wasn't words bad enough to describe her. I was done with her— never wanted to see her again—wouldn't stay no longer under her roof, nor accept her hospitality. Better to be wandering at large on the range, than even to breathe the same air what she did.

I climbed out of bed, and started to put on my clothes, taking care not to rouse up old Ursula; and laying on the dresser I found a letter addressed to me from a firm of lawyers in El Paso.

I opened it and read it. Any other time, I suppose I'd been considerable startled and stirred up by what it contained but I was so seething with hostility, so full of black bitterness, that nothing didn't seem to mean very much. I just stuck the letter in my pocket, and crowding my hat down on my head, stole out of the room.

Going down the stairs to the patio, I met a Mexican girl coming up, one of the maids in the house. I stopped her as she was slipping past me with a little duck of the head.

"Where's the señorita, Miss O'Beirne?" I growled.

Gone to town, she tells me; and that suits me fine, since it meant that Gerta wouldn't be back before evening. I'd have plenty of chance to make my get-away without seeing her. That was just the one thing I felt I couldn't stand—to see or speak to her. The reason I'd asked where she was, had been so that I could avoid her and sneak away from the ranch unbeknownst.

Her being at Yavisa, though, and thus giving me free swing, so to speak, made a difference. Since I was leaving the place for good, I might as well take all that belonged to me. There was several little things of mine in the drawers of my desk, that I wouldn't care to lose—a extra revolver and cartridges for it, and a gold nugget stickpin that I'd won in a poker game, and some photographs.

Also—although otherwise, I wouldn't have paid no attention to it—I was glad of the chance to set down somewhere, and sort of pull myself together. My legs, I found, wasn't altogether seaworthy yet, and there was a swimming in my head. That sure must have been some lick I got on the old dome. Why, I'd had to clutch at the handrail all the way downstairs, and I reeled and staggered now like a drunken man as I crossed the patio over to the office.

Strangely enough, the big open space was deserted. There wasn't no coming nor going, nor none of the ordinary business of the ranch being transacted. It was more like Sunday. But this couldn't be Sunday. According to my reckoning, it was on Sunday, the sixteenth, that I'd got back from the mountains; and this certainly wasn't the same day, 'cause it'd been at least two hours later than now when Henry was shot.

I checked off the days on my fingers to make sure, starting back at that Sunday afternoon at the Yavisa racetrack; but I couldn't make the tally come out no different. It was one week later, Sunday, the sixteenth, that me and Henry had come down that ravine, and straight into the jaws of disaster.

Finally, as I puzzled over it, the thought occurred to me that this might be a Mexican *fiesta* day, which would account just as well for the general inertia. That must be it—a *fiesta* day—and probably a Monday, since I was sure that no mere clout over the head could put me out for longer'n twenty-four hours.

Anyhow, the thing wasn't worth muddling my brains with. I had matters of more importance to attend to.

It was cool there in the office, and the sun didn't glare in my eyes like out in the open patio; and so t'wasn't no great while until I was feeling like myself again—that is, if you can call it feeling like yourself, when you're sort of holding a funeral overall for hopes and dreams.

I opened up my desk, and there right inside laid my account book for the ranch. At sight of it, the memory swept over me of all my plans and schemes and figuring to make the old slab pay, and of how proud I'd been to change them red-ink footings into profits; and it gave me a twinge like home-sickness. I hurried to close the book up, and shove it back in a pigeonhole.

Then I went to poking at the drawers, and I soon cleaned out of 'em what was mine. I stuck the revolver in my pocket, and fastened the stickpin in my shirt, and then I began running over the little sheaf of photographs to see which ones I wanted to keep.

But right on top was one of me and Henry Ford—a snapshot of us that Gerta took one day. And I remembered how she'd fed Henry a apple afterward, and how he'd nuzzled his nose against her shoulder. 'Twas a far prettier picture to my mind than the one she took. And it kind of brought back to me how thick her and Henry had always been—and I caught myself up. Damn her, she'd killed him!

After that, I didn't bother none with the rest of the photographs; just slipped a rubber band around 'em and stuck 'em down inside my shirt. I was afraid of running into some other among em, that might arouse equally harrowing memories.

Well, there didn't seem to be no sense in waiting any longer. It was quite a tramp into Yavisa—for I was fully determined that I wouldn't accept no horse, nor no other favors from this outfit—and if I was aiming to make the town by any reasonable hour, I'd better be starting.

So I wrote just a line on a sheet of paper, as follows, viz:

Miss G. O'Beirne, Voreza Ranch, Yavisa, Mexico.
    Friend Miss O'BEIRNE: I hereby resign as foreman of Voreza Ranch to take effect immediately. Good-by forever. I guess you know why. Y'rs resp'y,
                                    R.F. Conners

This, with my keys, I laid inside the desk, and closed down the top. But just as I was starting to get up, I seen something laying on the floor, and leaning over, picked it up. It was one of Gerta's riding gloves.

A fellow told me once about how a scientist could take a

single bone of some extinct animal—nothing more'n a knuckle joint, or maybe a toenail—and reconstruct the whole critter for you, same as when he was alive.

Well, it was likewise with me. The glove still had its fingers puffed out, and held all its creases, like it had just dropped warm offn her hand. And as I sat there, turning it over and over. I seemed to feel the sweetness and charm and the—the derned variety of her, and to be living over again all the different incidents that her and me had been through together.

She'd been haughty to me and melting; she'd been scornful and coaxing; smiling and tearful; teasing and indulgent. She'd been my gallant little comrade of the saddle; the stiff, unapproachable commander of the garrison, the girl who sang with me in the moonlight. She'd been heaven and hell. But through it all, she'd been Gerta. And there wasn't nobody like her.

"A heart of gold!" I didn't seem to say the words myself; it was more like somebody else was speaking with my lips. But whether I said it purposely or not, I had to agree with it. There wasn't nothing mean nor cruel nor bad in that girl's whole make-up. And I knew it.

How then could she have brought herself to kill Henry, I asked myself. She'd done it. There wasn't no chance for a alibi this time, like there was with the torture chamber.

But you never have no trouble in digging up excuses for a person, when you're not dead set on finding them.

Maybe—I smoothed the glove out between my fingers—she didn't really intend to kill the horse? Maybe she just shot in the air to stop us, and misjudged her aim and by one chance in a million the bullet struck Henry.

Pretty weak; what? But love has made men swallow even weaker stuff, and smack their lips over it.

That must be the explanation, I decided. Gerta wasn't to blame after all. T'wasn't her, but destiny that had finished Henry Ford.

So I opened the desk again, and tore up my resignation, and

put back the revolver, the photographs, and the stickpin; but the little, worn riding glove I kept and put it next to my heart.

A shadow fell across the door, and I looked up to see Pedro go swaggering by in full regimentals, even to wearing shoes. At the same minute he seen me, and came lurching in.

"Ah! The señor ees back," he says. "And, San Jose be praised, he has hees health once more. But there ees a matter I would bring to the señor's attention, since he seems in error, and—"

"No need of argument, amigo," I interrupts, for I suspicioned what was on his mind. "You are perfectly right; it is a small, low plant, and does not grow on trees. And now, that being admitted, tell me"—I looked at his feet—"why all this unwonted pomp and finery?"

"But eet ees Sunday, señor," he says.

"Sunday, hell! What Sunday?"

"Sunday, the twenty-third," says he.

I jerked around in my chair to look at the calendar hanging on the wall behind me. Sure enough, the date it showed was Saturday, the twenty-second, that leaf not having yet been torn off.

"Do you mean to say," I gasped, "that I have been laying dead to the world for one solid week?"

He nodded.

"The señor was ver' badly hurted. But," he grinned, "the señor ees lucky that he ees not dead. In thees ravine toward which the señor was riding, was ambushed a party of Esteban's men. The Federal troops were after them, but they would have got the señor, eef Señorita Gerta had not stopped heem."

Ah! So that was it? She had really saved my life when I was bent bullheaded on throwing it away. Too bad that Henry had to be sacrificed. I'll bet she hated it even worse than I did. But what else could she do. And here I'd been maligning and abusing her for everything I could lay my tongue to. In my humiliation, I wanted to kneel before her, to grovel and ask her pardon. I felt that I must see her; I couldn't wait.

"Jerusalem!" I groaned, with a glance at the clock. "I wonder how soon she will be back."

"But not until late, señor," says Pedro. "She rides in a race to-day."

"Rides in a race?"

"Of a certainty. Santa Maria! Does not the señor remember that to-day ees the big race between her and Señor Tyrell?"

Sunday, the twenty-third! How could I have forgotten?

"But what is she riding?" I scowled. "They say that black mare of Tyrell's can beat anything around here."

"Alas! I fear eet ees so, señor. But the Señorita Gerta would not give in. She rides her pinto pony."

"That little runt! Why, he hasn't a chance."

"True, señor, but what could she do? The rule is that the horse must be ridden by hees owner, and the pinto ees the fastest she has. I myself would not attend the race, because I did not wish to witness her defeat."

I dropped my head in my hands.

"Good Lord!" I muttered. "If only Henry Ford was alive."

"Eef Hennery Ford was alive?" repeats Pedro like he was kind of stumped. "Alive? And why not?"

For a second, I hardly got it. Then I was out of the chair and had him clutched by the shoulders.

"What do you mean?" I shook him till his teeth rattled. "Don't you dare lie to me, or I'll break every bone in your body. Henry Ford alive, you say? But it can't be. I myself saw Gerta kill him—saw him drop—saw—"

"But no, señor!" shrieked Pedro, almost as excited now as I was. "Señorita Gerta did not keel him. She only creased him to stop you from coming on."

Creased! I'd heard of that trick. But it required bull's-eye shooting, and at the distance Gerta had been from us, it seemed impossible.

"And you claim that he is now alive?" I stared at him incredulous.

"As I tell you, señor. Alive? Why, he ees better than ever. Only thees morning, he throw off three stable boys when they try to exercise heem, and—"

But a thought had struck me.

"And what time is this race with Tyrell?"

"At four o'clock, señor."

I shot another glance at the clock. Hot dog! It could be made.

"Pedro, get him up here!" I shouted. "Snap into it."

I flung off my coat and hat, jerked my feet out of my boots, tossed my revolver and everything else of weight out of my pockets; and wearing only my shirt and trousers, ran out into the patio stocking-footed, as Pedro came leading Henry up the ramp.

Just then old Ursula hobbled out onto a balcony overhead, and started jabbering down at me.

"She say," interpreted Pedro, "eet ees the señorita's orders that the señor must stay in bed."

I swung into the saddle, and Henry and me dashed for the archway.

"You and your bed kindly go to hell!" I shouted back at Ursula.

CHAPTER XXV

THE RACE

HENRY WAS full of zip as a bar'l of moonshine r'aring to go; but as soon as we got out on the trail, I gave him to understand that I was running this show, and not him.

"Look here" I says, "just because you've been pulling a Sir Oliver Lodge, and come back from the dead, don't imagine that you're any different from the low-down, flea-bitten goat that you always was. I notice," says I, "that history is discreetly silent regarding what became of Lazarus after he performed a similar stunt, and I judge the reason is, that he swelled around on the strength of his celebrity and made himself so generally obnoxious, that somebody put him out for keeps. Verbum sap," says I, "which you may think is a appropriate epithet, but which is really Rumanian for "It's a long lane that has no turning.""

"Pay attention to me now," I continues, "and I will outline the nature of the sketch in which you are to appear this afternoon. Firstly, you have got to get to Yavisa race track by four o'clock; but that don't mean you're to run your fool head off getting there, for immediately on your arrival you will have to race Jeff Tyrell's world beater for the honor of Voreza ranch, and twenty thousand cold smackers."

"What are you talking about?" breaks in Henry aghast. "I ain't no miracle worker. Breeze all the way to Yavisa by four-o'clock; and then, hot and blown, go into a race? Huh! It can't be done."

"Can't, eh?" I says. "Well, now hearken to me, little Easter lily, it's going to be done, whether it can be, or not. And further-

more, you and me is going to win that race, or else you'll wish
you'd stayed dead. So, if you take my advice, you'll not indulge
in any more of this pranking you've been showing; but while
seeing that we get to Yasiva in time, so conserve your energies
that you'll have enough and to spare to carry you through the
main bout."

Then thinking that perhaps I'd pitched into him hard enough,
I started in to jolly him by telling him what a super-horse he
was, and how the run in from the ranch wouldn't be more'n just
a breather to a equine of his abilities, and how fresh and fine he
ought to feel after a week's lay-up in his stall. I got him so perked
up, that by the time we reached Yavisa he'd have been willing to
take on Man o' War.

Henry was no darn fool either, let me tell you. Understanding now what was required of him, he saved himself in a dozen
ways that I or you would never have thought of. With a quarter
of an hour to spare, he landed me at the race track; and yet, if
you'll believe me, he hadn't turned a hair, and his respiration, as
the doctors say, was practically normal.

Leaving him in the paddock with one of the fellows from the
ranch I went over by the judge's stand, where Gerta and Tyrell,
surrounded by a group of listeners, was arranging the final details
of the contest. I managed to crowd in close enough to hear what
was going on, without being seen by either her or him. It was
to be a match race at catch weights over a distance of one mile,
for twenty thousand dollars a side, the stipulation being that
the respective horses should be rode by their bona fide owners.

So much, the announcer had got down on his pad, so that he
could spiel it to the audience; and now he asked the names of
the entries and their riders.

"Texas Queen is my horse," booms Tyrell, "and the rider is,
of course, Jefferson Tyrell."

"And the Voreza entry," says Gerta, "is Pinto Ben, with G.
O'Beirne up."

"Pardon me," I pushed in at this juncture, "but I'd like to

make a slight correction there. The Voreza entry is Henry Ford, with Roger Francis Conners as pilot."

Gerta turned, with her eyes almost popping out of her head.

"Red!" she screams. Then she grabbed me by the arm. But you mustn't," she protests. "You are in no condition to ride—unconscious for a week. Why, it's ridiculous. I told Ursula not to let you stir. And anyhow, what can you do with Henry Ford? You must have forced him at top speed to get him here in time."

"Sh-h!" I cautions. "You are giving away stable records. And"—I turned to the announcer—"You put that entry down just as I told you."

I guess he seen from my tone who was going to be the boss between us two, 'cause he finally done what he was told after Gerta had satisfied herself with some more useless kicking, and was induced to see reason.

Then, that being settled, Tyrell comes over to me. What he'd liked to do was to stick a knife into me; but instead, he held out his hand, and affected a fatherly smile.

You see, he had brought a lot of his pals—politicians and bankers and the like—down from Texas; and since they was all sure to find out that I was the guy what had rescued his daughter, he had to play amicable in spite of himself.

"My dear boy," he smears it on, "delighted to see that you have recovered from your unfortunate accident. I can't tell you how concerned we all were, when we heard of it. Also, it has prevented me until now from expressing my gratitude for your heroic deliverance of my little girl."

At this, the crowd standing around began cheering and slapping their hands in a way that made me feel like a fool.

"Aw, that didn't amount to nothing," I mumbled. "Forget it."

"But I can't forget it," he says. "Red—you don't mind if I call you that, do you, dear boy?—when I think of my precious Rosie in the hands of those unspeakable villains—"Here he puts a tremble in his voice, and has to stop and wipe his eye with his han'k'cher. "Forgive me," he says shakylike. "The very recollection of her peril unmans me.

"Of course," he says, swelling up and speaking loud for the benefit of the gallery, "such a service as you performed can never be repaid. But is there no way in which I can lessen my sense of obligation?" He pulls out his check book. "Isn't there something I can do for you, Red, in a monetary way? If so, you have only to name the amount."

Now, I ain't saying he wasn't cute. He'd read me well enough to know that I wouldn't stand for no tip for saving his daughter—not in front of all them people, anyhow. Even if I did, it was only a check he was offering, and he could stop payment on it. He was safe, whichever way the cat jumped. And at the same time he got credit for being big-hearted and generous.

For a minute, I was half tempted to take him up on it, just to see what he'd do. Then a better idea come to me.

"Well, now, that's mighty nice of you, Mr. Tyrell," I says; "but of course I couldn't accept any money for what I done. However," says I, "if it would relieve your mind any, there is a little matter you can help me out on."

"Anything, my boy," he beams. "Anything at all."

"Well, then," I says, "I'd like to have them phoney claims against Voreza ranch, that you've got hold of. They ain't worth a hoot and unless there is shenanigan of some sort, you can't never collect a cent on 'em. But it'd make me feel a whole lot easier to know they was in safe hands."

The smile slid off his lips, and his eyes narrowed. I could see that he was casting about quick for some way to wriggle out of his bargain. But I beat him to it.

"Or I'll tell you," I amends; "that sounds too much like taking a reward for doing my duty. Let's make it a sporting proposition, instead—a added wager on this horse race."

"How do you mean?" he asks wary-like.

"Why," says I, "if my horse wins, you hand me over them claims. If, on the other hand, your horse comes in first that settles any debt you feel you owe me on account of your daughter, and leaves you free and clear."

He looked down his nose, and hesitated for a minute, studying me from under his brows; then I saw a sort of sly gleam come into his eyes. He'd remembered what Gerta said about Henry having already come all the way from the ranch.

"But, my boy," he urged, oily as a porpoise, "that's hardly fair, is it?" As I understand, neither you nor your horse is in tophole condition. Of course, if you insist, I'll agree; but as a sportsman—"

"Then, that's settled," I broke in, afraid he might change his mind. "Just assign all them claims to me in writing, and put the assignment along with the money in the hands of the stakeholder; and we'll get down to business.

"Far as my horse being out of condition," I says boastful, "Henry Ford can race on three legs, and beat anything in this neck of the woods."

That was to hook him by making him think I was a crazy enthusiast, and it works.

"Done," he snaps. Fifteen minutes later him and me was facing the barrier.

On the way over from the paddock, I'd started to outline my plan of the race and give Henry his final instructions; but he cut me short with an impatient heave of his withers.

"Who's doing this job?" he demands rudely.

After that, no matter how I tried to broach the subject, he wouldn't have nothing to do with me; just kept looking over at that black mare of Tyrell's and working his ears.

"Pretty cute little trick, what?" I heard him mutter.

Well, I could describe that race for you stride by stride and furlong by furlong. Why not? I didn't have nothing to do but play spectator; just set there on Henry's back, and go through the motions of riding. But what's the use of descriptions? Guess you suspect by this time how it come out, and that's all that counts.

As old Henry flashed by the laboring black mare in the

stretch and led to the wire by a length, I shot a look back over
my shoulder at Tyrell. His face was working same as a man in
a fit and was all graylike, and his lips was drawn back from his
teeth like he was ready to commit murder.

He tried to claim foul, the cheap piker; but the happy, old,
blackjacking days of the Esteban regime was over, and his yelping didn't earn him nothing but contempt.

Then I forgot all about him and horses and everything else;
for Gerta, her face radiant, pushed her way through the crowd,
and threw her arms about my neck. It wasn't just the reconciliation scene I'd pictured, with the moonlight and the oleanders.
The sun was blistering down on us, and there was a thousand
crazy people yelling in our ears. But at that, I didn't have no kick.

"Then you don't believe none of that lying stuff about Rosie,
honey?"

"I never believed it," she says, and she gave a little ripple
of amusement; "not after I saw you that first night, when the
searchlight picked you up just outside the stockade. I don't
believe Joseph resisted Potiphar's wife harder than you were
trying to resist poor Rosie."

Later her and me did have a session in the moon-light and
after we'd told each other how it all happened, and when we first
began to feel that way, and all them usual things that passes on
such occasions, we got to discussing ways and means.

"It was clever of you, Red," says Gerta, "to secure those fraud-
ulent claims of Tyrell's. But," with a little sigh, "I am afraid it
will not do us much good. The honest and actual liabilities are
so heavy, that I doubt we'll be able to keep the ranch."

Then I happened to remember that letter from the El Paso
lawyers, that I'd stuck in my pocket and forgotten all about; and
I pulled it out and gave it to her.

Only a notification that these lawyers had been searching
vainly for me three months, but had finally succeeded in locating
me through the Rosie affair. And it was on account of my Aunt

Margaret dying without no will, which left me enough jack to buy a flock of Brooklyn Bridges, if I felt like it.

"But you are a rich man, Red!" gasps Gerta. "What are you going to do with all that money?"

"Well," I says, "the first thing I am going to do is to buy a wedding ring, and then I am going to put the old ranch on its feet, and then I'm going to college and get myself a education. We can't afford to have no scrambled grammar around the house, when the children is old enough to take notice.

Well, we talked for quite a spell longer, but finally she went into the house. As for me, though, I was too exalted to sleep, so I wanders down to the stalls to have a little chat with Henry, and tell him all about it.

I can't say, however, that there was any welcome flags displayed. He was tired and peevish, and after I'd only talked a half hour or so, he began to show his ill humor.

"Great man, you are," he says invidious. "Think you done it all, I suppose?"

"Well," I says placatingly, "to be fair, Henry, I got ta admit you won the race this afternoon."

"Won!" he snorts, "That race wasn't won. It was stole."

Then he starts to chuckling, and he tells me that him and the black mare had fixed it all up between 'em when they was over in the paddock together.

"She don't like Tyrell nohow, and she did—well, seem to like me," he says. "Most of the ladies do. So it wasn't difficult to arrange. Jeff, the poor fish, claimed a foul, but he never really knew what hit him."

"But, Henry," I says, reprovingly, "do you think that was sportsmanlike?"

"Shush," he says. "Where'd you been, if I hadn't? Tired as I was, that Texas Queen could have run rings around me. Why," he says, "all you are and all you've got is entirely owing to me. You'd never have got a second look from Gerta even, if it wasn't for the admiration I aroused in her."

"Sure," I says sarcastic. "All you need is a breech-clout and a bow-an'-arrers to be a regular Cupid."

"I can be anything I want," says Henry Ford.

I ain't sure but what he is right.